Triangle of Trust

by

Alexandria May Ausman

Book cover illustration by Alexandria May Ausman
Editor: Jon M. Ausman

Library of Congress Control Number: 2025908723-

ISBN: 978-1-963335-44-6 (ebook)
ISBN: 978-1-963335-43-9 (paperback)

Published By:
Ausman & Cousins LLC
1700 North Monroe Street
Suite 11, Box 284
Tallahassee, Florida 32303-0501

For author interviews: ausman@embarqmail.com

Das Kaiser Haus Series

The Collar King Series

The Most Brutal Man in Europe Series

Claus's Revelations (Chapters 1 to 8)
Priceless Changes (Chapters 9 to 16)
Silver Well (Chapters 17 to 24)
Book Four (Coming soon)

The Psycho Series

Cemetery Kid (Chapters 1 to 20)
Stop Calling Me Psycho (Chapters 21 to 33)
Motor-Psycho (Chapters 34 to 44)
Delusion of the Collar and the Key (Chapters 45 to 53)
Brutality's Prisoner (Chapters 54 to 64)
Aesthetic Akathisia (Chapters 65 to 74)
Metallic Burden (Chapters 75 to 83)

27 Masters Series

Anita the Benevolent (Chapters 1 to 7)
The Beast and the Witch (Chapters 8 to 16)
High Priestess of Schizophrenia (Chapters 17 to 24)
The Professional Dominatrix (Chapters 25 to 33)

Triangle of Trust (Chapters 34 to 41)
Book Six (Coming soon)

Stand Alone Books

The Grannybat's Weird Tales & Gothic Stories Volume 1

Book Five Characters: Triangle of Trust

Anita: deceased first Master
Arodia: High Priestess of the Green Ring
Bobby: a local beauty, deceased
Boyd: a deputy sheriff
Carla: Katheryn's secretary
Cathy: a deputy sheriff, dispatcher
Christian Axel: secret husband of Psycho/Rachel, trainer and original Master
Christopher: a Dominant
Cindy: mother of the sadist Julie
Circe: the third Mistress, a Priestess of the Green Ring
Colleen: Katheryn's daughter
Crystal: a former evil clique member with Julie, niece of Katheryn
Daniel: husband of Christine
David: one of Joyce's kinksters
Debbie: Psycho's sexual psychopathic and sadistic mother
Delilah: niece of Maiden Mary, caretaker of the nursery
Dennis: the county sheriff
Dude: a command hallucination, an aggressive anger shard of Psycho
Ginger Kirkpatrick: a FemDom, Mistress Ten
Grace: a friend of Katheryn
Greg: a high school classmate
James: spouse of Tracy, member of the Green Ring
Jim: a Vocational Rehabilitation counselor

Jon Ausman: the current Keyholder
Joni: a friend of Julie
Joyce: a Dominatrix
Julie: a previous sadistic Mistress who fled the law
Julius: a funeral home owner
June: a funeral home master embalmer, Mistress Nine, an interim
Katheryn: a lawyer, Mistress twelve
Kaylee: an alleged submissive to Joyce
Kick Start: a high school classmate and friend of Psycho
Leslie: Mistress eleven.
Linda: a deputy sheriff
Looper: a disembodied voice, Psycho's narrative hallucination
Maggie: Matthew's schizophrenic aunt
Mary: Maiden to Circe, takes care of Psycho's children
Mary: grandmother of Psycho, mother of Debbie
Matthew: a submissive
Mike: a friend of Psycho
Mindy: Katheryn's oldest daughter
Palkin, Doctor: a professor at the university
Pat: a master mortician
Phillip: prankster friend of Ginger
Psycho: a schizophrenic trying to survive
Randy: a Snake Pit staff rapist
Rebecca: a friend of Ginger
Roary: a High Priest, 3rd Level Initiate, also known as Richard
Roberts, Mr.: a deceased client of the funeral home

Ronnie: spouse of Circe, lives with Mary
Roy: spouse of Katheryn
Scruffy: a fire dog
Shannon: a friend of Julie
Shree, Doctor: a professor of psychology
Simon Brag: a command hallucination shard of Psycho, her lost inner self
Stacey: a high school and college classmate
Tammy: Master Eight, an interim
Timmy: Psycho's spouse
Victoria: a friend of Julie

Preface

A phone call on a chilly May morning starts a new awareness for the submissive pair of Matthew and Psycho. Their Mistress is easily bored. Try as they might, two are not enough to please this greedy Dominant. They have given her their hearts, adoration, and loyalty. Yet, she wants more. Matthew and Psycho want to be a family forever, the defense of their triangle is all that matters. It is their world. To protect their world, they will pull out all the stops, kick down all the walls, and even scheme against the one they love the most. Psycho and Matthew discover humiliation, fear, and pain are the answer to all their troubles. The submissive pair will eagerly grant Mistress Ginger their dignity. On their knees both pray she will decide that they are truly worthy of her undying love.

Everyone ready to live in a poly D/ss relationship for just a bit longer? Okay, follow me and stay three paces to my left. Now, kneel when told. Don't forget to address her as Mistress. Don't argue with commands and know your limits. Be ready to take all kinds of punishment to defend your honor. You must protect and defend your Mistress, brother and sister collars, and home no matter what you must give up doing it. Most important of all never fall in love with your family. Love is for vanillas.

Chapter 34: "The Mistress's Submissive Pair
Mistress Ginger and submissive Matthew

"Don't be silly, Psycho. Nothing can last forever. Face the facts. Dominants never truly love their playthings. Mistress Ginger has gotten bored of us like they all eventually do. She will toss or sell our collars sooner or later. We are not vanillas. We are submissive collars. When the day comes that our family is separated, try to remember that. I will do my best to accept it too. Although, I must be honest, I think I have done something very stupid. I have fallen deeply in love with you. I tried my best to correct that mistake, but so far, it is only getting worse."
Matthew's statement to Psycho – May 1995

Matthew was vacuuming the living room and I was cooking our dinner when the phone rang. He killed the machine then grabbed the phone. I watched as he looked at me appearing confused then he yelled for our Mistress. The call was for her as usual.

Matthew and I did not receive phone calls often. Our vanilla jobs and service at home kept us both too busy for friends, and other outside acquaintances. Our world was our Mistress and her needs. She, however, enjoyed many civilian relationships. Once or twice a week she would go out on the town with her girlfriends or just to hang out. Matthew and I didn't argue nor were we jealous of it. Mistress Ginger was not monogamous to us. If she had lovers outside our triangle that was not our business. She was the boss, and he and I were just the help.

That is the way it had been with almost all my Keyholders before Mistress Ginger. So, I was used to it. I never had developed territorial expectations of a lover that was mine exclusively. In fact, the very idea made me chuckle. The jealousy over the initial addition of Matthew to the household was my fear I was being replaced, not over the Mistress's affections for one or the other of us. Sometimes, it was better she found attention elsewhere. Loving a Master or Mistress is very time consuming, difficult and at times even painful (thudding, enforced humiliation, tons of labor with no rest). Matthew and I often really appreciated the break when she went out. Besides, we had each other to keep us, uhm, busy.

When she went out that door he and I behaved like children when the parents were out of town. We often did all the things forbidden us while the Mistress was around. Matthew would jump on the bed and roll around on it. I would laugh like hell at him. You see, he never got bed privileges because of the Mistress's continued bitching about his inadequate carnal congress with her.

He and I often pontificated that she was a closet lesbian but refused to admit it. When it came to sex with one of her collars, I was the preferred partner hands down. Hell, poor Matthew wasn't even allowed to touch her unit other than what had to be touched to play stud. That obviously made his attendance to her very hard for him.

I made that up to him by being his true sexual partner in every way possible. He and I had explored every avenue for a couple. Then we re-traveled every road many times. He was truly pansexual like me. He had boyfriends and girlfriends before being collared. Often, we would entertain each other with stories of our failed, and for me forced, sexual exploits with other lovers or whatever those people were.

Because neither of us had borders about gender or what was off limits for our units during sex, our lovemaking was truly no holds barred. That is how he knew what pegging was when I had made the foul statement the day he and I met. Matthew was an expert at lovemaking and a true sexual dynamo with no hang ups about his pleasures.

He even told me the secret of how he learned how to perform oral sex on a woman. As the story went, he oddly learned to do it expertly by the failed exploits of a previous boyfriend of his. The fellow hated giving blowjobs so Matthew learned to give them exceptionally well. His talents, like my own, were then universal since male and female parts are not that much different. Once you have the basics down you are well on your way to mastery of the act. In Matthew and me our Mistress had found the ultimate universal sexual partners.

Believe it or not, Matthew was right. Our Mistress was more vanilla than you know. Mistress Ginger never appreciated or truly employed either Matthew's or my own talents to their limits like she maybe should have. We could have rocked her world but she, like all his and my lovers before, was stuck in a routine of what she liked. Mistress Ginger never explored once. Matthew and I always knew exactly what she wanted and on more than one occasion we caught each other hiding a yawn during our attendance of her needs. The only thing truly deviant about her was her sensual sadistic side, and Matthew never learned a thing about that. That was solely my torture to bear. I would like to add, even that side was predictably blah.

PLEASE NOTE: *Matthew and I had several strict rules that both of us refused to break even at the risk of losing our collars. We both shared the no sex with non-consensual partners. In other words, rape is not okay, no kids, no animals, etcetera. Neither of us would tolerate nasty shit like fooling with blood, vomit, shit, piss, needles, or breath play. We loved sex, not gross stuff. Now I assumed all of you knew that but just in case you are wondering we were not that kind of weird. Just Kama sutra, sex toys or gender bending different. If you don't get that, then again explore your own sexuality and come back to read the above again.*

Now understanding all the above, with my long-term training in the art of carnal congress with both genders and his open minded, adaptable interests in both, we were quite the team. Sometimes, the Mistress would hear us doing our duty and come to watch. She told us seeing the two of us in action was better than going to the circus. Neither Matthew nor I ever figured out if that was a compliment or meant to be derogatory. It didn't matter, neither he nor I ever apologized for our animalistic sexuality, and I still won't even to the day I die. Matthew and I loved to orgasm, and we did what we loved every day for one year and eight months while never really losing steam.

Truth is we were following orders. Not that we minded that directive, but to be honest the Mistress didn't always ask for Matthew's stud favor. Yet, she never told us in advance. So, we engaged in carnal congress everyday just in case. She could have been merciful and given us a day off, but she never did. When you are a submissive, you do what you are told until you are told otherwise. Without indication to do otherwise, we had no real choice. If Matthew failed even once by being a two pump chump she had said he was out. By May), I couldn't fathom not having Matthew in my life. I would have done anything to keep him with me and believe me I did do anything. That is what this entire chapter is about.

Matthew and I were proactive in keeping our Mistress's needs met, no matter what it meant to us as individuals. The results were a wonderful season of peace, harmony and sadly, love. The four-letter word that is a no-no in our world. Soon enough you will see exactly why that was a mistake that to this day I have paid for. I learned my lesson so well, poor Master Jon twenty-five years from this time will suffer for it a bit in the beginning of our relationship. I almost lost my chance at finding happiness when it finally did come this time. So keep reading and ask yourself what could I have done differently to avoid the heartbreak that came from this seemingly glorious time in my life.

Mistress Ginger came into the living room to take the call. She directed Matthew with hand signals to get on all fours and she sat on him like a chair. I just rolled my eyes and went back to washing the dishes. I hated that furniture shit some of the Masters seem to love to do to us submissive collars. It is their right, but really?

I was ignoring her conversation till I heard the name Joyce.

"Oh, of course I would love to Joyce. Wait till you get a load of the fine submissive flesh I have collared now. Oh yes of course I still own Psycho and no she is not for sale. Neither is my latest acquired collar. I would love to show them off. Hey, can you bring some of your finest collars with you? I would like to look over your wares. No, just shopping. Either boy or girl, it doesn't matter. Okay, yeah, see you Saturday. Same place? No, I know where that is. Bye." The Mistress hung up the phone and got off Matthew.

She left the room without addressing either of us. I ran over to my brother. "Shit. Matt she is going to try to get another fucking collar."

He looked at me confused as he stood up. "What? Are you sure? How do you know that? This house isn't big enough for any more of us." He looked around the room.

"Matt, Joyce is a Dominatrix. She has a shit ton of wannabe Kinksters and they are usually just drugged out idiot kids. Not a one of them is the real deal, trust me. What are we going to do?" I was feeling my heart may explode. I couldn't deal with another fighting situation in the house. I had just accepted Matthew.

He had turned out to be the real deal, but he was not soiled by another poor trainer. He was born that way. I already knew Joyce was flush with young girls with daddy issues, and boys who had mommy issues (personality disorders like Mistress Ginger if you need that spelled out). Matthew may have been submissive, but he was not a Borderline Personality Disorder, Histrionic Personality Disorder, or a psychopath. If anything, he could have been a Dependent Personality Disorder, but truth is I never found out and now I never want to know. Whatever his issues they worked. The chances of there being another one of us was none. So, this was bad as it could get. A drugged out or personality disordered idiot in our home could destabilize all that he and I had worked so hard to build. Our Mistress was insane to even consider it or more likely she was addicted to chaos.

Matthew stood there appearing to think over what I had said. "Well, all we can do is wait and see the competition. If she tries to get one, we can create a plan to end that creature. Unless he or she is really good looking."

That statement startled me. "What? Are you serious Matt? Good or bad looking doesn't fucking matter."

He laughed. "Yeah, you are right. As long as they can suck a dick well. I really need someone around that can give a proper blow job."

Now I was pissed. "You asshole. I don't hear you fucking complaining when I give you one. Nor is your dick complaining. It seems to work just fine."

Matthew started laughing hard that he had teased me to anger. "You know practice makes perfect. I seriously think

8

you should practice more than once a day. Let's start the lessons right now in fact."

I realized at that point he was fucking with me as usual. "Hey tell you what, turn back on the vacuum and stick your dick in it. Since I can't suck it well enough for you then find your pleasure elsewhere pussy."

For the record. Matthew loved his blowjobs. It was maybe his favorite thing in life. He was nuts about the act and would bring it up in any conversation he could. Now the reason may have been that the guy was six feet, five inches tall. He was proportional if you catch my drift, so his male part was not only impressive it was downright frightening. Now you know why Mistress Ginger kept him around. Most of his previous lovers would not tackle, forgive that phrase, the task of oral sex with him because of that alone. Therefore, when he found I didn't mind, and could do the job properly, he tended to bug the hell out of me about it. Why did he keep bitching about my ability when even he privately admitted it was a lie? Actually, he was trying to get the Mistress to demand I practice by false complaining about my skills. A dirty trick? Yeah, it was but it never worked. She saw I was capable and despite his many attempts she never took the bait. Didn't mean the sly bastard didn't keep trying to get more than his fair share. He had learned that nasty little trick from me when I got him forced into belly dancing an hour a day. He continually tried to turn the tables on me in payback to get something he desired. Clever but he just wasn't clever enough. Men, hahaha.

9

Matthew got an interested look on his face then turned back on the vacuum appearing to take my advice as he acted as if he was going to stick his dick in the hose. I stepped back in shock. I mean we did weird shit, but this took the cake. I was impressed. However, just as he was almost at the zipper of his jeans, he turned the hose on my breasts sucking up my shirt into it while he laughed.

"Enjoy Matthew's nipple torture, Psycho," he yelled out in glee while forcing the vacuum hose to both breasts.

I smacked the hose off while it made horrid sounds from being plugged up. "You are a fucking idiot." I jumped at him and the wrestling began. I proved to him that the vacuum wasn't any match for my abilities. Hey look, we were just following the Mistress's orders.

Now here is how very weird, as if sitting on a guy like a chair wasn't weird enough an example right, it was in our house. The Mistress heard the commotion of our, uhm, adoration of each other. She came running thinking we were in battle again. She found the battle was not the kind she needed to correct.

"I thought you two were fighting again. Damn, get a room you two," the Mistress said laughing.

Matthew and I were already very engaged in our carnal act, so he looked at her and asked, "Uhm, okay, which one?"

Mistress Ginger shook her head. "Never mind. Just try to be quiet. I want to watch my show." She sat down on the sofa just a few feet from our tangled units and turned on the television.

Matthew looked at me and I at him. We shrugged and kept going. She didn't care, so we certainly didn't. Yeah, that is how it went in that house. As long as the kids weren't around to see the adult games, we did whatever, whenever, wherever without regard for who was there watching. That day the kids were off at Maiden Mary's playing with their little friends. So, the living room next to the sofa and vacuum cleaner was just as good as any other place to mate.

Eventually, Matthew and my moaning, yeah he was a screamer too, and carrying on turned on the Mistress who found our show more interesting than her television. After she saw Matthew was spent, we both got dragged by our collars to her room to perform for her pleasure. In the end, it was a wonderful afternoon with the whole family enjoying each other's company in carnal congress.

NOTE: *Now, I will take a moment to tell all of you a little bit more about the man I called a brother collar, lover and friend. He and I shared many secrets. Matthew asked for my confidence on several subjects about his history and life, and to this day I will honor him by keeping those secrets. He cannot give permission, so I will not betray him. He never once betrayed me. Service for service you know.*

He was college educated in the new technology of computer programing. New at that time in 1995. Matthew loved a variety of subjects, and history was his favorite thing to discuss, and of course human psychology. His

11

favorite music was gothic, heavy metal, anything dark and brooding. He like me was gothic in lifestyle tending to gravitate toward the dark, grotesque and even at times obscene. Black was his favorite color.

When he and I met he was twenty-eight years old, and when we said goodbye, he was just shy of his thirtieth birthday. His relationship with his biological family was a lot like mine in that they never spoke, not much anyway. He was on his own very young, and not from that state or little town. Matthew, like myself, had been displaced from our biological places of origin. His was due to a job, not because of guardianship issues. His only love in his biological family had been his Aunt Maggie who was schizophrenic. She had apparently raised him until she became too sick to handle a child.

I will say that for those of you who wonder what Matthew looked like, I can tell you all this, the late great Peter Steele of Type O negative and he were very similar in build. Matthew resembled him so much he often got misidentified as the fellow until the person got close enough for a good look. He had long hair but his was dirty blond, not black like Peter's. His eyes were deep set and light blue not green and Matthew had a softer face shape in general. Peter's was very square. Other than that, the resemblance was creepily uncanny, and really kind of cruel. For years after the end of the relationship I had to see Peter Steele and be reminded of Matthew. They were not exact doppelganger but close enough to be unsettling, that is for damned sure.

Matthew was intelligent, fair, good hearted, fun loving, good looking, loyal to a fault, and never took himself too seriously. He unfortunately was also very sensitive, anxious, and had a low pain tolerance. This very enigmatic character in my life slowly won my frozen heart over. He never forgot that I am a human just like him that made mistakes. He never made me feel bad for being myself, and I gave him equal respect by never judging him either after I stopped being a bitch when I discovered he wasn't acting or there to displace me.

That is all I will ever say about his background. Due to his request I stay silent about it.

Sadly, the respect we shared began to blossom into the dangerous territory called love over time. Submissive collars must never ever fall in love with another submissive. We can be sold, tossed or traded away. Our units belong to the Mistress or Master and no real relationship can exist between the submissive for those reasons alone.

More than that, a submissive can never totally fulfill the needs of another collar because of their nature to follow someone stronger than themselves. Each submissive has a weakness so destructive they need a powerful Dominate to keep them from failing at life because of it. We trade our freedom of choice for protection from ourselves. The submissive are not free to love anyone. Love between the submissive collars is often a deadly disaster waiting to happen.

Yes, I know the name of the demon that forced Matthew into that collar, but I am not willing to share it for reasons stated above. That is for all of you to decide from his story. I will never divulge it just like I promised him the day he told me more than twenty-five years ago. I will only say the collar for him was like it is for me, a necessity. His issue was valid and just as deadly as my own.

I had taught him those lessons in our first months of training. It was truly tragic that both of us forgot our hearts were not our own to give. I am not a submissive. I am a schizophrenic with a delusion..

That Saturday the Mistress commanded Matthew and I to put on the clothing she had laid out on her bed for us. We both groaned when we saw them. Mine the same fully unzippable black cat suit that barely fit my unit. Matthew had a black mesh see through shirt and his black latex pants were so tight I almost had to get out the Crisco to help him get them on. His sexual organ and mine were outlined leaving nothing much to the imagination. She had red cuffs laid out for both of us too. That made me breathe a sigh of relief. Those cuffs meant she was warning Joyce that Matt and I were not up for grabs and belonged to her. I explained it to him, and he sighed gratefully too. We always were afraid she would ditch us.

He looked at me laughing and I did the same after we got our outfits on fully. We taunted each other about how horrid we appeared in our obnoxious outfits. Matthew said we should just have painted ourselves black with a satin based house paint. It would have been easier than trying to get those tight outfits on. I had to agree with him on that.

Matthew watched as I put on my makeup. "Psycho, can you put that make up on me too," his reflection asked.

I looked up stunned. "Are you fucking with me Matt? Makeup? Really?"

He nodded. "Why not? I love the look. I am a submissive like you. Everyone is going to be staring at my stupid ass anyway. May as well give them something to look at."

I laughed but nodded motioning him to come sit in front of me. It took only half an hour but when I was done he looked amazing. Matthew admired his new look asking if I could train him to do it himself. I agreed to do so and indeed from that day forward when he was not at work, he wore his own pale face and black-eyed look. The handsome Matthew was even more stunning.

To this day I never can say why he started to wear the makeup. He never told me. Maybe he felt like me, it was a way to warn the normals to stay away. We were not like them nor could we tolerate them well.

When the two of us walked down the hallway to follow the Mistress to the car, she almost died laughing at her painted submissive pair. Now, Matthew and I did appear to be related. Only our size difference and gender appeared different.

Mistress Ginger yapped the entire trip to meet with Joyce about how much we appeared cut from the same cloth. I think Matthew was very proud of her pointing that out. I too was grateful to know she approved. I wanted Matthew to be as happy as possible given our station in life. If a little makeup made him feel better in his skin, awesome. If the Mistress was going to permit it, even better. She did in fact grant him the right to wear it. Despite our destination that little kindness made our moods lighter.

Of course anything that made heads turn and tongues wag, our Mistress was happy to permit. Big ass Matthew wearing white makeup and his little sister wearing the same look would certainly do just that. It caused a minor stir before we got to the restaurant to meet with Joyce. People could see into our car at stop lights.

Several carloads of folks were laughing, pointing, screaming, yea they did, and freaking out when they saw the two ghoulish looking subs in black sitting together in the backseat. It happened every time we were stuck at an intersection for more than a second.

Mistress Ginger was in heaven. Normally she would have had Matt or I drive but today she wanted to make sure her submissive siblings were displayed together like evil twins. It had worked better than she had hoped. She loved all the attention we were drawing.

Matthew shot me a we won her approval look. I smiled and nodded back. If all it took to make our Mistress happy was silly pony tricks, Matthew and I were totally up for it.

I tried to ignore the feeling of anxiety growing in the pit of my stomach as we approached the parking lot of the chosen restaurant. This was a different one than the one the Mistress and I had met Joyce at before but still far to swanky for our dressing style. I also worried that Christopher would be there. I was in no hurry to ever run into that idiot again. More than that, I hated to be anywhere around Joyce who had on more than one occasion tried to purchase my collar from Mistress Ginger. My deepest fear (and Matts too, was that Mistress Ginger would sell us to this old harpy.

Matthew reached out his hand and took mine while Mistress Ginger parked. He squeezed it while looking at me silently mouthing, "It's gonna be okay I got you."

I had told him about the Christopher ordered rape and about Joyce calling our kind 'it.' I cannot tell you how much Matthew's tiny gesture of kindness meant that day. In my chest I felt that odd feeling of sickness that sometimes I felt lately whenever I thought about Matthew.

At first, I thought it was my old heart issue acting up. When it got stronger, but I didn't have the heart attack I expected, I thought maybe it was heartburn. That day before meeting with Joyce after Matt did that, I realized with terror. I was falling in love with my brother.

That possibility simply was unacceptable. I made a mental note to stop acting like a child. He was just another stupid submissive like me. It was pure silliness to get all moon eyed over this big moose. He was such a pussy he couldn't even take a little thud.

Yet, the evidence was starting to mount up. I had deflected the Mistress from thudding him the day of Ostara when I got home. I was engaging in mock battles to save our collars. I was fucking him, happily I have to add, daily and starting to really enjoy it. I was such an idiot I had taken the position of house thudder to spare him the torture. Yeah, I was more than falling in love. I was in love with Matthew, damn me.

Worse still he was very obviously in love with me too. We were both idiots. I decided to have a stern talk with him later when we were alone. Matthew and I were forbidden to have that kind of love for each other. It was dangerous and sure to lead to big trouble for both of us down the line. I was sure he would understand, and once we applied corrections, we could fix this growing problem. *So, did I ever tell you how out of touch with reality I am? Sheesh, what a bonehead I am.*

Mistress Ginger waited while I got out and let her out of the car. She got out and told us both to kneel. We did as commanded while she reached into her purse taking out two chain walking leashes. I could hear Matthew gasping as she clicked one end to each of our collars, then told us to follow in high protocol until we got back in the car.

I nodded, "As you wish Mistress. Matthew follow my lead, brother."

He nodded looking at me with the face of a scared child. He had not expected to be humiliated in public by being forced to walk on a leash behind Mistress Ginger like a puppy dog. This was his first real outing with the overly dramatic, histrionic Mistress. He was about to get a real lesson in psychological pain that day. Submissive collars are not viewed as anything more than property by their Dominates. Matthew never could deal with that fact any more than he could handle a thudding. He simply had way too much pride in him. This was going to be one super painful dinner date for my dear brother.

We followed behind Mistress Ginger three paces. I was on the left and Matthew on the right. The hostess at this eatery almost fainted when she saw our horror show walk through the door. I am sure she wished she had called in sick that night. However, like a good employee, she just motioned us to follow her through the very packed dinner hall. Everyone gasped, dropped forks, and a few 'oh my lord' exclamations, followed us as we followed our very satisfied Mistress to the back rooms.

NOTE: *Now for a quick explanation. When BDSM people meet for meals like this one to discuss subs/slaves/and other lifestyler shit, it is often called a Munch. Joyce was the Dowager Dominatrix of the area so she would call other Dominants and set up these kinds of dinner business meetings on a monthly basis. They were always held in private back rooms with doors closed and pulled shades to keep out the prying eyes of the vanilla public. You'll see why that matters in a moment.*

Usually Mistress Ginger went to them alone. She only would drag us in is when she was showing off. The reason she wasn't showing us off every month was very obvious.

Most of the time either no one would show up or she didn't want her submissive pair to be pawed at by other Dominants.

While that kind of behavior is bad manners, the Dominants in the area were untrained, unmannered and honestly only wannabes. Only Joyce was the real deal like Mistress Ginger and the dumbass Christopher. So, to keep down the possibility of trouble she left Matthew and I at home safely tucked away.

Our being brought to this one made me incredibly suspicious that something big was going on. I assumed Mistress Ginger was up to no good. Buying another collar would not require our presence. Her red cuffs on my brother and I made me feel a bit safer, but I knew Mistress Ginger too well. She would trade one or both of us if she were offered a good deal. Thankfully, Matthew and I were such good quality submissive that most couldn't afford us. It also was not likely any could offer better. Still, I was most uncomfortable with this situation.

I stole a look at Matthew. He was walking with his sight toward the floor trying to block out all the horrified murmuring of the other restaurant guests. Matthew was very shy, introverted and this kind of public display was setting off his anxiety big time. Even at the risk of punishment, I reached out and took his hand. He looked at me with fear in his eyes.

I smiled while I squeezed his hand mouthing, 'It will be okay. I got you.'

He smiled back seeming to relax that I had repeated his promise from the car. We could do this together. Matthew now could be assured he was never alone. I let his hand go quickly. Luckily, that little display of affection was not caught. It literally would have been my ass had I gotten caught. See there I go again, love damn it.

We were led inside the back room. The hostess closed the door behind us, practically running away to be shut of this odd trio. I stole a glance up to see only Joyce and a skinny, young girl of maybe twenty sitting with her. The young girl had back short hair and sores all over her face. The thin child also had very obvious track marks on her arms. She was wearing a plastic cat collar with a bell around her neck. I almost choked realizing this was the so-called collar for sale that Joyce brought to the party.

I also noted that this thing was sitting next to Joyce and looking at the menu. She was even looking directly at the old hag and I heard her demand an alcoholic beverage. Oh boy, this little bitch was as much a submissive as our Mistress Ginger was in her little toe. I looked back at the ground already planning to destroy this druggy if the Mistress even considered bringing her insolent ass into our home.

I went ahead of the Mistress to pull out her chair, place her napkin and Matthew poured her water from the pitcher on the table. Mistress Ginger put our leash handles on her wrist that corresponded to our direction, then sat down. He and I backed up to our spots, arms behind our backs, heads down, waiting silently for further instructions.

The little cat girl gasped, "Oh man, that was some cool shit."

I could see Matthew hold his breath from my peripheral vision. I too was stifling a giggle. This little street rat was not only drugged out of her mind, but she was also really ignorant too.

Joyce reached over and pushed the girl back into her seat. She had been leaning on the table. "Enough of that jibber jabbering, Kaylee. This is Mistress Ginger. Say hello to her please."

Kaylee looked at our Mistress then reached out her hand to shake.

I immediately blocked the Mistress with my unit slapping Kaylee's hand away. "Insolent pig, keep your hands off the Mistress." I stood there fire in my eyes as Kaylee backed away in fear.

Joyce's face lit up like a Christmas tree. "Ah, Ginger you are right, she is well trained indeed. Kaylee this a head submissive. You would do well to watch her actions. She has well over fifteen years of experience."

Kaylee looked at Joyce. "She is scary looking and mean as hell. What is her fucking damage?"

Mistress Ginger hand gestured me to return to my submissive stance. I did as she ordered. Joyce again lit up watching the well-oiled team versus her very disobedient little shit.

The Mistress than cleared her throat. "Joyce, I appreciate your property, but could you ask Kaylee to either leave or shut her fucking mouth? I don't like her upsetting my submissive pair. I didn't come here to be fondled by the likes of an untrained little girl."

Joyce nodded. "Kaylee, leave and go home. You are not required any longer."

Kaylee looked at Joyce. "I haven't eaten yet. Damn, I thought I was getting some food at least."

Mistress Ginger stood up. I pulled back her chair. "Joyce, I am not kidding. Get this brat out of here. Matthew is still training and this bad behavior is a bad influence on him. If you don't move her ass, we shall leave."

Joyce grabbed the girl who started yelling, "Hey, stop it." Joyce pulled her to the door. She opened it and pushed her out. Kaylee had the audacity to turn around and stick out her tongue at Joyce, then stormed off to the front. Joyce returned appearing truly embarrassed by this piece of trash. Mistress Ginger sat back down, while I re-adjusted her to her proper status for eating.

"See that is why I need that head submissive of yours, Ginger. I have a ton of these little shits, all needing to be trained up right. When are you going to settle on a price for her collar," Joyce said while sitting down.

I almost choked and I heard Matthew suck in air too. Joyce had said settle on a price. That could only mean Mistress Ginger was toying with the idea of selling this bitch my collar. I wanted to strangle my red-headed Mistress. I had done nothing to deserve such indignity. What the fuck was she thinking. Then it occurred to me that maybe she really had collared Matthew to replace me once he was fully trained. I closed my eyes now terrified my days were numbered.

Mistress Ginger took a sip of water. "I told you Joyce, Psycho and Matthew are not for sale. Not now and not ever. I am loving having these two beauties. I mean just look at them. Well trained, easy going and beautiful. You are just jealous you can't do better than that thing you just called a submissive. Ha! I would have spilt that girl's gullet rather than stand for her to speak to me like that." She smoothed out her red cat suit as if unaffected if Joyce got mad at her very truthful statement.

Matthew and I let out a breath of relief hearing that we were not up for sale. I was sure that Matthew was feeling less upset over the leash now that he realized his head could be on the block anytime. Public humiliation was part of the territory if he was ever going to learn to be a fully trained submissive. He'd just have to get used to it.

Joyce and Mistress Ginger then began to discuss Matthew in some detail. I watched him carefully not to be caught keeping my eye on him. He was shifting nervously. The ladies were discussing his studding abilities, and other personal things that really was not very flattering to poor Matthew, such as his poor oral sex skills. Again that was bullshit but the Mistress didn't know that. I could see that Matthew was getting agitated. I was rocked and ready if I

24

needed to correct my brother if and when he made any stupid moves. Luckily, I had trained him well. He took the insults, the embarrassment and cruel discussion without flinching. I was damned grateful too. I didn't want to have to thump him where that old dust bag could see it.

Then Joyce did the ultimate no-no. She got up and approached Matthew. Looking his unit up and down she began to paw at his thighs and reached out and felt of his penis. Matthew began to pull away gasping.

Mistress Ginger felt his leash pull. "Matthew, let Joyce have a better look at you, damn it. You are embarrassing me."

I wanted to smack the Mistress in the head. This was improper. No Dominant can touch another's collared property like that. What the fuck was Mistress Ginger doing. Joyce didn't ask permission. She just took it upon herself to examine Matthew. Protect and defend, bitch.

However, I was not allowed to correct my Mistress in front of another Dominant. So, all I could do is watch the frightened Matthew who continued to wiggle and pull away from the claws of that nasty hussy trying to feel him up. Yuck. Poor Matthew, I did pity him but then again I was about to pity myself.

Joyce became irritated that Matthew wasn't just holding still for her to poke and prod him as she pleased. "Ginger this submissive is not completely trained," as if she had the right to talk given her example in Kaylee.

Mistress Ginger growled. "Matthew, watch your sister. Follow her example. You understand?" She looked at me., "Allow Joyce to examine you Psycho."

I nodded feeling immediately sick to my stomach. Joyce smiled at that then approached my unit. I held still with my arms behind my back as she grabbed my crotch through the cat suit harshly. She then unzipped my outfit and bared my breasts smiling while fondling them and roughing up my nipples to see if my parts responded correctly.

She told me to turn and spread my legs. I did as commanded and she slapped my ass hard. I winced but didn't respond nor look up at her. Joyce felt down both thighs and again grabbed my female organ but this time by reaching inside my clothing inserting her old nasty finger into me. I held deathly still wishing I had the power to strike her down with lightening.

I could sense the tension in Matthew as he watched this vulgar display made by Joyce. She was doing what they call a confirmation check. This is done when a Dominant is thinking of purchasing or trading for a collar. The potential Dominant will get a chance to look over the submissive and make sure all parts work, are real (no wooden legs) and no secrets are being hidden by clothing. I was lucky Joyce didn't strip me completely. Instead she only groped and fondled appearing to enjoy her bullshit a great deal. Now you know why back room with closed curtains are used for these meetings. Told you I would get to it.

I was not only irritated that Mistress Ginger was allowing this to happen but wondering what she was thinking. A confirmation check is only granted to potentials. I again worried that the Mistress was about to toss my collar to this old cunt. Or maybe she was planning to ditch Matthew. The terror within began to grow as the bitty continued to rough up my unit pulling and pinching as if I were a melon at the supermarket. I held still never looking up and only moved my arms when Joyce told me to reach up or out so she could check my range of motion. After a bit more of this humiliation she appeared satisfied I was the real deal and a healthy submissive.

She went by Matthew but didn't attempt to fondle him again. She also didn't replace my now exposed breasts or zip back up my outfit. What a lazy bitch. Mistress Ginger looked at me to see my unit in disarray.

"Adjust yourself Psycho," she said then went back to her discussion with Joyce while I quickly put all my part back into hiding.

Joyce sat down then looked at Mistress Ginger hard,. "The male is well endowed and would bring a good price despite his issues. That stuff can be taught. The female, on the other hand, I want. She is also well endowed, young, smart and I have plenty of kinksters that would love to have her on a leash for an hour or two. I think she could bring in good money until those looks fade. Then I could have her train others. She'd be worth a good sum of cash if you would just name your price, Ginger. I am sure I could make the money back off her in no time."

Matthew looked up at me in terror as he heard Joyce basically say she wanted to buy my collar to whore me out until worn down, then force me into training other poor females to do the same. This was always a possibility when you are a submissive, however, you do have the right to say no. I looked at him angrily motioning him to put his head back down. He had to learn his place.

I was not a child, novice nor a submissive to be fucked with. Mistress Ginger knew that. I was not worried when I heard that bullshit. Why? Mistress Ginger knew if she tried to sell me to Joyce who really thought I was just a slave like that I would kick her and Joyce's ass right to Hades. I waited to see if the Mistress was going to correct this error or if I would need to correct my Mistress later.

Mistress Ginger looked at me. "Joyce you are mistaken. Psycho is not a slave. She is a service for service submissive. You would play hell to get that one to do your bidding. Best you drop your bid for her collar. Psycho would eat you for dinner and Kaylee for dessert. Then she would likely use me for a toothpick. Matthew is the gentle one. Psycho, she is hell on wheels."

Joyce looked at me in surprise. "I thought you said she is trained? She has demonstrated extraordinary manners and protocol. You are kidding me, Ginger. I don't enjoy that kind of humor."

Mistress Ginger chuckled. "I am not kidding, Joyce. Psycho was trained in a rogue house since she was just a little girl, I told you that. What I never told you is she was not trained as a submissive. She was trained to be a Dominate by a sexual sadist. You can say it is in her blood. She can be beyond cruel and heartless when she sets her mind to it. Shit, she is better trained than you or me. I bet she has forgotten more about torture than either of us ever knew."

Matthew looked up in shock as did Joyce when the Mistress said those words. I wanted to kill the bitch spouting all that shit about me. I was no Dominate or a sexual sadist, nor had I taken the steps to get behind the whip. That statement, while true, was unfair. I had given up my beloved Scruffy and my mind to prevent those things. How dare she?

Joyce smiled. "Oh I have to have that collar, Ginger. I would make her into an amazing Dominatrix. She could be my own heir apparent. Look, you want to go back to California. I can make that happen. I will take the pair off your hands. Just think, you can go home, and I can use these two to regain my own house. It would be a great end for both of us."

Mistress Ginger laughed. "No way, Joyce. I told you I don't want Psycho pissed at me. You should see what she did to the last Mistresses who got on her bad side. I am damned lucky she keeps that collar on. If she ever took it off, she may burn down the whole fucking town to feed that sadistic side of hers. Joyce, just drop it. I only wanted to show off a little, but you are likely upsetting my siblings. I think maybe it is time to go home before I end up with a silt throat and the house burning down around my head."

I stood there fuming about those lies she was spinning. I never hurt anyone who didn't have it fucking coming. Equal service for equal service is not sadism. Grrr, I wondered if now Matthew would maybe not love me anymore since he heard about my wicked little secrets. I started to worry he would turn away. Eh, wait, what was I doing. I was worried that Matthew the pussy wouldn't love me anymore. Oh shit, I had it real bad for him. This had to stop. I did my best to get ahold of my stupid feminine wiles. I really needed to cool it. Matthew and I could never be. What the fuck was I thinking. Goddess help me.

Mistress Ginger stood then jerked our leashes demanding we follow her out. We did as commanded, but I did notice that Matthew almost stumbled several times trying to steal glances at me as we left the stupid old lady behind us. I wanted so badly to kill both those bitches right there.

The ride home was quiet except for the Mistress giving Matthew a warning about minding her when she says to hold still. She also told me I did a fine job allowing the old bat to look over my unit. Matthew was told yet again to keep his eyes on his sister to learn proper protocols for future outings.

He just nodded appearing upset. I felt my chest getting heavy. I was sure he hated me now that he knew I was trained to be like Mistress Ginger, only even meaner and more twisted. I wondered if he was thinking about our daily carnal congress and wondering if any of my aggressiveness was due to my previous training.

Seriously, I felt I may just die from heartbreak. It had to be that way; I knew that. I couldn't ever be with Matthew and honestly should never have been with him. It was not only irregular for submissive pairs to have sex with each other, it was bad manners and poor protocol. No matter what the Dominants try to say, they know we are humans too. Sex always gets the heart involved. Since relationships among submissives is forbidden, you shouldn't allow it to ever happen. At the very least, you don't order daily sexual congress with two house subs for sure. You are asking for this kind of trouble. Matthew and I were not any stronger than any other person. If we had constant intimacy, we were bound to fall for each other sooner or later. That is human instinct and natural law.

Once we got home the Mistress dropped us both off and headed back out to meet with a friend. He and I walked inside together silently. He turned on the light then sat down on the sofa appearing deep in thought. I decided to just clear this air, finish this bullshit and be done with it.

"Okay brother, what is on your mind." I sat down in the floor cross legged across from him while sighing.

He shook his head. "The way that woman treated you and me. The leashes, Psycho. They treat us like animals. How is that okay?"

I let out a sigh of relief. He was upset by the confirmation check not by the news of my upbringing.

"Some Masters and Mistresses don't see us as anything but property. Honestly brother, we are their property. I thought you understood all that. We talked about this. However, Joyce did show very bad manners tonight. A Dominant worth her salt would have corrected Joyce touching you without permission." I leaned back on my hands.

Matthew nodded. "You know Mistress Ginger will sell us eventually, right? I don't think I can handle that Psycho. I am not like you. It would kill me to never see her or you again. I couldn't stand having to kneel for that monster woman tonight. Can you imagine how awful it would be to have to attend to some old hairy woman?"

I looked at the floor upset at that statement. I didn't have to imagine it. It had happened to me more than once already. Matthew suddenly realized his mistake. "Oh Psycho, I am sorry. I forgot. Look, you are a trained Dominant. Can't you just be a Mistress yourself and cut bitches like Joyce down? Mistress Ginger says you could if you really wanted to."

I frowned. "Mistress Ginger exaggerated, Matthew. I have schizophrenia remember. She is right. I am not a submissive, but I am not a Dominant either. I am mentally ill. I must play submissive or I will not survive. We discussed this. That training I got was all submissive stuff. I never took up the other side or finished my training as a Dominant. So, please can we drop that idea?"

Matthew looked at his hands appearing pensive. "But what if you had the right submissive? One that could help you and you could help them. You could be the Dominant then right? I mean if you had to be?"

I suddenly realized why he was asking this question. "Matthew, we need to talk about our relationship. I think it may be getting out of hand."

He nodded. "It is. It always has been out of hand. Psycho, I can love two women at the same time. There is nothing in any books that say I can't. I love you and I love Mistress Ginger. I need you both and I think you both need me too. That is why this house is so happy."

I nodded. "Yeah, I adore you and Mistress Ginger too. That is possible, but I need to know you are not falling romantically in love with me. That will never work you know. I told you why." I held my breath waiting for his answer.

Matthew looked up at me. "Do you want me to lie? What is the difference between romantic love and submissive love for a sister? I think about you all the time. I want to be with you. I see you in my dreams, at work, everywhere I go. I could not imagine my life without you by my side. Is that the thing you are worried about, Psycho? Because if it is, I am screwed. I do love you like that. Why should that be forbidden? We are a submissive pair, siblings, and now lovers too. Even if it was against our will, we are lovers. Look at me and tell me I am wrong. I have tried to stop but I cannot."

I couldn't look at him. "No Matthew, we can't be lovers like that. We have sex to spend you for the Mistress, which is all."

He got up then walked over grabbing me by my waist. He leaned down kissing me deeply pushing me to the floor. I tried to stop his kissing, but I didn't want to, Goddess help me, so I was unsuccessful. He straddled my unit careful not to put his weight on me.

Then when he let go his kiss he looked me deep into my eyes. "Tell me you don't love me, Psycho. Tell me it is just sex to spend me for the Mistress. Let me hear you say it and I will believe you and stop loving you. I can't take not knowing anymore. Are you really just fucking me without feeling my heart?"

I felt I was coming apart. I couldn't speak as my throat closed. His eyes burned through my soul, searching for the answer that I had tried to hide so deeply even though I was unaware. I had denied Greg, Boyd, Mike, Linda, and Roary. I refused to get involved with any of them. I belonged to the collar and Key. I was not free to love someone outside of my delusion.

Yet, I looked at Matthew, my handsome brother collar. His heart so much like my own. I felt my chest aching so bad I hoped it was a heart attack. The emotions that I was sure Simon held flowed up to my eyes as tears began to well. I did love Matthew more than anything in the world. He was all I ever wanted; all I would ever need. He was my world. I was wishing I could just die because of my stupid mistake of loving one who could never save me from me. Matthew was the wrong match. He needed a Keyholder too. I was helpless against what was forbidden and all because Mistress Ginger didn't think before she forced us to become lovers. She had again failed to protect and defend me as she had promised.

Matthew leaned down and kissed my eyes tasting my tears. "You do love me. I can see it, taste it, feel it, sense it. I knew it the day you sacrificed yourself to the Mistress to protect me from her whippings. I am not wrong. I need to hear you say it, Psycho. Please end my pain. I need to know the truth."

I nodded. "Yes Matthew, I do love you. I am so sorry, please forgive me brother. I tried not to. It was an accident." I looked away damned ashamed for the first time in my whole rotten life.

Matthew was surely doomed now, and so was I. We could never be together. Neither of us would survive.

He smiled with his own tears beginning to well. "I know what you are thinking. This can never be. I have thought that too. I have been thinking we can be together Psycho. All we must do is make sure Mistress Ginger never lets us go. If we always stay together as a family, we can love each other romantically. I would die for Mistress Ginger, and I would die for you Psycho."

Matthew started kissing me again rubbing his hands over my unit, then very slowly undressed me. We copulated but this time it was not wild, aggressive, or experimental. It was slow, gentle and very loving. He took his time as we kissed and touched each other the way a groom and bride would on their first night together.

NOTE: *For a moment in time, I forgot I was Psycho. I forgot he was my brother collar. I ignored my horrid history, the shock of his touch, the ravages of my disease and the foulness of our position in life. I felt his emotion of pure love fill me instead of his unit's parts. I finally knew what it was like to make love. I had my very first experience with it at the age of twenty-four with a fellow submissive whose amour was forbidden and punishable by a type of death. If Mistress Ginger found out, she would sell us away or toss our collars. Either way, Matthew and I believed we could no longer live without each other or without Mistress Ginger.*

The trap had been set. Our destruction was assured. All because we dared to want what we had forfeited the day we gave up our freedom to a circle of silver around our necks: the choice in who we could love. Our hearts were not ours to give, but we stole them back on the floor that night and promised each other what it was not ours to give. We both understood that a clock was now ticking, and eventually our time would run out. Part of me wishes I had slapped him and lied about my feelings. Part of me knows it was his only chance at happiness, and at the time I thought mine too. Matthew and I would be together through thick and thin for the next year and three months in one epic secret love affair. Do remember sex is not always because you love the person. Matthew and I had to hide our true feelings despite our ordered daily sexual congress. That was going to be difficult to do, but believe it or not, Mistress Ginger never found out. If she had, then the story of Matthew would be shorter than it already is.

No, that is not what ended this story, not the way you think anyway, but it did play a part, nonetheless. Sadly, we get ahead of ourselves. Back to the happier times.

Since I was already married (yeah still legally married to the asshole Timmy until 2004) and because Matthew was also a submissive we never would be capable of marriage even if I had legal right. He and I didn't have the psychological ability.

So, after our lovemaking, Matthew gave me his ring and I gave him my ankh. We went outside and under the night sky swore our undying love to each other while we held each other tight. Matthew and I promised to never love another of our kind again. We would be faithful for life, a monogamous submissive pair forever. That was the best we could offer each other. Our lifestyle would prevent us from saying no to a Master or Mistress, but we did have the right to say no to another sub. To this day, I have kept that vow and Matthew did too. Matthew never betrayed me, and I will never betray him. Equal service for equal service. He understood that like no other before him and only one after him ever granted me that mercy.

That night the Mistress came home to find us working on chores as if nothing had happened. She didn't suspect a thing. However, she brought a surprise home with her, Kaylee.

Uh oh. Shit, what is that meth head doing with our Mistress. Matthew and I had better start working fast before the damned fleas jump off this stray cat onto our carpet. Yikes.

Note: Matthew deserves to be treated with respect; I am going to give it to him by telling my secret (just did) that I held for all these years. I never have spoken of him, and soon I will tell the reasons. I believe you will all agree I did the right thing keeping him all for myself all this time.

Now that I have found Master Jon, it is okay to finally let him go. I can now smile when I think of my foolish youthful antics and of my poor Matthew. Master Jon is aware of this whole story and gives his blessing for me to tell it in the entirety so you can all just enjoy the great stories of one insane, beautiful moment in an otherwise horrid existence.

I will go ahead and tell you so you can all prepare yourself for it. I will grant you the mercy I did not have. Matthew died of suicide in August 1996. Mistress Ginger's reign ends in October of the same year. How he died, why he died and the circumstances that led to his untimely demise will be discussed. You will be most unhappy to know the truth of it, I did not find out all of it until after the Mistress had sold me off.

I will also tell you he didn't tell me he was going to do it. He didn't tell me he found out he was being sold off. If I had known, maybe I could have helped him. I also was not with him when he died but was the last person, he saw in this life. My last words to him were I love you, come home soon. I will be waiting and missing you every second you are gone.

I can also tell you he also wasn't being sold because Mistress Ginger found out about us. She never knew. She tired of her family. We just were never enough for her. She had already sold me off too, I just didn't know it. It wasn't to the same house as my brother collar. Matthew once told me he was not as strong as me. He couldn't live with the life of constant stress of being sold or tossed from home to home, but he couldn't give up his collar either. In a no-win situation, with his family being ripped apart, I do understand why he chose to do what he did. I respect his decision because I have as usual no choice.

His death nearly took me to the grave with him, and had it not been for the children, well this story would never have been told. I am telling this partial ending now while I am strong enough to admit it.

I will have to tell all of you the exact situation, the way it happened, and what the aftermath was. However, just admitting it now had relieved a great burden from my heart. I didn't blame myself for his death. I blame the one who did cause it, Mistress Ginger.

Once you hear the whole story you will see I am right. She didn't have to break us all apart, we did nothing wrong except love the wrong Mistress too much and believe in fantasies that she loved us back. In the end, Matthew paid with his life. I paid with my heart broken so deeply, I never loved again until Master Jon and he had to fight hard to get it. Master Jon is a Dominant. So, I kept my word to Matthew, and trust me, I never break a promise.

Chapter 35: The Summer of Love and Fall of Loyalty: 1995
Mistress Ginger and submissive Matthew

Mistress Ginger is shaking things up around the house. She is feeling bored again. Matthew and Psycho will have to design new and amazing ways to delight their Mistress and engage her interests. On the surface, the two appear barely able to stand each other, but behind closed doors forbidden love has blossomed. Secrets are a part of their dark world. The submissive pair know the game they play is dangerous. However, when it comes to taboos both are well trained. Yet, keeping the truth from sight is not exclusively Matthew and Psycho's domain. Mistress Ginger is also not what she seems to be.

Ready to close the shades and listen to another rumor on the wind? Ah, then lean in closer, closer, now remember to whisper. We can't let the Mistress hear what we really feel. If she knew, the punishment would be worse than a thudding. Now, try to pay attention because I can only tell you this one time. If you miss any of this call for help, errrr, romantic tale you won't get there in time to save the Prince of our heart. These things can never be repeated sadly. That is because in our world there are no second chances.

"Are you sure about this Psycho? I mean lately I have been wondering if Mistress Ginger really loves us like she says she does. I mean, if she did, why does she keep on trying to bring in new collars every damned time we turn around? Have you ever thought maybe we will never be

enough   for   her   no   matter   what   we   do?"
**---Matthew to Psycho when discussing the Loyalty Dog
– September 1995**

Matthew's mouth had dropped further to the floor than my own as he stood there staring in disbelief at Kaylee standing behind our Mistress. The dumb girl was peeking around Mistress Ginger's back as if engaged in a childhood game. I saw this intruder and immediately left my sink of dishes to demand explanation. I walked past my beloved Matthew marching right up to the Mistress.

"I need to speak with you immediately, Mistress," I said glaring at the red head who had a very sheepish look on her pretty face.

"Oh? What about Psycho? I wanted to introduce you both to your newest probable collar Kaylee, so can you just make this quick please?"

I shook my head growling. "No I will not, Mistress. I need to have audience with you alone. I don't believe that protocol would dictate I have this particular discussion in front of my junior and this thing." I was using my position as household head submissive to demand my Mistress grant me my privileges.

The head submissive has the right to politely demand to be seen privately by the Master of the house when there is an extreme issue with lesser level or submissive collars in training. Mistress Ginger could ignore my calling her out but to do so would allow me the right to correct her bad behavior later. She knew better than to fool with me. I knew protocol

41

better than she ever did. I was far better trained in both her and my own position. The Mistress also knew I tend to live true to my service for service clause. Not smart to make me angry you know.

She blew out her breathe. "Okay Psycho. Let's go to the bedroom. Matthew make Kaylee at home. I want to test her out when I am done with this drivel your sister is pushing on me. Have her strip down."

Matthew appearing horrified. "As you wish, Mistress."

He looked immediately at the needle tracks on this scuzzy wannabe's arms. He was thinking what I was thinking, HIV, HEP C and other nasty disease. This is a threat to our home and our lives. Matthew and I had STD tests done every six months without fail. I had been doing that for years. It is the usual life of a submissive to prove you are without disease. Matthew always wore a condom when with Mistress Ginger due to her refusal to take birth control, and of course for extra protection from her catty ways. He did not have to use such protections with me, however. I was sterilized and since he and I were exclusive to the household, no need to worry about catching bugs from each other. Kaylee was not producing her clean STD testing I noted. This was unacceptable.

Mistress Ginger headed back to the bedroom.

I started to follow but went up to Matthew. "Hold that bitch. Don't undress her. I don't give two fucks what the Mistress ordered. That trash is out of here. Whatever happens play along." I whispered in his ear.

He nodded.

I went after the Mistress, entering then closing her door. "Just what the fuck are you doing, Mistress? This thing has track marks on her arms, is a little shit and ugly as sasquatch's foot to boot. You shame yourself and this house allowing that foul thing through the door. Furthermore, you allowed that bitch Joyce to touch your property without asking, and for fuck's sake she stuck her nasty fingers in my twat. Are you drunk?"

Mistress Ginger glared at me then ran across the room backhanding me with all her might. "How dare you question my judgement. Matthew was a mess too when he first came. Now look at him. You can train this one too. I want her and that is final."

I tasted the blood in my mouth then suddenly figured out what to do. "You want that? Why? Because you feel like slumming. I suppose I shouldn't be surprised Mistress. You always had a need to punish yourself. Tell you what. Get over there, I will tie you up and use the crop on that milk white ass of yours. I can make it as red as your hair, baby. Then maybe you will no longer feel the need to kill that emptiness inside you. I know just how to fill it," I said laughing in a mocking voice.

She was beyond livid. Mistress Ginger reared back and hit me with all her might busting my lip in two, sending blood spurting all over her face. Rivers began to roll down my chin.

"You insolent bitch. Get out. Send Kaylee in now. You will wait till I am done with her, then return for a thudding, the shock collar, and maybe even the fucking vampire gloves, asshole. Who the fuck to you think you are?" She was screaming red in the face clearly beyond controlling her anger.

I smiled allowing the bloody gore to pour freely. "Who do I think I am? Why Mistress, have you forgotten who I am? I am the Devil's Daughter. I will be back shortly for our date." I blew a sanguine kiss at her leaving the room closing the door behind me.

I tore off my wig then reached up and dug my fingernails into both sides of my head ripping the flesh with all the force required to make it bleed well. Then I did the same to the top of my noggin. I now looked like a bleeding, hardboiled egg with deep crisscrossed thick scaring and streams of crimson everywhere.

I rubbed my eyes until they began to water then ran down the hallway into the living room appearing to be afraid and crying.

Matthew and Kaylee were still standing where I had left them. Likely they had heard the fighting. When I came fleeing around the corner of the hallway the girl backed toward the door horrified at the sight of my condition. Matthew knew I was bald, but this girl had no idea. I was about to use that to my advantage.

"Oh dear Matthew, help me. The Mistress has cut off all my hair again." I dramatically fell into his arms as if in much pain and terror.

Kaylee backed closer to the door. "Oh my God! Ginger did that to you?"

Matthew looked up from my fake weeping unit in his arms at Kaylee. "The Mistress doesn't like to be talked back to. Psycho has been punished like she deserved to be. You can go ahead and strip now. I think that Mistress Ginger will still be pretty angry. As long as you keep your mouth shut, she likely will only pull out your pubes this time. It hurts but it keeps it from growing back too fast. The Mistress likes a clean-shaven pussy and a smooth bald head."

That was all Matthew had to say. Kaylee opened the door and ran out without saying goodbye. He and I went to watch as the girl took off down the street headed for wherever. She had decided not to submit to our household after all. Too bad. I am sure the Mistress would have been happy to keep the stupid bitch. Too bad her submissive pair did not approve of pond scum.

Matthew and I high fived each other. Then he looked at me in terror. "Oh shit. The Mistress will be pissed, Psycho. Kaylee is gone, what are we going to do?"

I smiled bitterly. "I am going to put back on my wig. Then I will go to her and take the beating for this, and for talking back to her. It is okay, I know you will help to clean up the mess when it is over my love."

Matthew kissed me despite the now drying gore on my lips. "I can go in your place if you want me too."

I shook my head. "No Matt. This is what I do. I am okay, I promise. Just make sure to get out the alcohol and bandages. This is going to be a long night. She is in a rare humor. You and I are going to need to be working on some plan to create some chaos around here or I will be taking more of these. Better this beating than HIV, right?"

He nodded. "Yes baby, it is. Thank you for doing this for us. That girl was scary as hell. I love you. Did I ever tell you that?" He kissed me again.

I laughed. "I heard a rumor about that downtown, but you can't believe everything you hear. Just so you know, I will need that special bath service of yours by tomorrow. I am sure to be a mess."

I winked as I headed off leaving my handsome submissive lover smiling slyly at me. He would have to attend to the rest of our chores. I was going to be too busy to attend mine for a bit.

I picked up my wig and readjusted myself best I could. I silently entered the Mistress's room to find her sitting on her bed naked. She was beyond furious when I told her the little cat girl ran away.

"Why did she run. What did Matthew do to cause that. Tell me the truth, Psycho, or so help me," she yelled at me.

I dropped to a kneel before her. "She was there when I went to get her, Mistress. She refused to strip and Matthew was informing her this was unacceptable. The girl looked at me and demanded drugs. I told her we do not do drugs in this house and she said, 'I don't fuck old hags without a hit' and then took off down the road before we could stop her. Would you like me to send Matthew out to find her?"

Mistress Ginger was now fuming in extreme anger. "Old hag? Fuck that slut. Let her walk home." She was now shaking she was so full of rage.

I nodded, "As you wish, Mistress."

She looked at me with hate in her eyes. "You will make up for this insult. I will take out my anger and fuck you till you wish for death." She kicked my unit backward.

I kept my eyes down. "Of course, Mistress. Whatever your pleasure."

Mistress Ginger got up then pulled my arms behind my back till I yelled out in agony. "God damned right it is my pleasure, you whore."

Well, I would like to say we kissed and made up but nope. Mistress Ginger was true to her word. I did wish for death more than once that night, trust me. Even as an old experience hand, that beating and torture was righteous in all the wrong ways. Mistress Ginger had lost her cool and my ass paid big time for my defense and protection of the household. She finally wore out her foot on my backside but after a quick rest, leaving me tied up while the bitch rested, she woke up and started again.

By morning I was pretty sure I could go for the dirt nap without regrets. The big problem with the Mistress going ape shit on my unit like that is it put me out of commission for her thudding pleasures until I healed up a bit. That night she did not mind her own rules of safe play and I was cut and even burned bad in a few serious places. Poor Matthew would have to pray she didn't get into a thudding mood for at least a week or he would be paying the price in my place. Yikes!

Despite her enforcing of several bouts of carnal congress with me through that night, when she unbound me, I was told to spend Matthew. She was in the mood for her stud. I could barely walk much less fuck my lover. My mouth was busted up too. I groaned but limped from her bedroom to find Matthew for our daily sexual romp. I was sure he would go easy but damn, no matter how big my sexual appetites, pain was not a sexual stimulator for me. I really couldn't have been in less of the mood even with my beautiful Matthew as my partner.

He was making breakfast when I staggered out of the hallway. He had been worried watching the room door all night even sleeping in the floor outside the door hoping that the Mistress would release me early. When he saw the mess she had made of my unit he gasped and came running.

"Oh baby, fuck. What has she done. Let me sit you down. Can you sit? I knew I shouldn't have let you go in there. Shit. Shit. She was just too angry." Matthew held up leaning my unit on his waist.

I winced. "Matt, we have to go fuck somewhere. She wants you in there within the hour. I am sorry. I will do my best for you, but I am a bit sore and definitely not pretty to look at."

He gasped. "Are you fucking serious? You cannot fuck in this condition."

I laughed weakly "Uhm, yeah I can and yeah I already have been. So, buck up buttercup. Time to put your gun in the cock holster."

Matthew glared at me. "Psycho stop that. You are much more than that to me and you know it."

I nodded, "Yeah I am Matt, which is true. But to her, you are nothing more than a human dildo and I am just her sperm dumpster. I want to believe she loves us more than that but sometimes when she hits me like last night, I think she beats some sense into me. I know you would never use me the way she does. I know you love me, and I love you. So, what is it that she does to prove her love? Force me to suck your dick so she can practically ignore you when you fuck her?"

He shook his head. "Psycho baby, please. You are just tired and hurt. Look I can take care of this myself. You need to rest. I won't force myself on my injured lover. That is not okay." He softly stroked my swollen face.

I looked up at his handsome face. "Oh, no way you are getting out of this gorgeous. I am practically there already just looking into those beautiful eyes of yours. Besides she won't let me out of my part in the bedroom when you go attend her now will she? Let's go, just do what you did last night. Take it slow, and easy."

He nodded then picked me up as if carrying me across the threshold. We went to our favorite spot, the bathroom. Matthew did as I asked, but before we even got half-way there our sex drives kicked into high gear and as usual shit got knocked off the walls and we broke a soap dish.

So much for slow and easy. It wasn't entirely his fault, I helped set him off as I always did. We just couldn't help it. When together, it was so damned wanton and urgent. Maybe we knew our time was short, so we always seemed to be in a big hurry to get as much love in as possible. I like to believe that is what it was and I am sure if I had asked him he would have agreed.

I think back to that morning and wish I had not said what I did about him being nothing but a human sex toy and myself just a place to dump his seed. This set Matthew into stress that he never told me about in life. My beloved began to question our Mistress's love for us when I so vividly pointed out the truth. I was right, that was how she was viewing us.

She had ordered my unit to spend Matthew for her own pleasures and my mouth to get him ready to enter her too. These tasks should not have been unpleasant for the Mistress. He was awesome and beautiful. A lover should want to be so intimate with her partner. Instead she sullied these pleasurable acts by enforcing him to use me like a masturbation machine and as tissue to catch the mess caused by his orgasm. Then to further insult Matthew, he was not allowed to touch her, only to thrust and he had to do that until she was satisfied. She didn't care one damned bit about his own sexual desires. He was indeed just a stud. This apparently had either never occurred to him or never bothered him before. Now it did.

Unbeknown to me he began watching her secretly. He made sure to follow her around quietly and listened in on her phone conversations. My beloved was too smart for his own good. I couldn't have done the recon he was doing. I had to work full time, went to school full time, and had the kids, him and Mistress Ginger to attend. Matthew only had the one job so he was home more often than I was.

To his credit he never told me, while alive, what he was starting to figure out. Nor did he ever tell me what the outcome was going to be. Unfortunately, he knew almost a full six months before the end that it was over but he took that information to his grave. Had he not cleverly written me a letter, stashing it in the right spot, I would have never known the full story. However, that is for the future, not yet.

I am truly grateful for his return to me of my gift of mercy. I had given him the same by taking all the thudding. In true submissive style, he provided me perfect service for service. I was blissfully unaware of the truth about Mistress Ginger. However, I did suspect it from the beginning. Matthew already knew it by the end of this one single perfect summer of our lives.

May ended hot and lazy that year. I finished my classes in college with my four point intact. Stacey and I said goodbye for the summer. By now she believed I had gone straight. This had caused our rides back and forth to become quiet and peaceful. No more accusations of whoredom or being a lesbian.

This was probably because often Matthew would sneak out front to kiss me goodbye before he headed to work and myself to school. She often caught us in a lover's embrace. If you saw us together there was no mistaking our love. He and I were super careful to never let the Mistress see us behaving this way.

Stacey was likely the only person who knew that Matthew and I were more than just housemates. She was not supposed to be privy to our adoration of each other but it was hard to get any privacy. Matthew and I would utilize our precious alone time for private words of affection not carnal congress. The sex was nice, but it was not what we both wanted from each other. As true lovers, it was the little chats, embracing, and concerns for the other's welfare that we fought to find a bit of secret space to enjoy from each other.

We were super careful. Maybe a bit too paranoid that Mistress Ginger would catch our weakness. To make sure she never suspected us, when the Mistress would catch us involved in the carnal act, he would start to behave harshly as if I were just a unit to fuck. I would loudly bitch he was being too rough. He would often tell me to shut up and do my duty and I would respond, "then hurry up idiot." We both had our acts together pretending to be annoyed we were having to fuck each other much less be in the same room. It was hard to keep up the act sometimes. Matthew was always making faces or saying stupid shit trying to trip me up. I suppose it was a way of relieving the constant stress of carrying on a deep love affair in our prison without being caught by the warden.

Make no mistake. Our home was a type of jail and our collars were our handcuffs. The Mistress would not even let he and I out of the house unattended, except for work or school. She would question us about who we spoke to, who we saw and what the nature of all conversations were. Mistress Ginger was a micro-manager type who made sneaking around very hard indeed.

I have often viewed this social isolation policy along with the enforced sexual congress as the two major factors in the causation of Matthew and my falling in love so deeply. We were lonely, under stress, in our youth, a lot alike in many ways, and intimate. Plus he was fucking hot. All a perfect storm for our accidently falling into the forbidden. In a way, I think she intended for that to happen. However, once it did, we never gave her the satisfaction of selling us out over her setting us up like that.

How do I know she would have sold us down the river had she found out? Simple, she told us so many times. Mistress Ginger tried to catch us adoring one another. So, to combat the possibility she would find out she had successfully coupled us, we actively appeared to be annoyed by the other's presence. We even continued to fake battle the rest of our lives together. Once a week, randomly, Matthew and I would have to be broken up due to verbal altercations or accusations of the other not pulling their own weight.

This always kept the cruel Mistress from suspecting there was anything more than the following of her commands when it came to our sex life. However, I have to say, despite all that, Matthew was the most wonderful lover, friend and submissive I could have ever wished for. To this day, I weep when I think of what happened to my beautiful, gentle giant. Our love was very real and so is the never-ending heartbreak.

Ask Master Jon that I am not lying. Matthew can still affect me twenty-four years later. You must realize how sincere my feelings for him really are. I was crazy for Matthew, there is no doubt. However, it is unclear if it was the horror that ended his life, the loss of a good heart, the helplessness at being unable to save him, or just the total loss of a first love that drives my grief to this day. Likely it is all of that and more.

NOTE: *I had always been a hard hearted, cold, unfeeling person. My life had been harsh, brutal and beyond cruel. How the holy hell Matthew had softened me into a purring kitten I shall never know for sure. I suppose when the right soul touches your own, it is just what happens. I do understand I had avoided falling in love with anyone because of my disease, and the lifestyle that I was forced to live to combat the ravages of it. Yet, I really was dead inside when I met Matthew. I know because when he brought me to life, I had never realized how much romantic love mattered. It made any amount of pain I would have to* *suffer worth just feeling it for even a moment. For that wonderful gift, I will always be grateful to him. However, when I got caught at long last by love, I fell so deeply it was in fact deadly, at least for Matthew.*

I finally understood the normals' apparent need to cling to those closest to them. If the world had been full of more Matthews I would have wanted to hang on to those around me too. However, Matthew was like me, not normal. He was a rare creature, and he didn't belong to this world any more than I don't. Sadly, that was ultimately his fate. When you belong nowhere and don't manage to wall up and grow cold like me, you don't last long. Poor Matthew never learned to stop caring. He never could let go of his pride. Worst of all, he had managed to keep his heart in one piece. You can never wear the frozen circle of silver around your neck if you don't let go of your belief you are human. My poor beloved Matthew, who was going to be his doom. Mistress Ginger had no right to collar him. I had been right all along. Now it was too late and his time would eventually run out.

The Mistress was all too happy to help him along on his journey to failure. I have often speculated this was also a way to torture Matthew and me to the hilt. Mistress Ginger knew I was one tough bitch. She knew Matthew had serious issues that were dangerous and potentially deadly. The Mistress managed to break me by adding the good looking, easy going Matthew to the mix. She was able to cause Matthew to find what he was looking for only to take it away from him. This may have been her way of ultimate sadism.

I do believe with all my soul that is what she intended to do to Matthew and me, it worked sadly, from the very beginning in a sinister mind game of epic proportions. The borderline personality disorder loves to hurt others by destroying their world, their happiness, and their future. She did a perfect job of it. In the end she managed to weaken and wound me deeply, kill Matthew and rip apart a world of joy, beauty, perfect service and intense love. Think on that just a moment, now let's return to the story.

Matthew and I had been successful at running off the drug crazed Kaylee, but we knew the Mistress was again showing signs of boredom. As June began, he and I started planning a type of teamwork long game. We had to find a way to cause constant entertainment and drama to keep the ever-empty Mistress from deciding to go back to California by selling our collars to fund her trip. She kept telling us if she went back, she would take Matthew and I, but neither of us believed her. He had a good job, and so did I, where we lived. It was unlikely either of us could do so well in another place. At least not for a few months.

We were all too aware that her going back to California would mean one of two things for her submissive pair. Prostitution of us to support her expensive tastes or selling our collars to the kinkster pimp Joyce. This was something he nor I could stomach so we decided to sacrifice ourselves in any way necessary to remain a family. Matthew hated thudding and public humiliation more than anyone can know. However, he was willing to do both to keep our Mistress happy and his beloved sister at his side.

I told him during our planning of the long game I would be willing to put sparklers in my ass, then march naked down main street singing the Star-Spangled Banner to keep our triangle safe. He of course laughed then offered to march behind me shooting Roman Candles out his rear end. We would have done it too. That is how much we wanted to keep our home in one piece. If only the fucking Mistress had loved us as much as we adored her, and each other. Then this story would have likely ended much differently or maybe not at all.

Finally, we determined her favorite thing in all of life was an audience. She loved to horrify, shock and incense strangers. Working together he and I managed to maneuver her to take us out for a lunch date on the first weekend of June. Matthew drove with the Mistress sitting shot gun. I took the backseat. He watched me from the rearview mirror smiling. We knew our roles, so now it was showtime. Our Mistress had no idea just how far we were going to humiliate ourselves that day for her pleasure. I only hoped Matthew the introverted, shy one could handle the dirty task of terrifying the masses.

Mistress Ginger chose an eatery just on the outskirts of a large town of around sixty thousand souls nearly forty miles from our own home. I could tell Matthew was a bit anxious. He tended to bite his lower lip when he was panicked. I watched him chewing his mouth that day like he was starving to death. Poor Matthew, he did so hate big crowds. I didn't like them either but I was still in residual so I could handle them fine. Without psychotic shit, I am shameless.

Thankfully, I was the head submissive of our pair. All he had to do was follow my lead. He was extremely gifted at taking orders or shadowing behaviors. Had he been given a few years, his abilities as a pure submissive surely would have rivaled my own. Matthew was a true diamond in the rough.

Mistress Ginger had no fucking idea of the amazing quality she had collared, nor did she ever truly appreciate my own incredible experience in the lifestyle. Even with schizophrenia my collar was worth a minor fortune if auctioned in the right circles. Even to this day, believe it or not. Mistress Ginger was a damned fool to never appreciate what she had in her grasp in 1995/96.

I have often wondered if later in life when she was trapped with wannabe's, liars, and SAM's [smart ass masochist] did she ever think back to these glorious days when she had the world on her leash and feel remorse that she killed it. I hope so, and I hope it kills her wherever she is to this day. Well actually I hope she died of something that took a long time and was horridly painful to be honest.

When I let the Mistress out of her car, I closed the door suggesting we sit at the outside tables since the weather was nice. She smiled and thought that a fine idea. I shot a smile at my brother, he smiled back. Our trio took a table in the center of the crowded, covered outside eating area. Matthew and I were dressed like BDSM nightmares with our signature white makeup. Mistress Ginger had brought a book so she could seem unaffected by all the murmurs, stares and laughter caused by her submissive pair's very odd physical appearance. She was already loving the minor commotion we were causing.

I pulled out her chair and Matthew did his task of pouring her water much to the amusement of the unwashed public watching the show of our attendance to our Mistress. He and I took our seats next to each other. We allowed her to order our meal, then I kicked his leg under the table. It was time to put our plan into action.

"Keep your fucking hands on your side of the table pussy," I growled at Matthew.

He looked at me angrily. "You don't own the table Psycho. Scoot over. Did you brush your fucking teeth? You stink. How am I supposed to eat with that smell."

I tried to look incensed. "Well if I smell it is because of that nasty cock of yours. Maybe if you'd wash it occasionally, idiot."

"Oh yeah? Couldn't be my cock causing that odor is coming out of your mouth. You suck at blow jobs, but not in the right way." He pushed me gently by my shoulder.

I pushed him back. "Fuck you, Matthew. You are just jealous I can eat pussy better than you."

Yeah foul but remember in order to get the crowd upset we had to pull out all the stops. For the record, Matthew and I made sure no children were in earshot of these most disgusting comments we were making at each other. We did care that kids didn't get an unexpected education in nasty shit. *Mistress Ginger wouldn't get her rocks off with the public display of chaos. Sad, but this is the world of the submissive. He and I were college educated, well-mannered adults, reduced to disgusting vocabulary, childish, brutish altercations to please this cruel woman. So, there it is. I would ask you to deal with it since Matthew and I had to.*

We began to lightly push each other making rude accusations regarding each other's abilities in the bedroom. The crowd cruelly enjoyed our childish antics. All around us giggles, derogatory statements about our looks and statements broke out. Our Mistress was loving the negative attention. She sat there smiling as Matthew and I practically came to blows.

Finally, the Mistress did what we knew she would do after tiring of the public's responses to this minor battle, she barked feigning anger, "You two are embarrassing me. Go sit elsewhere now."

Matthew and I responded in unison, "As you wish Mistress" while both pretending to be ashamed at making her upset.

We got up and picked a table three paces from her own. We watched her open her book and start to read alone. Matthew and I had successful deployed the first half of our plan to cause disruption geared toward pleasing our Mistress.

He and I sat in silence. We were watching as the other patrons started to finish their meals and leave. New customers quickly replaced the ones who were privy to our original bullshit battle. We saw the Mistress pay for our meals, then we knew we were in the clear. Matthew looked at me smiling then nodded that it was time for phase two of our plan. I nodded back that I agreed.

"You son-of-a-bitch. Did you just look at the redhead's tits. You are a bastard." I threw a napkin at Matthew.

He gasped looking very incensed. "Hell no. Why? Are you jealous? I was looking at that car over there. What redhead?"

I pointed at Mistress Ginger who looked up startled at our yelling, as did every other patron there. "That one right there. I saw you looking, asshole. You think she is prettier than me, don you? Admit it."

He shook his head looking at the table as if embarrassed. "No, I wasn't, baby. You are the only girl for me. Why do you got to be a bitch? I wasn't looking at her tits."

I stood up and smacked him in the shoulder. "You are a lying sack of shit. You want her, admit it. Well dog, go get her." I made a motion for him to get up and go for it.

He hung his head. "No, baby I swear it, you got me all wrong."

I laughed in disbelief. "Yeah? Well, let me tell you something right now, you couldn't please her if you want to."

He looked up shocked. "What? Oh, fuck you, like I could."

I crossed my arms, "Yeah, I could limp dick. Just watch me." I walked over to Mistress Ginger grabbed the back of her hair and planted a deep kiss on her.

Everyone gasped including the Mistress who didn't know what to do. Matthew jumped up knocking over his chair.

"You bitch. Get your fucking hands off her. I saw her first." He came over and pushed me back then also grabbed the Mistress by her hair and planted a deep kiss on her.

Matthew pulled up and I slapped him hard. "Bastard! She is mine."

He held his face as if it hurt. "Fuck you, I am taking her for myself."

He grabbed the Mistress by her arm, I grabbed her other arm (carefully by the way) we lifted her from the chair and drug her to our car putting her in the shot gun seat. Matthew got behind the wheel and I in the back seat. He took off leaving everyone there stunned into silence unsure if they should call the police or what just happened there.

The Mistress sat there silent in shock for the first few moments as Matthew started driving us home.

Then she began to laugh loudly holding her sides. "Oh my God, you beautiful brats are wonderful. That was so much fun. You both deserve a treat. Geniuses, the both of you."

Matthew smiled at me in the rearview mirror. We had pleased our Mistress by publicly humiliating ourselves. She praised us all the way home and told us that from then forward we would all go on trips to town once a week for more of this kind of acting. You couldn't have made two submissive collars happier that fine day. Our Mistress was so pleased she called us to her bedroom and while Matthew still didn't get to have bed privileges, he was permitted to stay the night on the floor next to the bed.

That night after the Mistress fell to sleep, Matthew and I held hands in the darkness sleeping cuddled up on the floor next to her bed. It was one of the best nights of my life, with only our promise at that time to love each other under the night sky being higher on my list.

We didn't have to fuck. We didn't have to hide. We just got to be two lovers holding each other in the inky blackness, heartbeat to heartbeat, skin to skin. There are no words to describe the joy of it. Only someone who has truly loved can understand. With Matthew it wasn't the sex, it wasn't his good looks, it was his always being there for me, and me for him. Partners fighting together, pulling in the same direction the weight of the world, sharing the heavy load. That is what love really is. The rest is just bullshit, and fluff. I was his rock, and he was my heart. Together we were more than just lovers, we were one person.

The next week our outing was in a park. Matthew and I did the same act. There were fewer there to witness our couple fighting over the red head scene but it did get a bunch of stares and even one park watcher tried to stop us from dragging away our Mistress. Matthew took the brunt of the young woman slapping at him telling him to let 'the lady go.'

Our Mistress laughed even harder over that little unexpected response. Matthew seemed a bit upset that the woman chose him to attack when clearly I was also involved in the fake, kidnapping. I told the Mistress we had to be careful before someone called the cops. She of course initially disagreed but finally relented telling us to come up with something else.

Matthew and I asked her for suggestions. She happily told us, "Well I think next week I will walk both of you on a leash around town."

I saw Matthew about faint, but he knew we had to do what she wanted if we were to placate Mistress Ginger. So, he and I agreed to behave as her leashed pets. He worried the entire week leading up to the day of our outing. Poor Matthew really hated being treated like an animal or less than human by his Mistress or anyone for that matter. Next to thudding and bondage it was his biggest pet peeve. I did my best to teach him how to go to a secret place in his mind so these things didn't affect him, but he never could get that lesson ingrained well.

When the day finally came she made sure to pick the worst place available in that large town. Matthew parked us at the city mall. Even I was a bit apprehensive about this kind of public venue on a fucking leash. Matthew was about to piss his pants. His eyes searched me wildly from the mirror. He was clearly terrified. poor baby.

I smiled and mouthed, "it will be okay relax."

He nodded as I got out to let the Mistress out of her seat. She immediate leashed us both by lock on two separate chains. We followed behind her keeping our eyes to the ground. Despite our best efforts to block it out, the gasping, laughter, jeers and comments were impossible to ignore. The Mistress walked ahead of us enjoying our complete and utter humiliation. She of course reveled in every nasty statement made about the two whackos on a leash. Matthew and I were in complete hell. However, we knew this was what we had to do to protect our collars from Mistress Ginger's boredom.

Not long into our 'walk of shame' a couple of nasty teenage boys came walking up next to us. They asked us if we were stupid, retarded or just high. Neither Matthew nor I responded but continued to walk in silence keeping our gaze to the floor. The boys looked at each other laughing as they jerked our chains hard yelling out 'freaks.' They ran off laughing and high fiving other teens who likely had encouraged that rude behavior.

Mistress Ginger started laughing wildly at that saying, "looks like my brats have many admirers."

I stole a look at Matthew and saw a tear fall from his downturned face to the ground. I winced. This was getting to him. Shit, that was not good. I should have known he couldn't handle this indignity. I wanted so bad to hold him and tell him it was going to be okay, but it would be risky to even try to grasp his hand for a second. Trying to openly console his pain would only give Mistress Ginger the ammo required to sell us both out to Joyce.

I took the chance of getting punished later by pretending to get out of step. This caused the Mistress to have to jerk me back into my place. She didn't even turn around to see why I was dragging for that few moments. Mistress Ginger was having too much fun to care.

However, Matthew looked up to see what had happened. I smiled with adoration at him noticing he was openly crying. He shot back a weak smile, but I could tell that small gesture of love helped to buck him up. I watched as he straightened his back took a deep breath, closed his eyes and reached deeper for strength. I let out a sigh of relief knowing that he would be okay for now.

This was a tough trick to pull off even for me. The witnesses were most cruel, and as we got further into the mall, more started to follow us to get a closer look at the odd scene. The Mistress got to the fountain display that was in the center of this huge place. There were benches for the patrons of the many boutiques and shops to sit for a rest all around this impressive aquatic display. Mistress Ginger selected one, then sat down. She used hand gestures to command Matthew and I to sit on the floor in a kneeling position on each side of her like a pair of human bookends. We both did as ordered keeping our head down, and we both sucked in our breath. Nothing worse than being in the center of hostile territory on a fucking leash.

Mistress Ginger began to read her book as if ignoring the gathering group of people who came to look at us with curiosity. Some were openly making foul remarks. Others just shook their heads or laughed. A few asked her what the deal was with the creepy people on a dog leash.

She laughed out loud and said, "Oh. These two think they are dogs. I am just helping them out. You see I am their therapist" or "they are really kinky, and this is how they get their kicks."

I must be honest. I wanted to kill the red-headed cunt. I could take this kind of bullshit, and had I really adored her, likely would have done it happily to make her happy. Matthew, however, was obviously under a lot of stress. She didn't bother to take his feelings into account. I was there when she promised to protect and defend him during his submission. I could see very well he was not feeling either of those things kneeling there on that mall floor.

Had I been the Mistress I would have taken him off that leash immediately. I also would have either made him a stay at home submissive for life or released him from his collar. Public humiliation was obviously something beyond his limits of endurance. Breaking a spirit to create a submissive is to be expected, but you can go too far. If you break someone too much, they will become hopeless. We all know where that eventually leads to now don't we?

To my absolute horror, it was not enough to push Matthew to his edge by walking him through that mall. Mistress Ginger waited till we had a large group of jeering onlookers. She then reached into her purse and took out a dog bowl with a can of dog food. She even remembered to bring a handheld can opener. The Mistress poured the wet mess into the bowl then set it just in front of her.

"Matthew go eat your dinner. Crawl for it," she said sternly.

I looked at him as he was startled into terror. He looked at me his eyes wild with fear. I knew this was just too much. I could see he was shaking from my vantage. The crowd was gasping, giggling and waiting for the human puppy to get to his trick for their amusement. I prayed he recalled as a submissive he could say no. It would result in punishment, but Matthew could take punishment, as long as it was short and quick.

I gave him a quick, barely noticeable shake of my head. He saw it.

"No Mistress, I will take the punishment," he said weakly still quivering with anxiety.

The Mistress growled, "You will go eat that dog food now Matthew or I will thud you when we get home. so help me God."

He sucked in his breath. "As you wish Mistress. I accept the punishment."

I closed my eyes in great relief. He stood his ground. I knew he would have a rough time with the thudding, but I knew that if he had crawled out there in front of those people to eat that dog food it would have ended him right there. My poor brother chronically suffered from Major Depressive Disorder since he had been very small. He also had Social Anxiety Disorder. With that tag team of significant psychological problems this kind of cruelty would assure a downslide into the dangerous territory of suicidal ideation. Luckily, this time, he had managed to take back some control and avoided the trap she was setting for him.

The Mistress was super pissed now that the crowd was irritated not getting to see the taboo of the big guy eating dog food like a nutjob. She jerked his chain hard promising she would make him sorry. I looked with desperation at my beloved Matthew, then to the crowd. Without another thought I crawled to the bowl. I knew damned well my stomach could not handle the digestion of this item which would force the Mistress to get us out of there rapidly. It would cost me my dignity. For Matthew's protection, as the head submissive, his sister and lover, I would willingly pay the price.

The laughter and gasps spread through the watching audience like the sound of cicada on a hot summer day as I made it and began to eat using only my head like a dog to eat that horrible stuff. The Mistress who had been occupied with her verbal threats to Matthew looked up to see me doing what she had ordered my brother to do. Later, Matthew told me her smile was huge as she watched everyone freaking out that I was doing this stupid trick. I managed to save his ass from her anger, for a bit anyway.

Hell, I only cared that I was going to be sick to my stomach. Those people watching could kiss my ass. I didn't know a fucking one of them. Nor did I care to. Since none of them had any bearing on my continued existence, let them look. I hope they enjoyed it. Gave them something to talk about in their insignificant little lives, the fucktards. I had certainly done worse for a crowd and by the age of twenty-four I really had no shame any longer. I was beyond jaded and in my own way stronger than I had ever given myself credit for. More than that, I committed this act for the mercy of another. My heart was not cold at all. Not many people out there would sacrifice themselves in this way to protect the one they love. I demonstrated I had more humanity in me than any of those people watching or Mistress Ginger by behaving like a fucking dog. Think on that for a moment.

Not too many people could have the balls to crawl like a dog on a leash, eat dog food from a bowl in front of at least twenty-five or so strangers calling out insults and laughing. I know that later Matthew told me if he had ever loved me before, that one act made him love me beyond anything he ever felt for another. Matthew did understand very well what I had done for him. His aftercare later made it so worth it, I would have done that a million times to get more of his gentle affection, and heartfelt adoration. I had been starving all my life for that kind of attention and my gentle giant was all too happy to give it to me till I was sated. By the way, I am not talking about sex here. Just hugging and sweet words of love.

He said he found my inner strength and resolve to survive incredibly attractive. He told me that night it was that very thing that caused him to call Mistress Ginger and ask for his own collar. He thought that if he could learn to be tough like me, he could beat his own desperate issue and save himself from himself. Matthew had a long history of serious suicide attempts. One year before he met Mistress Ginger he had nearly been successful in his bid for eternal peace. When she had invited him to look at her book collection he had been planning another significant attempt. Had he carried out his plan there would have been no return. Thankfully his collar and submission to our house had successfully ended his plans to carry that bloody plan out.

He and I had the misfortune of wanting to end our pathetic existences in common. I had a few of those brushes as you all know (right, just a few, hahaha). Neither of us should have been there in 1995, given the seriousness of our will to end it all in a previous part of our lives. He had hoped against all hope, that training by my side and the love of his Mistress could stop him from his fate. Sadly, it only postponed it for my sweet Matthew, but we are not there yet.

While I munched away on the nasty dog food the mall police approached our Mistress and informed her that the show was over. She initially complained to them that we were not breaking any laws. However, the security personal informed her that this public disruption would not be tolerated. She could take her fruit loops and leave voluntarily or they could arrest all three of us and remove us by force.

Obviously, we packed it up in a hurry. Mistress Ginger stormed off in a hurry. Matthew and I almost had to go at a jog to keep from being drug out by our leashes behind her. All around us there was clapping, and loud jeers made by our audience of so-called admirers, assholes.

Once in the car she smacked Matthew on his shoulder several times while hurling insults at his insolence. He took her weak blows never even swerving the car while she railed at him.

"You are in so much trouble, you little brat. How dare you disobey me. If I tell you to strip naked and stroke your cock while standing in the middle of the state capital, you will do it. I own you, you stupid prick," she screamed at him.

He just kept his eyes on the road. "Yes Mistress. I apologize for my behavior. I accept the punishment."

"You sure as fuck will get it too. When I am done with you, you'll beg to be taken on walks. You will learn to love your leash, or I will find someone else to deal with your unruly ass," she growled.

I saw terror flash in his eyes. He and I were both thinking the same thing, Joyce. Matthew would never again get upset when the Mistress leashed us from that day forward. Not because of his punishment that night, but because he decided no matter how bad it made him feel to be treated like a dog by Mistress Ginger, it was better than being treated like a whore by Joyce.

Mistress Ginger true to her word took Matthew to her bedroom the second we got home. She thudded him within an inch of his sanity that night. I paced and sat on the floor outside the closed door stressing for him. Matthew just couldn't handle the thud. I admit it brought tears to my eyes hearing his wailing and screams while the Mistress took out her aggression on him. I knew deep in my heart she had set him up for this. She knew he would balk at eating dog food from a bowl in a crowded mall. My only real solace is the mall personnel made it clear we were no longer welcomed. She would not be pulling that bullshit on us again. At least not there anyway. I wanted so badly to kick in the door, kill Mistress Ginger and untie Matthew. I wanted to run away with him, far away where no leashes, whips or ropes existed. No more collars, no more fucking kneeling, no more fucking Masters, but that could never be. He and I were losers at the game of life. People like Mistress Ginger were always going to be there to make sure we never forgot just how unfit for life we truly were.

We were condemned. In order to survive our lives would play out only one of two ways: complete exploitation from random assholes around us who accidently discovered our secret weakness, or controlled exploitation under a circle of silver. Matthew and I had already tried the first version. It had nearly killed us both. So, I sat there fuming angrily at the Mistress's cruelty but didn't break down the door to save Matthew from her thudding. I knew it would only result in destroying us both the second we shucked our collars. He and I were a team unit, but neither of us had a fucking head. That was ultimately why our relationship was forbidden and to be honest, doomed to fail.

It was early morning when the Mistress finally threw Matthew out of her room. She had tired of his crying and pleading. I was there waiting when he staggered out. I helped him down the hallway straight to our bathroom. There I treated his cuts and bruises, bathed him and held him while he cried over his inability to handle this harsh part of our daily existence. I did my best to convince him that in time he would toughen up. Yet, he and I both knew this was a serious hang up for him. He never could handle it, and likely never would have even if he had lived. Every submissive has a single or a few hang ups about the regular things expected of them in any given D/s relationship. Even me.

I told Matthew my secret that night to help him understand his lack of tolerance for the thud did not mean he could never wear his collar properly. When he heard it, I saw the look of gratitude in his eyes. He held me tight letting go his pain grateful for the gift of understanding. He finally could accept he was not failing at his training. Just because we are submissive doesn't mean we are not human. He had found out it was okay to not be able to master everything expected in the lifestyle.

NOTE: *I would tell all of you the weakness I confessed to Matthew that night, but you see I still wear my collar. I have a current Master, and he is a sadist (not the bad kind but a sadist none-the-less) so now way am I putting it into writing. Once the Master or Mistress knows your weakness, they can't help themselves but to pick on that when you are being punished or just for kicks. So, you will all have to just guess. Just be aware mine is just as serious as Matthew's inability to handle thudding and bondage. Sorry Master Jon, I am crazy not stupid. LOL.*

Once a submissive knows their weakness, then we do what we can to become better at the other shit and stop trying to beat what we were not cut out to handle. A good Master that discovers the submissive weakness will withhold asking for such a thing, and it becomes the ultimate punishment instead. Too bad Mistress Ginger was not a good Master. She did use the thudding properly that night, but she tended to thud Matthew more often after that night just for 'the hell of it.' I was the house thudder, but when it came to the Mistress's pleasure, there was nothing that we could do when she got a hankering for Matthew's ass under her crop. Her terrorizing him with random, spontaneous thudding sessions would eventually get to him but again we are getting ahead of ourselves.

The entire month of June, July and all of August was peaceful as any D/ss household could ever boast to be. Matthew and I were now very accustomed to our Mistress's weekly public displays of her submissive pair to a jeering public. She was still sticking to the leash trick and the angry couple bit. By September, Matthew and I knew it was time to come up with new and horrid plans to up the kick. She was showing signs of boredom yet again. Mistress Ginger was thudding Matthew more often and coming to watch and direct our daily sexual trysts. She was quite cruel when playing porno director and neither he nor I appreciated her bullshit. Bad enough we had to do it, we didn't need the added pressure of someone telling us how to do it. Ugh.

These were always bad signs. It was clear she was wanting more from us. So, he and I started to talk over new plans for her amusement so she would stay out of our sex life and stop dragging him off to tie up and beat till he pissed himself. It was during one of these thinking discussions that I recalled my Loyalty Dog. I had promised the Mistress I would submit my lifelong loyalty to her authority if she lasted a year as my Mistress. I told Matthew about this little token of my undying affection and he was against it from the start. I had no idea he had found out things about our Mistress by then.

To his credit he didn't tell me the truth as to his misgivings. I know Matthew could already see our triangle was doomed. He wanted so badly to just be happy while it lasted, even though he knew that our time was fast running out. So, he just warned me not to do it but stepped aside when I argued it would buy us more time.

In reality, it actually did. Had I not called her to a meeting about it that day, we likely would have been sold off that winter. My granting my Loyalty Dog accidently raised my collar price. Mistress Ginger was no fool. She intended to get top dollar for our collars and now that she had proof of my true worth, she would not just take any old bid. So, I am not sorry to this day I granted her my Loyalty. It bought me more time with Matthew, even if only a little more. By then, I would have sold my soul to buy even a few more hours of that kind of happiness with my brother submissive and ignorance of my Mistress's lack of love for us. I think Matthew understood that too. He never criticized me for it even when he finally told me the whole story, again another chapter.

I called the Mistress to a meeting just after wake-up service completion on September 2nd, 1995. When she came, I knelt before her and held out the little black dog that Master Anita had given me years before. She looked at the token in my upturned hand and smiled.

"I thought you had forgotten me and your promise, Psycho." She took the dog from my palm.

I shook my head. "No Mistress. Just as I promised. You have served me, and I you for the agreed upon year. I grant you my undying Loyalty as your submissive for life." I looked down in reverence feeling more secure that Matthew and I would be safe for many years to come at her feet.

She cooed. "It is so pretty. This is a wonderful day, Psycho. I have waited so long for this, my beloved." She reached down and grabbed my collar.

I was hauled to her room to consummate this new union for life. I dealt with her thudding and cruel affections stoically. It was her right, and I had just promised to serve her for life, no matter what her pleasures. I take my Loyalty seriously. Far as I was concerned, she was mine till the day I went to the Summerlands and I was hers.

Surely, now with Matthew having already granted his and now the Mistress had mine too we be forever safe. I was sure she did love us. Why would she take the Loyalty Dog if she never planned to keep our D/ss family forever? That would be beyond cruel. No one is that heartless, right?

Well, I will say it once more. I am schizophrenic, and reality is one thing that is completely broken for me.

Chapter 36: Hopelessly Devoted
Mistress Ginger and submissive Matthew

Mistress Ginger has captured the hearts and undying loyalty of her submissive pair. The triangle is a strong, loving, and safe place to be. The fall and winter of 1995/96 is a time of joy for the greedy Mistress and her collars. Her pets are working as a team to keep her entertained. However, the hole inside her is too vast to ever be filled. Her wandering eye cannot help but behold all she thinks she is missing as the world passes the isolated trio by. Mistress Ginger can never get enough adoration. The town is just too small for her outrageous appetites for the obscene.

Matthew and Psycho complete each other. Together they are a beautiful sight, one male, one female, pulling the weight of their world equally. Two tormented souls have fused into a circle to create one. Their unified powerful psyche will titillate their Mistress but never capture her heart. They kneel in unison to the irresistible red-haired demon, trapped like moths in her flames. As their desires for her adoration grow so does the price of their collars. Like the alchemists of old, these two have turned silver into gold...

Okay I am going to walk ahead, but you stay by my side. I may need to hold your hands on these next few chapters. I am truly afraid to travel these most devastating memories for the second time in my lifetime. I know the end of this road is just ahead, we are almost there. I can see it clearly from here. There is a river and a bridge. We will have to cross both very soon. I don't want to lose anyone else that I love in those muddy waters. So, stay close and hold me tightly. Please whatever you do don't stray from this narrow path. I am here to protect you from the fate of the one who lost his way and never returned. I know the pitfalls. I learned them painfully well a long time ago.

"Did you know ever since I was a little boy, I wish that I had never been born? I used to wish that almost every day. You know I was going to kill myself. Then I met Mistress Ginger and you. I love my collar, Psycho, I can't live without it. It has given me everything that makes life worth living. Since the Mistress had me kneel to put it on, I had stopped wanting to die. Being a submissive helped to focus the pain outward away from my heart. No matter what you may think after reading all the truths in this letter, being with you and this last year and eight months has changed my mind. Now, I am glad I was born. The beautiful life I have known at your side made it worth all the pain, but I know nothing lasts forever.

Then last summer, I started waking up from the same nightmare every night thinking what happens when…"
--**Excerpt from Matthew's suicide letter to Psycho, dated August 27th, 1996.**

"I am telling you Psycho she is going to bring another God damned collar into this house," Matthew yelled turning red in the face with frustration at me.

I shook my head. "No way she is going to do it, Matt. We don't have the room. I think she just likes to stir us up is all. Besides, she has our Loyalty now. Not even Mistress

Ginger is that crazy. You and I fight enough as it is." I was just so damned sure of myself that she was not that crazy.

He threw up his hands. "Okay, you will see. That is where she is now. I heard her talking to Joyce about some sub wannabe named David. Psycho, I swear I am not sucking his disease riddled dick. And I have news for you, neither are you. You know if he is one of Joyce's he won't have clean papers. I won't stand for this bullshit. It is not dignified. I don't care if she is our Mistress." He pointed at me harshly.

I snorted. "Damn right I am not. Are you sure, Brother? I just can't believe she would be so stupid. Wait, you heard a name? Okay maybe just in case we had better come up with a plan to rid this house of Joyce's street rat." I realized if Matthew heard a name, we had trouble coming through that door.

He nodded. "Finally you are making some fucking sense. Now I do have a plan so hear me out." He smiled diabolically.

The entire month of September had gone quiet and normal (our normal) after I had granted Mistress Ginger my Loyalty Dog. October had started somewhat sleepily too with nothing unusual. Every week Matthew and I were drug out of the house into public to perform tricks at the end of Mistress Ginger's leashes as her pets. Every day Matthew and I performed our services and duties to the household, our collars and with each other. Our lives had become predictable and comfortable. Well, as comfortable as our lives could ever be.

The second week of October, Mistress Ginger had started to seek us out then interrupt our daily carnal congress. She would demand we perform sexual acts on each other, or bond one or both of us and direct the whole show. This behavior was always a bit too much indignity for both Matthew and me. Worse yet, we both knew that random, spontaneous, or even violent thudding sessions for either or both of us were next if we just kept allowing her emptiness to build. When she started that shit, we would try to plan a new trick in public to keep her sated in other ways.

This time before he and I could start our planning, Matthew had overheard the Mistress talking to Joyce shopping for fresh collars again. Kaylee had taught us that Joyce's submissive flesh was not much more than drug addicted youngsters looking to fuck in order to feed the habit. He and I were disease free and intended to stay that way despite our Mistress's lack of concern for her own welfare. A submissive with an STD is doomed to become nothing more than a skid row ho. Their collar is worth very little to anyone. Neither of us could stand for such a fate. Dominants could still find a submissive with a sexual disease since they are the bosses and control the submissive. Though no submissive worth their salt gets involved without checking first. We can refuse to submit in the first place.

We both knew the Mistress cuts off all your hair trick would not work with a male submissive. He and I would have to dig a bit deeper to scare this next asshole away. Matthew and I would also have to decide who was going to take the beating when the creep flew the coop. Mistress

Ginger would want to thud someone all night. She never tolerated being denied.

"Well it is a male, so I guess, you got the girls. I will take the boys." Matthew took a deep breath to steady his nerves.

I nodded. "You sure Brother? I mean she is going to beat the piss out of you. We may not even be able to scare the shit head off, so maybe it won't matter. But if we do, she will tear off your hide. Maybe you better let me handle it. You are such a pussy and all." I chuckled bitterly.

He glared at me. "Psycho, you know I love you. I admit I am a pussy about this thudding business, but you can't keep catching my fall. You are right. I must learn to deal with that our life is going to be hard. If I can't buck up, I am finished. We both know that. I appreciate you always trying to protect me, but one day when this is all over you won't be there. Then what will I do?"

I looked at him with a start. "Stop talking like that. You and I are not going anywhere. She took the Loyalty Dog, Matthew. Mistress Ginger is never going to sell us or toss us. Unless you keep on pussing out all the time. I told you the dog food wasn't that bad."

He laughed. "Bullshit, that stuff was horrible. I almost puked before my first bite. If I had eaten it in the mall instead of the park, I would have messed those marble floors instead of that begonia bush behind the park bench. Damn, I am glad she isn't into that shit anymore."

We both had a good laugh at that most hideous fact. Matthew did eat the dog food the very next week when the Mistress ordered him to do it in front of the jeering crowd at the park. This time he didn't hesitate, but like me he got very sick from it. So, Mistress Ginger never repeated that foul humiliation again. I am sure she wanted to, but puking submissive collars were just not her thing. I was green for almost six hours and Matthew for a good four. Dog food is just not for human consumption. We were not dogs despite what she seemed to think. At least we did not have the digestive tract of one anyway.

We had managed to change the subject, but I think both of us had figured out that our Mistress's chronic emptiness was a challenge that continued to threaten our existence as a family. It was getting harder and harder to please her. Matthew and I were to the point of planning public humiliations that could get us arrested.

We both assumed eventually we would have to resort to bail outs and embarrassing charges at the rate her appetite was increasing for the horrific looks on the weekly crowds we drew. That was not good for either of our chosen careers outside our D/ss household. Mistress Ginger, as usual, was thinking with her desires and not her brains. It was a problem neither Matthew nor I had resolved. We still had hope that one of us would figure it out before anyone did any jail time over our antics.

In the other areas of my life things had been going smooth as silk. My grades were top of the class. If I finished in the spring, I would just need a signature of recommendation from my course advisor. I would be sent to my final year to finish up my education and licensure as a forensic pathologist. With a four point, I was the number one student in the program. I was almost to my goal of being viewed as a person that everyone viewed as credible and important.

Simon was more than proud of us. He would speak to me from time to time, but in residual I could no longer see him. We had acquired all he had ever wanted, a home for our children, a Mistress who helped us attend our daily needs, a family in our brother Matthew, an important job and now almost a degree in Biology/Forensics. No one in the little town had seen me running as a fool for more than a year. No arrests, no hospitalizations, no psychosis. If we had gotten a fire fur baby, it would have been perfect. At least our perfect, we are not normal, so this was as close as we could ever get.

Sure, we were wearing a collar, calling our girlfriend Mistress, living in a poly relationship, having daily carnal congress with our brother submissive, had no access to our own income and totally banned from any outside friends or influence. It was true we were often bruised and battered from our Mistress's thudding, and we spent more time on our knees or back than upright.

However, we weighed 110 pounds, had started to grow hair, were taking our medication like clockwork, cleaner than ever in our dirty life, and were corrected when delusions or hallucinations did crop up by the very observant Mistress Ginger. I spent any free time I had, not that there was much, trying to find ways to please her rather than find ways to end my existence.

Matthew had also gained a few pounds and was healthier than ever in his life. He no longer was suicidal and spent his time writing bad poetry rather than suicide notes. He had gotten a promotion at work. He had finally found the family he had sought for all his years. His happiness was written on his face. Matthew had even conquered his social anxiety through our constant public humiliation. He also reported he was no longer depressed. He honestly didn't have the time to be sad and introspective. Mistress Ginger was always looking for a reason to thud his ass. So, he stayed super busy making himself useful any way he could to avoid her crop.

On the surface it did appear the overly cruel, insatiable Mistress Ginger had cured my schizophrenia psychosis, and Matthew's chronic bouts of major depression and crippling anxiety. We absolutely loved her for it too. Despite all she had done, and was doing to us, we did nothing when together but talk about ways to show her how much we loved her.

To the normal that seems odd, maybe a bit crazy, but for those who live by the collar, it was as natural as breathing. She had our respect, our adoration and our loyalty for her service. We saw what she demanded in return. Yeah even eating dog food and having sex with each other was part of equal service for the life she had given us. Both Matthew and I were beyond grateful to her for saving us from ourselves. We would have done anything for her, she only had to ask, and we would make it so.

However, our love for Mistress Ginger now made us both extremely territorial. We viewed our protection and defense of our triangle as paramount to our continued survival. The addition of another collar to the mix making the triangle a square would threaten to destabilize our barely balanced secret world. Mistress Ginger's continued threats to add another confused us and made us super paranoid. Any visitor to our home was a potential threat in our very brainwashed minds.

NOTE: *Make no mistake, Mistress Ginger had brainwashed Matthew and me into believing this was a wonderful life and only she could grant such a mercy. Ultimately, that is what killed Matthew, this very bullshit of isolation, constant telling us only she could love us, and keeping our spirits broken by chronically treating us like her pets rather than human beings.*

She had eroded my feelings about myself by forcing Matthew to treat my unit like a piece of meat. It was the very thing I had tried to not believe prior to her collaring me.

She had broken Matthew by eroding his code of conduct. She did this by forcing him to become the rapist he detested. He had to have sex with me even when I was hurt or he would be thrown out. He viewed our forced sexual congress as rape and she knew that.

She made both of us walk a leash, perform stupid pet like tricks both in private and public, and she kept us from talking to anyone but each other and her. We never saw our checks, where our money was spent, nor were we allowed to ask. Matthew made that mistake once and she thudded him till he couldn't walk for two days.

We were told by her that she slaved day and night just to attend our varied and difficult needs. Our Mistress constantly insisted that our care was almost unbearable. Mistress Ginger stated only her love for us kept her from ripping out her hair and running away screaming. She said both of us were worthless, incapable, useless, and only with her constant work able to stay out of a mental institution where we both truly belonged.

Over time, we had fallen for this slow overtaking of our dignity, minds, life, income, futures and all faucets of our lives. By the end of her reign, neither Matthew nor I saw us as anything other than helpless babies who likely could only have made it as far as we did in our life before her by sheer accident. If what she did to us is not brainwashing, then I don't know what is.

He and I had and have serious psychological disorders that were disabling and made us easy marks for exploitation. Our higher intellect didn't protect us due to the severity of our diseases. Our Mistress had used our weaknesses against us in most effective manners. Why did she do it? Well, obviously to keep us from escaping her clutches, or even realizing we were being systematically dismantled until she had gleaned the most income off our employment and our collars as possible.

If you know anything about abusive and toxic personalities then you will agree what she did were typical manipulation tactics seen in typical vanilla abusive relationships (i.e. battered wives, lovers, et cetera). The most come types to harm others in this fashion is the Psychopathic predator, the Antisocial Personality, and yep, you guessed it the Borderline Personality Disorder. Now back to the story.

The night Mistress Ginger brought David home, Matthew and I had been nervously watching the door for hours waiting for her return. We knew she had gone to one of Joyce's so-called Munches. If she was going to try to ring in a new collar, she would bring the dead cat home with her. By ten that night, she made our fears realized. Mistress Ginger walked through the door followed by a skinny, male who appeared sallow in pallor, never looked up from the floor and from what I could tell couldn't be older than myself in his early twenties. He was shaking all over and not from nerves. This fellow was tweaking no doubt. Matthew shot me a look of terror.

I just nodded to him that our plan should go into action immediately. He and I approached our Mistress and knelt before her in reverence, waiting for our chance to attack the intruder where she would not see it.

"Ah, see David. Your brother and sister already have accepted you. You will love them, and they will love you. Psycho there is very well versed, and she can take care of all your needs, but if you prefer Matthew is also very good. Or have them both. But first you take care of your Mistress.

88

Psycho, you will get him bathed and ready for me." She walked off to her bedroom to get her toys out in preparation for David's consummation.

I stood up flashing a look to Matthew. He nodded then headed to the bathroom without a word. He knew his role. I then looked back at the quivering David who was smiling at me.

"Nice tits baby. I am going to enjoy this a lot. Sexy Mistress, hot piece of ass to fuck when she is not available. Damn, how'd I get so lucky," he said rudely looking my unit up and down.

I frowned then spoke forcing my voice as low as possible, and that is low trust me. "Well you see the Mistress paid big bucks for these boobs. It was only fair since she cut off my dick and balls. I figured if I got to be a girl I may as well be a big boobed one."

I shifted my breasts then grabbed my crotch as if to adjust myself. "Oh shit, I keep forgetting the boys are gone now. Oh well, strip down there baby cakes. Hope you like anal. Oh, won't matter as the Mistress will get you used to that real quick. She likes her boys slick if you catch my drift. If only I had known that then I would still be drilling instead of getting drilled."

David's eyes were wide with terror. "You used to be a boy?"

I nodded. "Yeppers, but that was a bit ago. Hell, I barely miss it. Now Matthew he just started his surgeries. The

Mistress will be pleased getting a discount now that she has two of you for the doctor. Well, he isn't really a doctor, but hell the with the drugs he has, you'll be too fucking high to feel it, until later anyway."

Matthew came back to find a very upset David looking over my unit with fear rather than lust now.

"Hey, Bruce, I mean Psycho, is David about to look good with tits or what? I mean I am a bit too tall but shit, didn't stop the Mistress. She does love her girly boys." Matthew looked at David's crotch longingly.

I laughed low and then said deeply, "Hey, David drop your pants so Matthew can see a pair. He has been missing his so bad."

David glared at Matthew. "Okay, so this guy over here, yeah I can believe, used to have a dick, maybe still does by the sound of him, but you fellow are you trying to tell me she cut your dick and balls off too. No way dude."

Matthew feigned a look of sadness. "Yeah buddy. I love her man. When the Mistress says cut off your boys you do what you are told. Here let me show you. Now the surgery was pretty recent, so it is still a bit gory." Matthew dropped his pants to revel a bandage that appeared bloody and clotted.

I was impressed, the bandage appeared flat, as if nothing was under it. Matthew had done an amazing job tucking his boy parts so it looked fucking real. Matthew even winced as if in much pain as he pulled down his pants.

David let out a gasp, "Holy shit. Where is your dick, man?"

I growled low. "Fuck man, clean the shit out your ears. The Mistress don't like meat and potatoes fool. She wants a Ken doll. Now get your pants off so I can get your measurements for the doctor. Not that it will matter once she bashes it with her hammer tonight you will be glad to get it off by morning. Hurts beyond your wildest dreams, man."

David had heard enough. He took one more look at me then Matthew. "Fuck this shit. I ain't cutting off my cock for some old whore. I am out of here. See you sissies." He opened the door and slammed it on his way out.

Matthew and I looked at each other then broke out laughing. He and I high fived just as we did with Kaylee. Then I looked at his crotch curiously.

"Okay, I will bite. How the fuck did you do that brother?" I went to poke at the bandage.

He backed up. "Whoa there, baby. I used duct tape and it is going to hurt like hell to get off. I know we agreed I would take the thud but I am going to need a moment to deal with hell on earth here." He looked at me while taking a deep breath.

I shuddered. "Uhm, duct tape? Yeah, I guess you are off the hook. I will take the thud. If you move too fast, then next time we pull this trick you won't need to fake it. I would suggest getting into a hot bath and soaking that shit for a bit before pulling. Shit brother, you have my respect. Damn." I figured if he had risked a raw dick the least, I could do is take the punishment.

He nodded. "Are you sure? It is my turn. I can do this, I swear it."

I laughed as I started down the hallway. "I know you can, Matt. But I got this one. Go take care of yourself and my chores for the night. Catch you on the flip side. Oh, you better get my earplugs. I have a feeling I will be yelling for Jesus, the saints and all the Gods and Goddesses tonight at the end of her whip."

He chuckled. "Maybe you should just call on the devil. I believe he is related right?"

That made me really laugh. "Nah, besides Matt the devil is a woman. I should know she gave birth to me. No reason to call my Mom in. She would only complicate the sex."

He let out his breath laughing hard at my very dark humor. "I love you, Psycho. Mary me creepy woman. I need you in my life forever."

I looked at his fake bandage. "Sorry Matthew, I must decline your offer. I see you don't have the right parts anymore. Lesbians can't get married. It is illegal." I winked then headed to the Mistress room leaving him behind in spasms of laughter.

Mistress Ginger was beyond pissed when I told her David left and had called her an old whore. She nearly broke the bedroom window throwing her brush at me calling me a liar.

I stayed knelt at her feet despite her attempt to brain me. "Mistress, I am not lying. I would never dare. Would you like me to get Matthew to find the dirty mouthed, ungrateful brat for your whip?"

She sat there staring at me. I tried not to look back at her handsomely dressed in a red see through bra and panties. I wondered why she did that for David but never for me, or Matthew.

"No, let the fucker walk home. I guess you will have to do, Psycho. Get Matthew too. I will have my fun at both of your expense tonight. I think it may be fun to get more involved with my two brats. I am so bored. Watching you two suffer will cheer me up. I am not old, and I will prove that tonight. Go now. Get Matthew then both of you get your asses back in here pronto." She pointed at the door.

I felt my stomach do flip flops. This was a very bad sign. However, I knew better than to piss her off more than she already was. I did as she told me to do. I found my brother soaking in the tub. When I told him we both had to go I could see the look of terror in his eyes that I was feeling in my heart.

"Oh, shit Psycho, this is bad." He said as he pulled off the duct tape trying to move quickly before she got any angrier.

I looked at the floor. "Yeah it is. I am sure it is going to be worse than either of us can imagine. Just so you know, whatever happens, I forgive you."

He finished undoing his trick, then he also looked at the floor. "Psycho whatever happens, I apologize."

I nodded. "We had better hurry up. She was pissed Matt."

He grabbed my arm as he got out of the tub and pulled me close kissing me deeply. "I love you please remember that."

I looked at his eyes which were filling with rain. "I love you too. Nothing she makes you do will change that Matthew. Please just pretend like we always do. It is not us. Close your eyes if you must but it is not me and it is not you. I will try not to upset you by yelling or crying."

He leaned his forehead on the top of my head. "I will do my best to ignore it if you have to do that."

We held hands then walked to her room. Taking a deep breath, we went inside to face the wrath of our thwarted Mistress. I will not sully his memory by retelling the events that night. She was beyond cruel to us both. I did my best to keep my promise, but I did yell and cry, and so did he.

In the end, it took a lot of holding and many weeks for either of us to get over that horror show. She knew our fears and she knew our baggage. That night she made sure to force them on us and each other. David cost Matthew and I a piece of our soul. We did have some trouble being intimate after that for a bit. Memories of the trauma of what she made us do, bondage folks not just command here, kept one or both from our usual devil may care performance plus. I had been minorly injured to top it all off.

However, in true submissive style we got over it, moved on and did our very best to forget. One promise we did keep to each other is we never blamed the other. Because of that, in a very short time, we managed to get back to 'our normal' love life. We knew she would make us hurt each other sexually before we went in there. That is why we apologized to each other in advance.

Mistress Ginger was unable to break apart our paring because we knew if we had the choice, we would never hurt each other. Matthew always theorized that it was her plan, to cause a serious rift between us so that we would fail at our daily duty of spending him. He believed it was a way to justify selling us off for insolence.

I continued to defend her bad behavior to him. I just kept saying no way the Mistress was that devious and cruel. I argued she was just angry, and we were easy targets for her to take out her aggressions. I mean she was only human and shit rolls downhill, right? Again, reality is not my strong point…

QUICK NOTE: *So, I guess I am saying Matthew, you were right Brother and I apologize that I didn't believe you.*

When I am wrong, I admit it. This was another time I was wrong. Despite her many attempts to get a good excuse to sell one or both of us, we continued to work as a team never giving her the satisfaction of a just cause for what she ultimately did.

The very next week after we ran off 'David the tweaker' our Mistress surprised us by saying that she was going ahead of us to wait at the park. This was most unusual behavior. We normally went to our family outing together with Matthew at the wheel. We were not allowed to inquire why she was taking her own car and making us wait a full hour before we followed. Matthew and I just accepted we were to mind her directive. She left with a strange smile on her face that, frankly, gave me the skeevies.

Matthew and I watched her drive off. Once she was out of sight, he grabbed me by my hand and demanded I take him to see my beloved Darlin. He had never been there but had heard all my stories about my old outhouse home. I was a bit nervous that the Mistress would catch us somehow but got on the Motorpsycho behind him to give directions and get to hold him while we traveled.

When we arrived at the old iron gate, I got off and opened it so we could drive inside. We didn't have too much time before we would have to race off to the park almost an hour drive away. Matthew marveled that I was able to live in that little outhouse, survive the weather and the torturous people who came to drag me through those dilapidated headstones for sport.

He shook his head sighing. "People are shits, Psycho. What else can I say? They all pretend to be cultured and civilized but they leave a little girl to rot in a cemetery like a corpse or come to use her like a piece of meat. You know, all around the country and maybe in the world, there are

Psychos out there and most will die in their graveyard hells."
He stepped into the outhouse appearing truly disgusted.

I looked at the handsome Matthew standing in the doorway of my old home. His silver collar caught my brother the sun just right. It looked like it was shining around his neck. Matthew's long black jacket and beautiful long hair framed his face just perfect to make him appeared to an angel fallen to Earth. He seemed like a dream I had once laying there as a teenager, lonely, longing and lost. I realized Matthew was one of the Psychos he was talking about. His life had been harsh and brutal like mine. Well not just like mine but bad, nonetheless. Somehow, he had managed to keep his honor, code and heart in one piece despite all the pain he had known. For just a moment I thought maybe he and I could just stay there forever. We would never need to go back to Mistress Ginger or to the world that didn't understand or even want us. We could dance with Simon and watch the sleeping Giant.

Then we would never be alone again. We could just live for each other until we accidently or purposely killed ourselves. I shook it off as I woke up from my hallucination fantasy to the cold harsh reality. Matthew was exactly like me. His halo in my vision was his fucking submissive collar.

We couldn't survive without someone directing our actions. If we threw off our collars and ran away we wouldn't last a month. Neither of us could decide anything other than how to run off a fucking intruder or please our Mistress.

If you asked us to choose what we wanted for dinner, you'd starve to death before one of us stopped saying, "I don't know, what do you think?" Matthew and I worked beautifully as a team when given a directive, but alone or without a purpose, we failed.

He saw me staring at him longingly. "Psycho baby, what are you thinking?" He smiled.

I looked down feeling sheepish. "Nothing that matters, Mathew. Only stupid delusions and hallucinations. The tapestry fools me sometimes. I forget which world I am in."

Matthew nodded at that then chuckled. "You were thinking we should run away together and get married."

I looked up in shock, wondering how he had read my fucking mind. "Whaaa what? I wasn't. I was just, uhm, I am crazy Matthew. That's all." I felt I may cry at that truth for the thousandth time.

Matthew came over and held me tightly kissing my forehead. "I was thinking it too. I was wishing that we had met before we got sick. I wondered for a moment what our life could have been like. What would our children have looked like? I thought what happiness it would have been, Psycho? I wished it too. We were not meant to be lovers. We were meant to be siblings, but just like everything else in our life the wires are crossed. Sooner or later, one of us will have to go. Just know this, you are everything I would have wanted in a sister. I have never felt more loved, safer or more peace then when I am in your arms."

I kissed him deeply. "I feel the same way my brother. I am just so sorry it all happened this way. Maybe one day she will tire of her games and stop torturing us like she does. Then she will see the love we have for her, and for each other and all of us can be a family in the right way."

He snorted then looked deep into my eyes appearing very serious. "Now you are hallucinating, Sister. But since you are off your rocker and no one is around, how about practicing that blow job. You really need to work on your technique."

I punched him in the shoulder. "You pig. Damn Matthew. I was trying to be serious here." I started laughing.

He looked down at his feet still sounding very serious. "I was too. Come on. When will you ever get a chance to do me a favor in a cemetery again?" He started laughing unable to keep up his act.

I punched him again as he almost fell while laughing his ass off at his horrid attempt to get a blow job in Darlin.

Now the story behind this is when I told him what we all called that cemetery he said his big dream was to be able to say, "I put my dick in a Darlin at Darlin."

It was the simple things that made Matthew smile. I watched him giggling wildly at his stupid joke. You have no idea how much I adored this man. His kind heart, his readiness to laugh, his loyalty, and his honor. It was maybe because of those things or maybe because neither of us ever seemed to get what we wanted. It is hard to say what drove my next move. I really believe that it was just once I wanted to see Matthew have a wish come true. Even if it was just a silly one.

Of all the things Matthew and I did together, this is the one I put as number one. To this day it makes me smile to remember the look of total surprise that spread across his face when I dropped to my knees and undid his pants. That day I fixed it so he could say his stupid saying for real. Hey, in my defense we had to do it every day so why not in Darlin. I sure didn't hear any complaints, not from Matt and not from the residents.

We had to rush like the wind to make it to the park in time thanks to my moment of, ehmmm, kindness? Matthew had the biggest dumb smile on his face the whole trip. I just held him feeling his heartbeat in my ears. I pretended this was my boyfriend and we had just consummated our love after our Senior prom. He was driving me home. I had just given him my virginity, and in his pocket was the engagement ring that he was going to give me in return. He was planning to drop to a knee and ask me to wear it in front of my approving mom and dad.

NOTE: *Yeah, I wanted that kind of mundane life. You may think that is silly, but I never had the chance to have such a mediocre and normal existence. For that hour ride, I pretended I wasn't Psycho, and he wasn't my brother collar Matthew. That day we were just two dumb kids about to make the biggest mistake of our lives, that we would live to regret in our old age, instead of the true regrets I would have till old age. I like having to fuck my submissive trainee* *in my old cemetery to meet our quota for the day. Like hiding our love for each other as if a dirty secret or like losing this beautiful man to suicide instead of divorce. When put that way you can understand why I did my very best to make our relationship a delusion of the normal kind.*

He and I made it to the park right on time despite our little indiscretion at Darlin. Immediately, Matthew and I saw Mistress Ginger was in trouble. She was sitting on a park bench and a man had decided to sit next to her. Even from our vantage we could see Mistress Ginger was not appreciating his very bold advances. This guy was pawing her, and she was trying to push him off while yelling. Matthew barely killed the bike before both of us had jumped off to run to aid our troubled Mistress.

Matthew ran at the man, I ran to our Mistress. Matthew grabbed the masher by his shoulder dragging him off her easily. The fellow was a shrimp compared to our gentle giant. He couldn't have been more than five foot nine. I pulled Mistress Ginger into my lap and covered her with my own unit, holding her as she continued to yell as if the man were still trying to put his hands on her. I did my best to calm her by petting her back and telling her she was safe now.

I watched as Matthew pushed the man to the ground telling him to beat it before he kicked his ass. The man was looking at Matthew as if frightened.

"Get away from me you freak," the little man yelled.

Matthew kept coming at him. "I will knock your ass into the ground creep. Get out of here now," he growled back.

I felt the Mistress shuddering. "It is okay Mistress. I have you. Matthew is getting rid of the man. He can't hurt you anymore," I whispered to her gently feeling angry that we had let her go alone.

She could have been raped or killed. We should have been there. I was damning myself for our failure to protect our Mistress when I suddenly realized she wasn't weeping. She was laughing.

I looked down at her. "Mistress?"

She sat up with tears of laughter in her eyes. "Phillip. We got them. They really thought you were trying to grab me. Matthew, leave Phillip alone. He is a friend of mine. Get off him. Now Matthew. Get over here and kneel idiot," she yelled becoming mildly annoyed when Matt continued to try to push the man away as he tried to return.

Matthew looked at me, I shrugged feeling anger burn my ears. We had been set up. This was a cruel trick of some kind. Matthew returned and knelt in front of her.

She looked at me. "You get down there too, Psycho. I told Phillip here that you two are great belly dancers. You and your brother are going to dance for us." She reached into her purse and threw our belly dancing outfits at me and Matthew kneeling at her feet.

I looked at Matthew who was turning seven shades of red and green too. The damned woman was going to humiliate Matthew and me in public in those hideous outfits she made us wear around the house when we were forced to practice every day. It gave the Mistress great delight that mine was too reveling and Matthew's was a woman's outfit.

Matthew looked at me and then we said in unison, "I will take the punishment Mistress."

He and I already knew there was no fucking way I was going to have my tits hanging out or he in a dress in the middle of bubba land park. She could thud us. We were not going to do it.

Mistress Ginger smiled cruelly. "Oh okay, so you are both willing to embarrass me in front of my friend Phillip. Well, I guess I will have to give Joyce a call. I think I have two collars for sale." She didn't get a chance to finish, Matthew and I had already taken off for the public privy to change into those awful costumes.

Thudding, vampire gloves, shock collar, the strap, those we were okay with. A short life being whored at the end of a leash to old nasty kinksters, forget that nightmare. Matthew and I returned in short order both very upset over this latest indignity.

To our horror Mistress Ginger had managed to gather a crowd along with her little balding friend Phillip. Matthew looked at me appearing ready to pass out from the anxiety.

I hazarded a quick whisper to him, "Try to think of something else. I have my boobs hanging out everywhere so unless they are chicks, they will not be looking at you. Just think of something else and it will be over soon I promise."

He nodded back letting out his breath then whispered, "Thank you for the mercy."

The laughter, jeers and eye humping were almost intolerable even for an old schizophrenic like me. I am sure Matthew was deep in the pit of hell. To his credit he took his place next to me and as the Mistress started our music, we did our dance for her pleasure, eventually shutting the crowd up from laughter to silence. We had been practicing a long while by then. Matthew was not a bad dancer and at that time I had my shit together too. Much to our Mistress's surprise we got applauded instead of made fun of when the horror finally ended. Several of the watchers tried to approach to talk to us, mostly the fellows trying to get a closer look at my assets. Still it was better than the lynch mob we expected.

The Mistress was pissed off that Matthew and I managed somehow to be a hit rather than a joke. She made us go change back into our horrid BDSM outfits immediately. Honestly, we couldn't have been happier to do just that. She then ordered we go home and leave her alone with Phillip. Neither my brother nor I were happy about that. This guy was not very attractive, in his forties, and appeared very creepy.

At first we worried he was a new love interest for her. I admit it, Matthew and I were very jealous. However, when the Mistress arrived back home right behind us, we realized Phillip was likely one of the many males Mistress Ginger was using by teasing him into believing he had a chance. She tended to lead these hopeless types by the nose while taking their gifts, monies and attention but granting nothing in return but a broken heart. Phillip was only one of those poor slobs. Our Mistress thought far too much of herself to settle for a middle aged nobody. To top it off he was vanilla. Matthew and I should have known our Mistress better. In fact, instead of worrying she was interested in that fellow we should have been worried about her wrath over our failure to humiliate ourselves.

Luckily for us she was there to remind us of that most astounding fact. That night Matthew and I had to apologize to each other again thanks to her nasty abuse of us in her bedroom. We both were aware that we had to start working harder fast or this kind of torture was going to make it to our new normal schedule. Matthew and I couldn't tolerate a future where we were used as sexual pawns in her sick twisted bedroom games. Plus, the thudding was painful for both of us. Mistress Ginger was upping her kicks to violent and psychologically damaging levels.

Despite our best efforts this horror continued through the month of November and December. Matthew and I had started to show signs of strain by the New Year. Our little staged battles seemed more real, though it likely was all in my head.

Truth is I was becoming afraid of my lover. His forced antics were painful, and all too familiar from my sorted past thanks to Mistress Ginger's knowledge of my history. Matthew did his very best to show love and attention after these horrible scenes, but for a moment I began to have a few flashbacks over the ordeals. I even began to try to avoid him or winced whenever he would try to touch me.

Our daily congress was getting harder and harder to engage in. Even with my ability to fantasize reality into unreality, I was starting to behave like a rape victim. Matthew couldn't miss my pain, and it was hurting his feelings of confidence too. Thank the Gods my brother was clever. By early 1996, he found the answer that ended this type of nightmare for both of us.

He told me of his plan. I must admit, I was in awe of his ability to think outside of the box. I knew right away this one would placate our cruel Mistress for some time to come. His idea was multi-faceted, adaptable and brilliant. In a word, perfect. I knew that right away the second he told me. It was too. From that day till the day of our bitter, sad end, this original act was able to keep our Mistress from ever pulling he and I into her bedroom circus show again. He and I went back to our comfortable, even boring, routine with our Mistress when it came to sex.

To this day, I am grateful to him for saving me from sending me back to the hell of hating and fearing the beautiful act of carnal congress. Had Mistress Ginger kept that shit up, I would have had to join a nunnery or worse would have been useless at the management of providing special services of the collar to the Keyholders of the future.

NOTE: *It is interesting to realize that despite all the nastiness I had already encountered, nothing had* *completely broken my ability to enjoy an orgasm. However, being forcibly and painfully raped by my own lover (not his fault by the way, he was bonded too) was the thing that threatened to end my ability to perform this most important service. One must understand with a woman, most of our sexual interest is psychological. Mistress Ginger's forcing Matthew to become my aggressor was damaging my trust that he would never hurt me.*

Over time that had begun to unravel my nerves to a dangerous level. It is my belief that Mistress Ginger was trying to create, and was nearly successful, a submissive who truly feared sex. I had already started showing behaviors she obviously was trying to incite. I would cry and beg during her cruel games of using Matthew to hurt me during carnal congress. That fear and pain was very real. I had even started to fear her advances as the terror within began to spread like a disease.

I knew from my childhood that some foul persons out there in the world pay big money for this type of behavior from a partner during sex. I had initially made Debbie a minor fortune when I was just a little girl. I was quite popular among the pedophiles because of my terror. It didn't help that Debbie allowed those people to do hideous things to a unit truly not ready for such an adult act. Over the years I had developed tolerance and apathy to such indignity.

Eventually, I was tough enough to tolerate rape of all kinds and high pain levels. I would barely raise an eyebrow unless there was a chance it would result in my death. I

viewed rape as a nothing. Take a shower, get over yourself.
So, what if they got their jollies, I would live to see the next
day. (*I usually trusted Karma to get them for me. I noticed*
sometimes fires happen, or other bad things when people
take what is not theirs. **I really had that attitude, as long as**
nothing got broken that is. I was one tough bitch trust me.
Remember besides Debbie there was Julie, Victoria,
Shannon, Randy, a near miss with Lee, Daniel, and let's not
forget the lovely Tammy. Rape was something I had come to
expect sadly. Let me say just for the record, no one should
have to live like that.

Mistress Ginger had found a way to cause me to revert
to a quivering terrified victim after all I had been through.
Had she been fully successful she would have literally
collected a pretty penny on my stupid ass. It is always about
control, so my terror would have allowed scumbags to feel
powerful while they paid for the pleasure of raping a
weeping, struggling young woman. Matthew is forever
owed my debt of gratitude that he managed to prevent her
from finishing this diabolical plan she thought out dead in
its tracks. Protect and Defend bitch. Just saying.

Now the reason Matthew's plan was brilliant was
because no matter how many times we pulled it, and no
matter what the venue, it always shocked, horrified and drew
audiences. To make things even better, it was something he
and I already did every day anyway. Matthew talked our
Mistress into no longer hiding our D/ss triangle relationship
in public. In our past tricks, we always tried to behave like
insane vanillas. Now, Mistress Ginger could wear her
obnoxious red latex cat suits, carry her crop and demand we

adore her to the surprised and curious public whenever her black heart desired.

In 1996, long before the idea of BDSM was a household word, this was a spectacular and rare display. We never wanted for throngs of laughing, jeering crowds while our Mistress had us do stupid tricks like act as furniture, walk on all fours while on leashes, or heavy pet to her command. Our Mistress was in sadistic heaven, and Matthew and I were just being ourselves. It worked out beautifully.

He and I were very careful to act as if this kind of humiliation was horrible for us, so she never got wise to the fact that we no longer cared. Let them look. We were not normal. We were never going to be normal. If this stupidity made our Mistress smile and kept our collars safe, then we were all too happy to engage in such trivial behaviors. The important thing was our cruel Mistress had stopped using us against each other. Our life together finally settled back into one of trust, love and adoration.

I must be honest, it was a close call. It was the fear that one day she would tire of this all in behavior that kept both Matthew and me up nights with worry. It had not even been two years and already we had to pull out all the stops. If she grew bored now, there was simply nothing left for us to do to bring her a new quickening. Even running nude through the streets or fornicating on the mall floor would likely not have fed her ever increasing needs for public attention. Matthew had become incredibly suspicious that something would give and soon.

I was so busy trying to complete my final semester and prepare for my eventual completion of my program at another institution of higher learning, that I didn't have time for noticing the signs that our time was running out. All I knew is that Mistress Ginger seemed happy, my grades were straight A's, our income was holding strong, and I loved my family.

I look back on the Spring of that year as the final moments of my blissful ignorance to the coming storm of despair. It was my last and only moment of peace until 2015. I had found everything I had ever desired. Life was still hard, and sure I would have changed how things worked in the household, but it was as close to perfect as I would ever get. My future was assured. My loving Mistress was my world. My gorgeous brother collar was my secret lover. My children were strong and beautiful, and my disease was under control. A weekly park romp with my D/ss family that assured I would be sat on like a chair or being groped publicly by my brother at our Mistress's command was a small price to pay for so much peace and happiness. I believed that finally I had gotten lucky. I was no longer a failure, nor a loser. My life had been worth it after all. Simon was right, the Key and collar were the answer all along. What could possibly go wrong?

Then came May.

We have one more chapter before the really bad stuff comes. Some readers may have had siblings or others close to you commit suicide. Now I want to prepare you for the chapter after this one. I am going to lose my beautiful

Matthew to this horror. I don't want to open any of your wounds, because it certainly is going to open, has opened, a few of mine even writing about this time in my life. So, I would ask you to either skip it or at least take it slow when we get there. Some of you understand why your loved one did what they did. I do understand why Matthew took his life. In the next chapter, I will be honest about the signs he demonstrated, and the reasons behind his decision. You will find that while there may have been another answer, for Matthew this was his only good choice. You may or may not respect what, how and why he did it. No matter what you may think of it, I just want all of you to know he didn't do it to hurt me or the children. In fact, I think he was of the mindset he may save us by his actions. In many ways he did. That too will be discussed in detail. This was our last chapter of peace and happiness for a very long time. So, brace yourselves. I hope everyone enjoyed this brief moment in the sun. Like Matthew always said, nothing can last forever. I will add, this is real life. In the real world there are very few happy endings. My fairy tale does not belong in a book for children.

Matthew was always a true enigma to me. Though we shared deep intimacies and almost two years with full honesty about our pasts, I still feel as if I never understood why he got caught up in the collar. I know what he told me, and while it makes sense on the surface (I can't divulge it) I have trouble believing it to be the only reason. Over the years the question as to why he took the collar and suffered as Mistress Ginger's submissive has always plagued me. So, take a moment and answer why you think he did it knowing what you do about him from this story. I would appreciate your mercy, and viewpoint that is not tainted by both the memories of our life together, and the secret he told me. Since none of us can ask him, your theory is as good as anyone's thoughts on the matter. I simply am too close to this beautiful lost soul to ever see clearly.

Chapter 37: I Hear the Secrets that You Keep
The Fall of the Triangle of Trust
Mistress Ginger and the Death of submissive Matthew

We have arrived at the final chapters of our beloved Matthew. I have done my best to prepare all of you to take this final journey with him in the last few months of his life.

So, this intro and his chapters are the Eulogy I never got to give for him:

Over the years I have looked at his short life and how he managed to touch my heart so deeply in that brief time. I have wondered does life matter when in the end no one will even know you lived at all?

To this very day, if you went to those tiny towns and asked about Matthew, no one would know who we were talking about. For twenty-four years I kept the secret of his existence buried deep inside my broken heart. Funny how easy that was. No one ever asked about him in all that time. Matthew was introverted and shy. Almost no one ever knew him. Save for one lucky person. I am honored to have called him my brother, my lover and yes, my best friend.

A finer soul likely never walked this Earth. I say that not just because of my history with him. It is the truth. The man loved puppies, children, innocence, and peace more than anyone I have ever met to this day. His code of conduct was unbreakable. Matthew was fair, honest and generous to a fault. He chose death rather than betray his oath to his collar.

He promised his loyalty to Mistress Ginger and to me. Matthew made sure that vow could never be broken.

Until all of you met him in this book he was just a ghost, a shadow, a fleeting cloud across the moon of my soul. One I tried not to look at directly for fear of being haunted by things that were never meant to be. Now, we shall lay the tormented dead to rest at long last. Matthew's unit died that horrible August day, but his heart and soul live on forever within me. No matter what you may think, he is still here to this very day.

Matthew changed me and in his own way, he was the cure everyone said was not possible. I still have schizophrenia, but my almost two years of mirroring this amazing person allowed me to recapture the ability to love. Matthew also instilled within me the desire to share that with a Benign Master and a family of my very own. Had he never stumbled into my life I would have remained cold and uncaring towards all human beings.

Through Matthew, I learned how to trust when the person is truly good. So, let's all take a deep breath, and this time you go on ahead. I don't want you to see me cry for my poor lost Matthew. I will be right behind you don't worry. I have done this before and I always make it to the bottom.

"I can't stop thinking about your life Psycho. The constant struggle to serve hoping the Master serves you back and doesn't hurt you too much. I have finally realized that it was not being submissive I really needed. It was a family. This collar has given me that. I have a sister, and a

Mistress, children and a home. Now that I have lived this beautiful life, I can't go back to the emptiness of being alone ever again. I also can't live the way you have. I can't deal with constant heartbreak. I am not strong like you sister. I beg your forgiveness for what I must do, but I can't let her win. She deserves to suffer for what she has done. I intend to make that happen."
---excerpt from Matthews suicide letter to Psycho, dated August 27th, 1996

May started stormy and unsettled. In our D/ss household Mistress Ginger seemed a bit restless even more than usual for her normal chaotic state. I barely noticed. In truth, I assumed that whatever was eating the Mistress could wait till my classes ended. Then I would have the entire summer to deal with her greedy ass. Until then I stayed focused on my goal of becoming a pathologist. Afterall, Matthew was there to attend her until I could be around more to help him keep her placated.

I was about to end my final semester at that college. I had already sent my request to Doctor Palkin for approval to finish my education with a year of internship with the state coroner's office. There were only five in the Forensics program. I was the only female and with a four point, the top of the class. There was no reason for me to fret when my paperwork still had not arrived as classes ended. Doctor Palkin was a busy professor, that's all.

Then three days after my final class ended, Mistress Ginger called me and Matthew to the kitchen table for a meeting. He and I were always nervous when family

115

meetings were called. Normally it meant one or both of us were not pleasing her with our service, or worse yet, maybe she had decided to bring in another collar again. I could see by the look on my brother's face it was something much more severe this time.

He seemed to be hiding something but what, I couldn't be sure. I knew Matthew better than I knew myself. When he was worried about something, he tended to withdraw, rarely speaking unless he was pushed. It occurred to me that day, he was barely talking to me or the Mistress at all.

As I sat down at the table next to him to await her arrival, I began to count how many weeks I had noted his obvious anxiety. I could recall it began around the first week of May, so for the last two weeks, Matthew had been bothered by something he knew but I didn't. I felt the icy fingers of terror roll down my spine as I watched my sullen lover keep his eyes on the table never even flashing a concerned look my way. Shit, this had to be really bad. Had we been sold? What the fuck was going on.

"Psycho, Matthew, I have some news that will affect everyone here in one way or another," Mistress Ginger said before she even sat down.

I felt I may puke from fear. "Mistress, have we done something?" I looked at Matthew who never looked up or even winced at her announcement.

I was now sure our gooses were cooked.

Mistress Ginger reached into her purse that she brought to the table. She took out a letter and slid it across the table at me. I looked and it was addressed to my legal name, the return address was the college, office of Doctor Palkin. Mistress Ginger had opened it.

I picked up the envelop unsure what to think. "I don't understand Mistress. What is this about?"

She frowned. "Doctor Palkin has denied your request for internship. He has basically tossed you from the program. Psycho, your college career is finished. Without his approval, you have no way to graduate, and your classwork is null and void."

I started at her as if she had turned into an alien. "Wait, what? That can't be." I opened the letter to read it for myself.

There in black and white type was his reasons. "We don't believe with your history of mental illness this career choice is in your best interest. It is with regret that I must decline your request for my recommendation for internship blah blah and more blah."

I couldn't fucking believe this. I had just gone to college all this time for nothing. My classes were useless. My grades were perfect, this had to be a joke.

I looked at Mistress Ginger. "Mistress I don't understand how this can be. Vocational Rehabilitation cleared me. Doctor Palkin knew all this time I have schizophrenia. If he was going to deny me a recommendation, why did he wait till it was too late to do something else. This just doesn't make any fucking sense." I grabbed my forehead feeling I was hallucinating this whole nightmare. I had to be right?

She shook her head. "I already called Voc Rehab a few weeks ago when this letter arrived. They said Doctor Palkin is tenured and nothing can be done. Tenured Professors can't be fired or threatened, and the college is going to back his play no matter what. Jim from Rehab said he doesn't know why he waited till now or why he is not granting your recommendation. He said he suspects it is because you are a woman not schizophrenic. Doctor Palkin is a quite vocal about his dislike of women in the science fields. Jim told me you can hire a lawyer and go after the college because this is a case of clear discrimination due to disability. They believe you could win, but Psycho it would take years in court. In the end, you would still never get into the program, not in this decade at least. In a sentence Psycho, you are screwed. Which means this family is screwed. We all depended on your getting a good job with the coroner's office in the next two years. Now, you don't even have a high school diploma."

I looked at Matthew who now was looking at me with pity. "I am sorry sister. It is so unfair; I can't find the words. I know this was your dream, but now it is over. People like us don't ever get what we want, even when we have earned it." He looked back at the table and covered his eyes with his hands appearing very upset for my situation.

Mistress Ginger growled. "Well dreams or not Psycho, you have wasted tons of our money, and tons of my time on

118

this stupidity. I want to know how you plan to make that up to me? You have one hour to come up with some way to make this right." She got up and stormed from the table back to her bedroom.

I sat there feeling I had been hit with a hammer in the back of the head. Did she just say I wasted her money and her time. Seriously? Now I was to figure out how to pay her back for my misfortune. What the holy fuck was going on here. I felt as if I had somehow become acutely psychotic in a matter of moments. This simply couldn't be happening.

Matthew put his arm on my shoulder bringing me back from planet 'what the fuck.' "Psycho, I have been thinking about this problem since I found out Mistress Ginger got that letter. I think I know what to do but you are not going to like it." He looked at me hard.

I shook my head. "You knew about this since when? Why didn't you warn me."

He looked sheepish. "I wasn't supposed to know, sister. I overheard the Mistress yelling at your Vocational Rehab counselor Jim on the phone. I found out by accident. After I heard I went to your college handbook and found out you can still graduate but you will have to go an extra year and change your major right away. Psycho, you can never be a forensic pathologist. You'll have to give up your bid for the Bachelor of Science. But you can still get a Bachelor of Arts in psychology and it will only cost you an extra two semesters. You can graduate by 1999, if you hurry and start this Fall."

I stared at him in disbelief. "No Matthew, a BA in psychology is nothing more than a glorified high school diploma. You can't get a fucking job with that. I may as well major in basket weaving. Besides psychology, brother, I am a fucking schizophrenic. Seriously? Did the Mistress thud you in the head."

Matthew laughed bitterly. "No Psycho, I didn't get hit in the head. I know how you feel about psychology but if you went for your Masters or even a Doctorate you could be a professor or even a psychologist. How cool would that be? I mean it is like letting the fox guard the hen house when you think of the beauty of it." He sat back in his chair crossing his arms.

I stared at the denial letter as my vision began to fog up with my coming storm clouds of rain. I couldn't believe I was going to be forced to change my major to the subject I hated the most. Like everything else in my shitty life, I would have no choice. Now, besides wearing a collar to survive thanks to my disease, I would have to bow down before the very department that had labeled me in the first place.

I knew my brother was right. Psychology was the only major I could shift to and still graduate without having to start over completely. I would lose only one year but sadly would have to attend graduate school to even consider a real job even in the damned field. No one would hire anyone to work with the mentally ill or teach courses in it with just a BA.

Worst of all, social sciences assured I would have to work with the public. With my disease, which would be a tough sell to my attending Vocational Rehabilitation counselor. I had been forbidden to interact with the public by extensive psychological testing. This was really a full-on nightmare unfolding.

Matthew grabbed me holding on tight when the torrential downpour of tears finally hit me. I wept like a child in his arms. It was so unfair. I had done everything right, and fought so hard, only to fail at the finish line. Now, my future was lost to uncertainty. Where the fuck was I going to get the money for graduate school. My kids were going to grow up before I ever was able to get my first real job. If that was not enough, my fucking Mistress seemed to believe she was owed money. That was indeed pure bullshit. I had paid for my classes with the money I earned at my job at the funeral home. More than anything else, I was mourning for a degree that I now would never possess. My dreams were once again blocked by my stupid illness. It seemed I was never going to find a way to prove I was competent.

When my childish crying passed, Matthew handed me a tissue to wipe my eyes and fouled makeup. He looked at me smiling kindly. "Psycho, take my advice sister. It will not be the life you wanted, but it will be a life. You and I are not people who get good choices. Didn't you tell me a thousand times sometimes you just have to bite the bullet and endure?"

I chucked. "Yeah, you are right brother. At least there is an option. I don't know what to tell Mistress Ginger about the money though. I am not sure what she is talking about. I didn't realize she was out money over my going to school. I was enrolled before she came along. My job covers my costs."

Matthew looked up at the ceiling. "Sister, I will only say this once. If she pulls any bullshit demanding you do something nasty to make up the lost income for this then take the punishment. Mistress Ginger has already gotten enough money off both of us. I think it is time I find a way to take some of that income back from the bitch. She is a thief and she is a liar. That is all I have to say about it." He got up and left the table headed for the bathroom appearing very upset himself.

I sat there stunned. He had called her a bitch, thief and a liar. That was not like Matthew at all. He loved Mistress Ginger and would have clobbered anyone who said nasty shit about her character, yet he just accused her of the worst. I was beyond confused. Was I missing something here?

I got up to ask him, but Mistress Ginger detoured me back to the table. She demanded to know what I was going to do to repair my damage to the family income. I told her I would change majors and go an extra year. She was livid with anger at hearing my plans to continue my college bid.

"You are beyond stupid. No one is going to hire a stupid schizophrenic for anything other than corpse preparation or digging ditches. You would make more money whoring on the street corner, you loon," she yelled hatefully.

I shook my head. "Mistress, I can do this. I will have to go to graduate school but…"

She interrupted with heavy laughter, "You? Graduate school? Will Simon go too? Oh, I know you could get a degree in straight jackets or drooling. Oh my God, you are insane. Well, I forbid this stupidity. You will quit college immediately and get a second job. I believe they are hiring down at the VFW. They need a bar maid. I am sure that sexy little ass will make good tips around all those old coots. I will get you an application tomorrow." She got up and left me sitting there reeling in disbelief at her discounting my ability to gain an education.

Matthew eventually came out of the bathroom. He snuck off into the kid's room digging in the closet. I saw him go in there but didn't pay him much mind. I was in such psychological torment at my epic failure. He came out an hour later carrying the Advanced Genetics book I had been reading the day we met. The smile on his face made me smile back. He always was a sucker for sappy shit like 'first this thing' and 'first that thing.'

"Look at what I found, Psycho. Remember this?" He sat down next to me opening the huge book.

I nodded. "Yeah I do, brother. You should have listened to me that day and run like hell. I still stand by that advice." I reached out and flipped his collar.

He reached up and grabbed it. "If I had, then I would never have fallen in love with the most amazing woman on Earth. What a tragedy that would have been." He stared off as if deep in thought.

I took the book from him. "Mistress Ginger is incredible but surely there is a better Mistress out there somewhere, brother." I looked through the pages.

He snorted. "I wasn't talking about that idiot. I was talking about my beautiful sister. I would have never fallen in love with you like I have. You make everything worth it. In our next life, I am going to marry you and make you an honest woman, and myself a decent man."

I snorted back. "I am honest, Matthew. I honestly think you are a nut and I am a loser. Yet, I am glad you took that blasted collar too. Damn me for it, but I do love you. I never thought I ever would love, but there it is." I smiled at him.

He took a pen off the table then wrote on the inside of the book cover. "Matthew loves Psycho forever."

Matthew underlined forever several times then said, "No matter what ever happens, if you ever miss me or worry that I have forgotten you, open this book and read this. This is the truth, Psycho. It will always be the truth. I will never love another for the rest of my life. I never loved anyone before you either. I thought that I did, but now that I know what love really feels like, I know the difference." He pulled me close and kissed me deeply.

I was feeling very confused. He was talking like we were not going to be together for years to come. I pulled out of the kiss to study his face. Something was wrong. I could sense it, but Matthew was not telling me. He had just told me he loved me above our Mistress. This was not like him at all. I wondered if he was getting depressed again.

"Matthew, are you taking your medication?" I couldn't believe those words came out of my mouth to anyone.

He nodded. "Yeah. Why? I feel fine, and so do you. I think it is time to perform those special services of the collar." He winked at me.

I laughed. "You are not the Mistress. You don't get special services of the collar, fool."

He stood up trying to look powerful. "Kneel, Psycho. I am the Master now. I say you need to do what I say."

I almost fell of the couch laughing at his poor performance. "I will take the punishment, Master Matthew. No way I am submitting to a pussy like you."

He grabbed my collar and began to pull me toward the bathroom. "Well okay, punishment it is Psycho. I will make you scream my name." I allowed him to drag me to our usual spot to attend our daily duty.

That day three things happened. First, I did kneel for him. Second, I did submit willingly to my beloved brother collar. Last, I did scream his name several times. I believe it was the stress of the bad news, and maybe my inner knowledge that something was going on with him. Whatever the reason that day the carnal congress was incredible, loving and went on for quite a while. It is definitely in my top five list of beautiful intimate moments with Matthew. However, making the list to include only five would be very hard to do.

That summer, my brother was more romantic, loving and amazing in our performance of our daily carnal congress than ever he had been before. I often would be treated to rose petals in the bathtub, sudden deep kissing, and cuddling after our duty was completed. Matthew appeared to be adoring me more and more each day, not that I minded. I had never been treated so well when it came to the act of sex. Had I been more versed in such things maybe I would have realized that Matthew was now only in love with one woman, not two. I was getting all that he had been saving for his Mistress. Maybe all he had been saving for anyone he would ever love. He had become withdrawn and quiet around Mistress Ginger but with me, he was open. In the last months before he died, he gave me everything he had inside his heart and soul. I have to say it was the most wonderful experience in my young life. I already loved this man more than you can know, but that summer, I became one with him in every way. I wish that I had understood why. Maybe it was better that I believed it was because our love was meant to be and not because it was his last.

The Reason that Matthew was upset that day in May/Backstory

What Matthew was not telling me that day was the other thing he had overheard Mistress Ginger discussing on the phone. He had been working in the hallway dusting pictures. Mistress Ginger thought he was in the back-yard pruning, but he had decided to do his inside chores first. So, she didn't know he overheard her when the call from Joyce came in.

Matthew had learned his collar had been sold to the 'pimp Dominatrix.' He had also discovered he was not to be handed over until the unnamed person who had purchased my collar finished paying her off. She and Joyce had agreed the collar transfers would happen on November 1st. Mistress Ginger was making Joyce wait to collect her property so that neither of us would be alerted and maybe thwart the sale of my collar to this unknown person.

He now knew we had been sold to different houses, and he was to be used as a leashed whore for the pleasure of a never-ending list of cruel kinksters. His life would be short, thanks to probable disease and lack of care, and his mind crushed by complete exploitation.

To add insult to injury, Matthew listened in complete disbelief and horror as Mistress Ginger told Joyce how to submit him. Matthew overheard our Mistress tell Joyce that Matthew was a pussy when it came to bondage and thudding. All Joyce had to do is tie him up and beat him until he did what he was told.

I cannot even imagine what Matthew must have felt or thought hearing the woman he loved betray him like that. To this day, when I try to imagine how bad his heart broke, it makes me tear up. Matthew truly loved and trusted Mistress Ginger. He did all he had done to please her, even forsaking his own dignity and ignoring his fears. She had sold him out to be used up and thrown away like garbage. Our Mistress had not even granted him the mercy of selling his collar to a decent owner. That is how much she loved him back.

Understand Matthew was now trapped by his collar as much as I ever have been. Mistress Ginger had taken all his money and he had no family to help him until he could get back on his feet. He surely knew I would care for him if he refused to submit, but he also didn't know who got my collar. He already knew my new owner didn't want a pair. He understood that Joyce and her goons were poised to take him by force, bond him and thud him until he did as he was told, maybe indefinitely.

That is kidnapping right? Well, like me, Mistress Ginger had effectively ended his weak support system. Not likely anyone would come looking if he disappeared off the face of the Earth. He also assumed it was likely no one would believe his schizophrenic sister if she went to the cops with such a wild story either.

He could possibly recover financially in time, but he still had the issue that put him in his collar in the first place. Without a new Mistress of worth, probable homelessness and loss of his peaceful existence, Matthew was facing complete devastation. I was too, but he knew I had handled such things before. This was new and scary for him. He didn't think he could withstand the unknown future of his collar being passed from house to house with no one ever truly loving him. He also could not tolerate giving up his collar or submissive lifestyle.

Now the question is, why didn't he tell me? Well, you all know me. He did too. Matthew was aware if I found out, Mistress Ginger would have been on the five o'clock news as a homicide victim. He was right too. I would have killed that bitch for doing that to him alone, much less what she did to me. He truly loved me and the kids too much to risk my wrath on that demonic woman. He didn't think she was worth my losing my freedom and her death would not end the fact that Joyce now owned his collar.

So, he kept the secret, mourning the truth in silence. He was creating a plan, one that would save him from his fate and hopefully punish Mistress Ginger for what she had done to us both. Now on to the main story.

Mistress Ginger brought me the application for barmaid at the local VFW. I refused to fill it out taking her vicious thudding instead. Luckily, they hired some other dumb twat before the thudding went into its third day. Next, she brought home an application for waitress at a truck stop. Again, I took the thudding. This time it went on for a week before the position was filled.

I was growing angry at her continued attempts to put me to work at low level jobs where showing your tits and ass earned you better cash. I began to understand she was trying to backdoor whore my unit out. I eventually had a blow out with her.

"Mistress, if you bring home one more fucking application I would recommend you sleep with your eyes open if I were you. I am not a fucking whore. I will return to college in the spring as a psychology student. If you get in my way, I will provide you equal service for your efforts," I yelled at the top of my lungs as she sat there on the couch demanding I fill out a third shitty application.

Her eyes glowed with fire. "Kneel you insolent bitch. I ought to bust out your fucking teeth for raising your voice to me like I am some commoner on the street."

I stood there refusing to kneel in defiance. "You think you are froggy enough, then jump bitch. I am tired of this bullshit. You forget who you are dealing with here, I believe. I mind you because I choose to do so, fuck with me Ginger and I will show you how to dance." I was beyond ready to end this cunt, trust me.

Matthew heard the commotion and came running. "Mistress, Psycho, what is going on?' He was wild eyed in fear.

I looked at him. "The Mistress is being an asshole. I am correcting her mistake, brother. Best if you just stay out of this."

Mistress Ginger was observably scared. "Psycho, it is very clear to me that you are showing signs of psychosis again. You are irritable, paranoid and I noticed you have lost some weight."

I interrupted with a growl. "Fuck you, Ginger. This is not psychosis speaking. You are trying to undercut my abilities for a quick buck. You are aware that a career requires investment of time and money for a better payout in the future. If I didn't know any better, I would swear you're trying to collect cash fast as you can so you can ditch Matthew and I for greener pastures. I sincerely hope that is not your plan. I would not want to be you if that is what this is all about."

Matthew looked at the floor then dropped to a kneel. "Mistress, maybe it would be best to let Psycho handle her own college choices. She was involved in that before your collaring of her. Maybe it would work better to keep the peace in the household to stay out of it." He was trying to help without setting the Mistress into a thudding of his unit.

Mistress Ginger looked at him then to me. "Fine, if you are both going to gang up on me. You are useless brats both of you. Do whatever you want, Psycho. You'll go to college till you are old and grey no doubt. In the end no one would hire you on a bet anyway. When that day comes, think back to today and realize how much money you lost wasting your time chasing dreams of being a professional. The only profession you'll ever be is a professional whore." She got up and stormed from the room.

I started to chase her down to beat the holy terror out of her for calling me a whore one time too many times when I felt Matthews arms go around my waist.

"Let her go, Psycho. Who cares what that dumb bitch thinks? You are going to be a wonderful psychologist someday. I can see it now, Doctor Psycho." He kissed my neck from behind.

I snorted still angry. "Well, I don't see that ever happening, but one thing is for sure, I am not a fucking whore like other people I know," I yelled loud enough for the Mistress to hear me.

He kissed me harder. "Come with me, Psycho. Let me treat you like the lover you are and forget that old bag. No reason to get your blood pressure up. Tomorrow I will drive you to the college myself and you can change your major. Fuck her Psycho, I mean fuck me and ignore her."

When Matthew kissed me like that, I couldn't pay attention to anything else. He was successful at lobbying me into his possession. He gave me plenty of reasons to forget her bullshit for that moment. The next day true to his word he drove me to the college. I changed my major to Psychology and a minor in Biological Sciences to retain as many credits as possible from my failed attempt at pathology.

To my complete surprise, he stopped at a restaurant and bought us lunch out. For the first and only time in our lives together we had a meal like a real couple. It was the only time he and I had ever been out together without having to perform like a couple of monkeys at the end of the Mistress's leash. Everyone still stared at our odd dress and makeup but otherwise it was nice to be normal, sort of normal. He then drove us to Darlin where he and I once again entertained the residence with our romantic acrobatics. It was one of the finest days I could recall. There was nothing fabulous about the meal, the sex or even changing that major – I was actually pissed over having to do that – but Matthew made it all seem magical.

He didn't treat me different, crazy or like a piece of meat. Okay he liked to fuck but what man doesn't? He was my boyfriend so that was totally normal, right? It was a tiny taste of what life should have been like for me. I reveled in the mundane nature of it, the lack of weirdness (okay yeah maybe some would say cemetery sex is weird but not that weird, okay) and getting to live the dream of normalcy. It was completely worth the thudding he and I got for being out all day without permission. Yeah, Mistress Ginger was waiting on us when we pulled up on the Motorpsycho near dark that day.

She wasted no time dragging us both into her room. Our Mistress showed no mercy, but I noticed oddly that Matthew was unusually stoic. He didn't plead or beg like he normally did. In fact, he appeared to be angry or something. I couldn't quite place his emotionality. I could take the beating with only cursing and yelps. Without Matthew's wussy crying our Mistress rapidly tired of her attempt to make us sorry. After only an hour she cut us both loose telling us to get back to our chores and out of her sight.

I looked at my brother. "Wow, you have finally beaten your fear of thudding. I am impressed," I said while rubbing my wrists that were still stinging from her ropes.

He looked back at our Mistress's closed door. "Nah, I haven't. I still fear it just as much as ever. I just wasn't giving her the satisfaction. Fuck her. Stupid bitch had no right. We are not children, Psycho. If we want to go out, we should be allowed to go out. After all, we support this house. I have a job and so do you. What does she ever do."

I was startled by his anger. "Whoa Matthew, calm down. We will get thudded again if you talk too loud." I took his hand and led him off to our chores.

I should have recognized these strange behaviors in my usually calm, easy going brother. He was obviously disgusted with our Mistress. However, I was just so accustomed to him telling me everything on his mind I never suspected he was keeping a secret. I believed in Mistress Ginger that deeply too. My trust was complete for the pair of them. In all my life I had never had faith in another person, so this was something very special I had bestowed on the greedy Mistress and honorable Matthew. Perhaps it would have done me well to listen to my instincts this one time. I knew deep inside that our triangle was starting to weaken. Even as deft as I am, I could sense that Matthew and Mistress Ginger were no longer in love with each other.

As May turned into June, then June into July, Mistress Ginger almost never called Matthew to her bed like she used to. She also appeared to ignore him more and more. It was as if he didn't even live in the house with us. Matthew turned to me in response to her cold shoulder.

He and I spent more and more time in each other's arms, having sex (she never told us to stop so we didn't) or sleeping together on the floor when I wasn't working. Matthew and I grew closer than ever. I now could see nothing but him. I found myself wanting nothing else but to be his. Simon warned me I was beginning to mirror him deeply. This delusion was exclusive to a Keyholder not another submissive collar. However, when Mistress Ginger started ignoring Matthew, she also noticed me less as well. Matthew didn't need to tell me his secret. I was starting to suspect our Mistress was considering ending our family.

I even confronted her with my fears a few times. Each time I asked her point blank she would pull Matthew and I into her bedroom for a family bonding, appearing to enjoy being with us as she always had in the past. Yet, that seemly affectionate behavior would only last a day or two then she would go back to ignoring us again. It was right after one of these days of reunifying in our Mistress's bedroom that I ran into an old friend at Knight's station while I was getting gas.

I had just dropped the kids off to visit their friends at Maiden Mary's when I noticed the gas tank as usual was about to burn fumes only. I stopped and had just started to pump the gas when an all too familiar voice called to me.

"Well, I will be damned. If it isn't my own pet loony Psycho." I turned finding myself face to face with Julie.

My heart almost stopped beating right mid rhythm. "Julie? What the fuck are you doing here," I yelled out in surprise.

She looked like shit. My old nemesis Master was in rags, very slovenly, heavy and looked ten years older than she should at twenty-five. Life had not been kind to her, or should I say she had not been kind to herself. I noticed large bruises on her arms. She had been shooting up. Apparently, her little drug habit had become a much larger demon than she could control. I suppose I should have been pissed to see her, but I was so stunned, my anger demon had not even had time to find its way to my surface.

She chuckled. "Why I came looking for you Psycho. I see you have been handled very well. I am shocked someone hasn't killed you and buried you in Darlin by now."

I snorted. "Well after they ran you off there wasn't too many standing in line to do that. Maybe you could ask Dennis or Boyd about it. I think they are just down the road. I believe they have been looking for you for a while." I looked off in the direction of the local police's speed trap.

Julie took a step toward me, I stepped back unwilling to let her get too close. She smiled at that. "Oh wait. I have something for you, Psycho. I think you'll love it. I have held on to them all these years." She took off to an old beat up Pinto I assumed must be her car.

I tried to get the gas to pump faster. I was in no mood to be reminisce with this demon. I finally got the pump off and went inside to pay the old man. When I came back out, she was standing by my driver's door blocking my escape.

"Typical of you to get in the path of someone who wants you dead, Julie. I suggest you move the fuck out of my way and get on your own Darlin." I growled as I approached her now finally feeling some irritation at seeing this prick who had damaged my unit, mind and created my fucking collar delusion.

Julie stood her ground appearing unafraid. "Here Psycho, for you. I kept the good ones for myself. Joni says hi by the way. You can tell her hi yourself if you want. I am taking you back with me. I have come for your collar. You belong to me and we both know it." She smiled that old gotcha smile of hers.

I pointed at my neck as I took the photos she was handing me. "I already have a Mistress idiot. You want to have my collar perhaps you should take it up with Mistress Ginger. I am sure she will be happy to beat your ass while I watch."

She looked at my collar. "Yeah, I noticed that fancy collar there. I just assumed no one would be so stupid to put another collar on you. In fact, I am sort of surprised you are still wearing any collar. I suppose you always were damned stupid."

I nodded. "Not so stupid to stick around till you killed me. I am also still here bitch. Where you been? Hiding in ditches, under overpasses maybe?"

"Fuck you, Psycho. When I get done recollaring you, I will make Crystal pay too," she growled.

I laughed. "Nope, but thanks for the offer. I am happy with my current Mistress and I have had a lot better fucks since you. I am not in the mood to slum but if I ever get in the mood for suicide, I will call you. Just leave me a number and address to reach you?" I smiled evilly at her.

Julie spit on the ground. "Good to see you are still fucking insane as ever. Why don't you take a look at those photos, Psycho. I think you forgotten who I am."

I looked down at the pictures she had handed me. It was disturbing to see myself as a teen obviously in a lot of pain.

I suddenly recalled Joni had taken these while her the evil clique took turns dragging me through Darlin cemetery the day her house burned to the ground in May of 1988.

"Ah good times, eh? Hope you enjoyed them bitch. One day you will have to face the music on this shit, though looking at you that day may have already arrived. You are looking rough. Guess not having any luck collaring another poor soul, are you? Oh well, too bad. Looks like you will be wiping your own ass for a lifetime." I smiled as I threw the photos into Mistress Gingers backseat through the open window.

Julie looked at me appearing desperate for a moment. "Look Psycho, come back with me. It will be different this time. No one knows you like I do. I can take care of your medication this time, and make sure you eat and everything."

I pushed her back hard away from the door and got into the car. "No thanks Julie. I am crazy, not stupid. Besides I have children now to look after. Oh but you didn't know that did you? I also have college to attend in a few weeks. Hey, how is your college education coming along?" I narrowed my eyes smiling.

Her eyes went wide. "You are lying. You are not in college, Psycho."

I looked at the newspaper stand. "Check the paper, under dean's list. You will find my name as a straight A student Julie. Now I would say have a nice life, but I don't want you to have a nice life. I want you to die, painfully, alone and screaming for help that never comes." I rolled up my window and drove off leaving the raggedy Julie with a shocked look in my dust.

I would never see the bitch again after this one-time meeting. Of course, I told Mistress Ginger of running into her. My Mistress assured me if she saw the girl, she would call Dennis and Boyd immediately. I told my Mistress not to bother. It had been almost seven years. The statute of limitations had passed. Julie would never do a day in jail for what she had done to me. I was in no mood to dig up the dead memories either. I told Mistress Ginger seeing her impoverished, drugged up, and lost was punishment enough, only because that was the best I was ever going to get. That night Matthew had to wake me and hold me most of the night. Seeing her brought up my old nightmares of her bench and chair. Thankfully, my big brother was there to kiss away my tears and trauma.

By the third night of nightmares I realized with growing terror I was starting to change. My sleeping pattern was switching around. I found myself irritable over little things. My food had developed a metal taste. Even Matthew's touch was getting unbearable though I never told him that, thank the Gods.

Then on July 7th I saw Simon in the backyard. There was no longer any doubt. My prodromal cycle was beginning to onset. My longest residual ever recorded to this date of one year and six months had ended abruptly. I was due to become acute by December as I had done back during the early reign of Mistress Ginger and the reign of Circe. It was at this time I had to admit, most of my acute cycles tended to happen around Christmas, just as my very first onset had. July was a month of suspect for prodromal.

NOTE: *With a rapid cycle like mine only the spring seemed somewhat safe, though I had overtaken the church in June during Circe's early reign. She had not treated me and I was definitely nuts many months before the church blow out. During my twenties, this cycle was indeed very common, but since those early days now there is no guarantee that I will not get prodromal in the winter, spring or even fall just as commonly as I used to every summer.*

I debated if I was going to warn Mistress Ginger. I had become very expert at spotting my signs of going psychotic. However, I still feared letting Masters or Mistresses know when I discovered my return to madness. There was always an underlying terror that they would toss me over the impending stress of managing my children, household income/bills and psychiatric care without any hope of return service till I returned to residual, if I returned.

I had not missed any doses of the medication. This time I had been falsely led to believe my disease was adequately controlled because of that. Without any real stress, I didn't yet know we had been sold, other than having to change majors and having a stable home my disease was becoming active once again.

After seeing Simon, I had run to the bathroom to cry my eyes out for a good hour. I felt so damned helpless. I knew that every psychotic break meant more brain damage and eventually would lead to burn out. The psychiatrists had done all that could be done to slow down my rapid decent to perpetual madness that would one day come for me. Every break with reality drew me ever closer to losing my connection with Simon forever. When that happens, I will not ever have a residual again. I will be broken instead of just shattered.

NOTE: *Psychotic breaks are ongoing active brain damage. What that means is every single time I go acute my brain is losing more functioning. Eventually, the disease will create a type of Alzheimer's or dementia that I will never return from. Burn out is what they call a schizophrenic that has entered the end stage of this progressive brain disease. Notice that schizophrenia is progressive, which for those who don't know means it will continue to worsen over time.*

The older I get the more I understand my symptoms and can even resist some that I could not in my youth. However, the downside is the more I recognize the sickness the more devastatingly sick I am getting. I am far worse at managing my daily adaptive functioning than I was at twenty, or even forty thanks to this fact. If I live to sixty, I can expect my psychotic cycles to end and my connection with Simon forever severed. I will be mad as a hatter and weirder than even I can imagine. Most schizos who live to this ripe old age end up in nursing homes blathering to nobody, in word salads, completely retarded.

That may or may not be my fate. Since I don't have a natural schizophrenia, all we can do is wait and see. So far, it has behaved like the typical disease, so to be real honest, it ain't looking good for me if I live another twelve years. But hey, that is twelve years. A lot can happen in that time. I should know. This story shows how much can fucking change in only five months.

Matthew found me bawling like a baby in our bathroom hide away. He asked me what was wrong. I never could lie or hide anything from him. I told him I had seen Simon and was going mad again. He held me tightly apologizing that I was cursed to suffer such a fate. We just sat there on the floor holding each other for some time. There was nothing he could do for me. Sadly, I was about to find out there was nothing I could do for him either. We both had a shit storm coming that promised the end of everything we had ever dreamed. The good times were over now and the brutal cold world had come to claim our souls. I didn't know it that day, but this was going to be the last time Matthew and I would cuddle together on our bathroom floor weeping in each other's arms over things we could not change.

He and I would still have our daily carnal congress there, and we would hold each other in the night when I would sneak out of the Mistress's bed to be with him on the floor. But we would never share another moment of hopelessness so openly and pure as that day. The horrible month of August had arrived. By the end of that month, it would not only be my major that was different. My entire world was on the verge of collapsing.

My overly attentive brother had become downright clingy by then. I would turn and there he would be. I found him always putting his arms around me, stealing kisses or trying to touch me in some way or fashion. I didn't try to stop him despite my growing tactile pain at his affections. I was feeling so lost, his being there comforted me in ways I would miss more than I could ever say in the coming years.

My daughter's sixth birthday happened mid-month just before my classes and my new major began a few days later. Matthew was there. He bought her a stuffed horse and acted like the biggest child at the small family party. Our Mistress didn't attend. He made her a cake and I blew up all the balloons. Mistress Ginger never came around either of us much anymore. I knew she no longer wanted Matthew by now. I assumed she was not selling his collar for fear I would retaliate. I was so cock sure that she would never incite my anger. So, I did my best not to worry. I should have worried. I should have known better.

My first day of classes Matthew came with me. I was shocked but didn't complain. He had always been enamored with psychology. He wanted to see what it would have been like to be a student of it. I enjoyed showing him off to Stacey and walking around campus with him hand and hand. It was a fine and fun day. Again, it felt normal. My paranoia and budding symptoms held off allowing me to enjoy this final great moment with my first love, Matthew. To this day it is how I remember him best. Walking hand and hand, sitting with him in class, whispering secrets, kissing by the car while waiting on Stacey to come drive us all home. For one sweet day, I was just like everyone else if you ignore our weird clothes, makeup and collars.

September twenty-seventh, Matthew came to me mid-morning to say he had to leave that very afternoon for a family emergency. I was shocked by his news. He seemed agitated and nervous. I was unsure what was going on.

"What has happened Matt? I didn't know you even still spoke to anyone in your family," I said trying to wrap my mind around his statement.

"Yeah, it is personal, Psycho. I need to go right away. Kansas is a long way off. If I get going now, I can make the line by dark or close to it. I will be gone a while, but I know you can handle things without my hanging around." He started heading for the door without packing a thing.

I followed him unsure what to say or think. "Matthew, wait. Are you sure you must go? Sure, I can handle things here, but I don't want to. I need you here with me and the kids. Have you told Mistress Ginger?" I looked outside realizing she was out with one of her lovers likely.

He nodded. "Yeah I called her (a lie, by the way) she told me to be back in a few days. I told her I would be back in three or four at the most." He held my hand walking to his car.

I looked at the ground feeling shaky and unsure, something was just not right here. "Matthew, please don't go. I can't be here without you. I love you very much. Whatever the problem is let, them deal with it." I felt bad acting like a selfish child, but I didn't want him to go, damn it.

He turned around looking at me with a peaceful smile on his face., "Psycho you are the most beautiful woman I have ever seen. Did I ever tell you how gorgeous your eyes are? They say you can see the soul through a person's eyes." He kissed me deeply and held me tight for a long while.

We had already completed our daily duty. I had noticed he took his time with our lovemaking that morning just as he did with this kiss. Lingering, enjoying as if trying to record every second forever in his mind.

When he released his kiss I looked at him starting to tear up. "I love you Matthew. I will be waiting and missing you every second you are gone. Please hurry back."

He brushed away my tears. "I will love you forever Psycho, never forget that. I have to go now, before I am persuaded to forget why I am going at all."

I watched him get into his car back out and drive away never taking his eyes off me. I never took mine off him. As I watched him drive away in the distance, I felt an aching in my chest dull, steady and horrible. He had only just left and already I was pinning to be held in his arms once again.

Mistress Ginger got home a few hours later. She didn't even ask about Matthew. Finally, at dinner time when he was not there helping me cook, she noticed.

"Where is your brother, Psycho," she growled barely looking up at me standing in protocol behind her.

I was rather surprised. "He is dealing with his family emergency, Mistress. Don't you remember? He told me he called you for permission."

She dropped her silverware and ran to the phone. I became nervous, unsure what was happening. Mistress Ginger called Matthews contacts for his home. There had been an accident in his immediate family, Matthew had been called. She suddenly appeared to relax when she was told Matthew was expected to arrive the next day. Mistress Ginger hung up the phone and asked me how long did he say it would be before he headed back. I told her three or four days is what he had told me. She nodded then dropped the subject.

The three days of Matthew's departure were hell on earth. I watched the driveway like a puppy dog waiting for its person to come home. Every motor, car door closing, and noise sent me to the front window as I prayed it was Matthew coming home at long last. When day four arrived and still no Matthew, I was in full on panic mode.

Mistress Ginger had to thud me twice during the wait. I was distracted, irritable, insolent and inconsolable. My pining for my brother collar was beyond horrible. He was almost like a drug I had become addicted to. I was now in the middle of the DT's even breaking out in sweats worried that the hours would not pass fast enough for me to get my Matthew fix.

The afternoon of the fourth day finally Mistress Ginger became worried too. Neither of us had been contacted. She decided to call his family again to inquire his whereabouts. I hung around the phone hoping to get a chance to speak to him, though I knew it was a long shot.

I watched as the Mistress spoke to Matthew's mother. "Oh no. No, we had not heard. How may I ask? And when? Where did it happen?" I felt my heart start to sink as I watched the look on her face.

I didn't have to wait for her to hang up the phone. Matthew was never coming home. I felt like the air had been sucked from my unit. The world stopped and only the sound of the electrical grid filled my ears. Mistress Ginger hung up the phone and just stared into space appearing stunned.

She looked at me. "Matthew was killed in a car accident the day he left Psycho. He fell asleep at the wheel and his car went off a bridge. He was killed instantly." I heard her say but did not at the same time.

I fell to the floor unable to think, see, feel, hear, breathe. I couldn't be hearing this. It couldn't be true. Matthew was not dead. He can't die. I wouldn't believe it. He will be home in just a moment. There was a knock at the door. I knew it. It was my beloved, he had come back this was just a cruel joke.

Mistress Ginger told me to answer the door. A postal worker stood there holding a box. I took it blindly and closed the door on the man. Nothing seemed real. The box had Matthew's last name on it. I took it to Mistress Ginger sleepwalking in a nightmare that any second I would wake up from.

She looked at the box then opened it. My Mistress let out a growl of anger. She reached inside and pulled out a ring of silver.

"That son-of-a-bitch. Well, Psycho. You always wanted his collar. Here you go. God damn him." She threw the circle at me dropped the box and stormed off to her room slamming the door behind her.

At my feet laid a submissive collar. I picked it up and found the dent where I had once tried to cut it off my beloved Matthew's neck. It was locked close. Without any doubt it was the silver wedding ring that Mistress Ginger had put around my brother's neck the day he submitted his will to her. I stared at it unable to think or understand. Matthew would never have allowed this to be removed, not over his dead unit he said to me a thousand times. I began to walk without knowing why to the Motorpsycho. I got on my bike and drove to Darlin with my lost brother's collar on my arm like a bracelet.

I cannot tell you anything about the trip or even much about how I managed it. I was so deep in shock I was more robotic than human. Once I reached the iron gates and went inside. I stood there in the middle of my old home where not long before my brother and I had made love in the grass. I felt my heart split in two and my mind shatter into a thousand pieces as a wailing exited my mouth loud and long. I fell to my knees in agony unlike anything I had ever known. The pain was beyond hell. I wished my life would end right there while I gripped the dented collar tightly to my chest moaning like an injured animal. My beautiful Matthew was dead. He was never coming home. I now understood what it means to feel utterly alone.

There is not much more I can say here. I thought I was ready for this. I hoped I was, but it still hurts like hell. He was my only dream so long ago. Thankfully, I have found my Master Jon, but reliving this part of my life has been as hellish as it was all those years ago. We will hear from Matthew one more time in the next chapter but then he is gone forever from the story of my life except what he put inside my heart and soul. Do understand at this time, I believed he was killed in an accident. Soon, I will learn the Truth, and why it happened at all. The worst part is now over. You cannot bring back the dead.

It was because of this wonderful man I became a psychologist. Had he not done the research I would have quit college when I was kicked to the curb like that. You all now know he was sold to Joyce and Mistress Ginger never loved him. You also know that he knew this a full four months before his death. How exactly did Matthew's collar get back to Mistress Ginger locked, and exactly four days after his death. The postal service was not any better back then, snail mail you know, so most everywhere took three to four days when you mailed something out. Did his family do that? If so, how did they know to do it and how the fuck did they get it off his neck then relock it? The truth to this day is that answer is still a mystery.

We still have the cruel Mistress Ginger to put to rest, and Matthew's confession to find, then read. I hope everyone is ready for the hell that is coming. I know I sure as shit wasn't.

Chapter 38: The Key to Matthew's Heart
The Fall and Betrayal of Mistress Ginger, Part 1

We have now had to say goodbye to our dear brother Matthew. It is painful, believe me,, I do know. However, my brother was very clever. His is unit is gone, but he has left something powerful behind: The truth. Matthew also managed to give us one more very important thing. When this chapter is over you too will realize he is still with us to this day.

Mistress Ginger and her collar are in mourning for their lost triangle. Matthew has been taken from them in a tragic accident. The two hold each other tight in their grief. Mistress Ginger is worried she will lose her remaining source of income, errr, lover. Psycho is not taking the loss of her brother collar well. The Mistress will never leave her side showing the utmost in care for Matthew's grieving sister. Ginger is there to keep the broken hearted submissive from escaping, errr, following Matthew to the Summerlands.

Idle hands are the devil's playground. The best way to handle loss is to stay busy. Without the extra income from the late Matthew's job, the Mistress will be forced to find employment. She must keep Psycho under her watchful eye. Mistress Ginger realized that a new job, a change in the environment, which is the answer to keep Psycho from discovering her lies, errr, focusing on the death of her lover Matthew. The two of them will work together for a single goal, the end of this reign, errrr, recovery from the loss.

It is too bad Psycho is schizophrenic. She never was any good at recognizing reality.

Ready to end the days of glory, errr, reign of this horrid Mistress? Great. We are not as in a hurry this time. We know what is up ahead and this is not going to be a pleasant journey for a very long time to come. We hope you brought your reading glasses. Take a deep breath and remember the chant of the necromancer. Tonight, we are going to speak to the dead. Our beloved Matthew has returned one last time. He is going to tell us where we have been for the last two years. You are not going to like to hear what he has to say but be honest with yourself. All of us knew the whole time. We just choose to ignore it. Get going. We are going to dig around in this closet for a moment. There is something hidden there we will need to tell this story correctly.

"Mistress Ginger never love us like we loved her. I believe she never planned to keep us with her for very long. She set us both up Psycho, from the very start. We were always just a source of easy cash. Mistress Ginger was stealing our income the entire time. When I called her asking about the lifestyle in 1994, she saw an opportunity to double her profits in two ways. My job of course, but then she had you train me so my collar would be worth something. All that public humiliation and forcing us to have sex was her way of making me ready for sale and increasing your price, my love. My love, we were her ticket back to California. I fell for her trap and so did you. I had asked myself dozens of times, 'What will I do if Mistress Ginger sells me?' Please forgive me, my beloved sister, the answer has always been the same. If I can't be with the

ones I love, I would rather be dead. Now, I am faced with my nightmare come true. Mistress Ginger sold me to Joyce and you to someone who's name I never heard. Whoever it is they paid a fortune for your collar."
---**Matthew's suicide note to Psycho, Dated August 27th, 1996**

I could not get off the ground unable to catch my breath, not wanting to. My brother, the sun, set in the west. My father, the night, pulled his dark blanket across my weeping unit. I held tightly to the collar that I had gripped so many times in ecstasy while uniting with Matthew in carnal congress. I believed with all my heart I would just wait there until the boatman came calling for my passage across the river. I wanted to be with Matthew in the Summerlands forever. How could I ever face the brutal world without him at my side?

My mother rose high in the sky casting her gentle light across the cemetery. I listened to the nighttime creatures calling to each other in the inky blackness. Some found each other, some mournfully continued to call out for those they had lost. I understood them like I had never had before. I too was calling for one that would never return. Fresh anguish filled my usually empty inner psyche. My wailing began again, my tears more bitter than the ones before. It was clear I was completely devastated by the death of my brother, my lover and my friend.

Simon heard my desperation. He came running to save us before we walked down to the bridge and followed behind our brother by jumping off. It was all I wanted to do, just die too. He found me on my knees rolled up into a ball, Matthew's collar cuddled to our chest in a death grip.

He laid his hand on my back. "Psycho, you have to get up. Matthew would not want to see you like this. He believed you are strong, now here you are acting like the pussy you accused him of being."

I wailed out, "I don't care, Simon. I cannot do this anymore. I want to be with Matthew."

Simon sighed. "I know you do. I am sure he wants to be with us too. But he is gone, Psycho. The Gods took him to be with them. We have children who will need us. Do not assume they are not going to be grieving too. What about your Mistress? Psycho you have no time for selfishness now. Your family needs you. Matthew would want you to take care of them the way he did. You are working for both of you now. Get up. Get up now, Psycho. Don't disrespect Matthew by letting his dreams die. He wanted to see those children grow up. He told us how many times? Now he can't because the fates took him from this world. You must finish this for him. For us. For them." He grabbed my shoulder, hard shaking me out of my hellish torment.

I looked up at his concerned face. "I know you are right, but it hurts too much Simon. I just can't do this without him. I love him, Simon, I want to be with him forever. If I can't be with him, I would rather be dead."

Simon slapped my face hard. "Stop that shit. Matthew would never be okay with you saying that. Matthew is helpless now. You must take up his slack. He would do it for you."

I looked at the ground realizing Simon was right. The only thing Matthew loved as much as me were the children. His whole world was about them. To abandon them now for my selfish wants to escape my grief would insult his memory. I sat up feeling the horrid aching in my chest. I groaned against it.

"Good. Now you will need to heal the shattering or you will not be able to have the strength to pick up the pieces. The children are going to ask questions, you will need to be able to keep it together, so they don't suffer along with us. Their minds are far too young to understand death properly. So, you will tell them that Matthew has moved away when they start asking. They will ask you. When they are old enough to handle this, you will tell them the truth of what has happened. For now, I believe Matthew would want you to give them the peace of believing he is still out there and will come back someday. The truth of this loss would damage their ability to trust and love for years to come if they ever find out. You will not be able to grieve in front of them. That will not be easy." Simon stepped back so I could do my healing.

I nodded then closed my eyes. Slowly, I removed our borders allowing our father's blanket to move through our pores. We felt the smoothness of Matthew's collar in our hands. His smell, his voice, his eyes spread out running through our veins. We all shattered to tiny pieces as we turned to static then collapsed flowing across the ground.

Like a thousand locusts we traveled in every direction seeking the electrical grid. Matthew's residual energy from his collar merged with our own. For a moment, we and he were truly one holding each other for the last time. He gave us his strength to add to our own. We did not put our pain into the ground. We locked it inside our static, deep and secret. Matthew would be safe with us forever snuggled tightly within. We felt the vortex begin to spin, calling us back inside the unit. All that ever was or will be pulled back churning, mixing and finally solid once more.

I opened my eyes feeling Matthew inside me. He spoke to me from beyond telling me to forgive him. I didn't understand, but I knew that I did forgive him. Whatever he thought he had done wrong it was not important. Now, I had his love forever, and his heart was my own. This gift was worth all the pain.

Simon smiled bitterly. "Thank you, Psycho. It is time to get up and face what is coming. Pain is something we have always known. We have a mission to complete. One day you will be grateful you listened to me."

I nodded at Simon. "I already am my friend. Matthew is here inside with us. He found a way to do what you cannot. He unified with our soul."

Simon looked surprised. "He got in? How?"

I shook my head. "I don't know Simon. I feel him and hear him. He is with Looper speaking, don't you hear him?"

Simon listened for a moment but shook his head appearing upset. "No. I don't understand how that can be. I can't get back inside but he did. We must be getting sick again. This is not possible." He let out his breath angrily.

"Well, believe me or not, he managed it Simon." I stood up smiling as I heard my love on the breeze speaking of his love for me.

I took his now empty collar and buried it in my burial plot. I would not give it back. Mistress Ginger said I could have it. Now it was mine, just like Matthew, forever.

Then I got back on the Motorpsycho and drove home to the yellow house and my awaiting Mistress.

When I came through the door Mistress Ginger was hanging up the phone. She looked at me appearing relieved. "Oh my God, I have been so worried baby. Where have you been. Dennis and Boyd are out looking for you. Come here Psycho. Let me hold you. I thought, I thought I had lost you too." She held out her hands calling me to hold her.

I went to her and hugged her tightly holding back my tears. I could still hear Matthew calling to me. I had no need to cry. He never left me. He only left this plane. My lover was now inside my heart and soul. Mistress Ginger could never thud him again. No matter what happened, I never had to worry about being separated from him. We had become one.

She held me appearing to be crying. "Oh Psycho, our poor Matthew is gone. What are we going to do without him?"

I shook my head. "I don't know, Mistress. I think he would want us to keep going on. I am here now. I can take up his chores and service. You will not go wanting. I would ask the mercy of not telling the children." I looked down feeling bad that I would have to lie to them, but Simon was right, they were too young to understand.

She nodded. "Yes, you are right, Psycho. We will tell them he moved away to be with his parents. Now, we must talk about the money situation. Without Matthews income we will not survive in this house long. Things cost money baby."

I pulled back. "I don't understand Mistress. I am making good money at the funeral home. You have my check. Matthew's income was extra, wasn't it?"

She looked annoyed. "No it wasn't, Psycho. His income was a big part of why I asked him to move in with us in the first place. Damn you are like a child when it comes to the cost of living. We will have to get another job to cover expenses around here. No. You know what? We will have to consider moving back to my trailer. I need to move back there to get it ready for sale. Once we get rid of that we can move back in this house. Maiden Mary can take the kids in for a bit. I will find a job and get you another one too. We can work together and fix this mess Matthew has left us in together. It is just you and me now Psycho." She let me go then appeared deep in thought.

I sat there feeling strangely angry with Mistress Ginger. Our beloved Matthew was killed and all she could talk about was money. I could hear my brother whispering 'beware' from far away. Something was just not right here, but what exactly I couldn't quite get my mind to accept. My prodromal was onsetting rapidly thanks to the stress of Matthew's death. Had I been residual, perhaps I would have understood his warning in my ears.

However, I was too scattered to deal with the reality of this very nasty situation. I was starting to understand Mistress Ginger never loved Matthew at all. She only saw him as a piece of property and a wallet. That no longer mattered. He was gone and she could no longer use him for either. Lucky thing he was accidently killed before he figured that sad fact out right. Or did Matthew make his own luck?

NOTE: *That night even with my coming madness and weakening grip on reality I began to privately question if Matthew's dive off the bridge was because he fell asleep or if maybe he had finally awakened. Was his death an accident or suicide? How did that fucking collar get mailed back so fast exactly? Who would have known to mail it to Mistress Ginger? His lifestyle with us was a secret. Why and how did his collar get locked back after being removed from his unit? These inquires began to bother me a great deal, but for now, I had a mess to attend. Without my beloved brother, my workload had just become unbearable* *and nearly unmanageable. The answers to my questions would have to be put on hold for now.*

Due to the death of my brother, my Mistress insisted I drop out of college for the rest of the semester. She told me she would require my assistance in selling her trailer, living with her there until the sale was accomplished and of course we would have to find extra employment. I was of course granted forgiveness since Matthew was a close relative. Mistress Ginger helped me to convince the school he was indeed my biological brother.

Truth is I was in no condition to deal with Stacey, the course work nor did I have the time to keep my GPA up with my growing list of tasks ordered by my Mistress. I was happy to drop out. I hated psychology and unfortunately Dr. Shree was the department head. So, escaping dealing with that shithead while I was in deep mourning was maybe one of the only good things that came out of Mistress Ginger's refusal to allow me to continue going that semester.

She and I packed up her belonging and a few of mine. She hired a local group of fellows to haul her stuff home. We left Matthew's things (since she bought all of them for him, not really his choices), the kids' stuff and my own right where they laid. I was unwilling to tackle packing up my lost love's items to haul off to Goodwill. That would just have to wait until a bit of time had passed. My ability to hear him helped but I still missed seeing and holding him too much to chance setting off more pain by going through our memories together like that. I saw no reason to hurry. The tangible items would still be there waiting when I was strong enough to deal with them.

Only two days after finding out Matthew was never coming home, Mistress Ginger and I had abandoned the yellow house where we had all lived happily together for so long. Maiden Mary happily took the kids back into her home and I went back to sleeping at Darlin.

Yep, I couldn't stay with Mistress Ginger or with Maiden Mary. I couldn't tolerate living in the yellow house alone without my beloved Matthew or my loving Mistress. So, Darlin became my home once more. I did travel between the kids and Mistress Ginger's trailer. When I did sleep, which was not often, I did it in the outhouse as I had done in my teenage years. I consoled myself with this seemingly hard fall back to square one as only temporary. Mistress Ginger would sell her trailer and small acre of land soon. Then she, the children and I would go back home. Maybe by then I could be in that house without always seeing the ghost of my lost love around every corner or behind every curtain. That is what I told myself anyway.

September rolled along cold and cruel. Mistress Ginger was overly attentive. She would not let me out of her sight. Her excuse was that after the loss of her Matthew she feared losing me too. I believed her. I was scared beyond my wildest dreams. I grew closer to Mistress Ginger than I ever had been. In my deep grief, she was there to hold me and say it was going to be alright. We became the lovers we had been in the beginning. I spent many hours attending her carnal needs and attending all her needs outside the bedroom too.

She praised me often, held me a lot and even appeared to be in love with me more than ever. I had always loved her from the very beginning so now my love was growing to extraordinary levels. I could not imagine my life without her in it. I was fooled completely that she could not see her life without me too or maybe I just needed to believe it. Without my beloved Matthew, I was lost and almost broken. Mistress Ginger was there to catch my fall. The bitch! Grr.

By the end of the month Mistress Ginger had secured a job as manager at a quick stop gas station. This little place had been built just down the road from Night's Service Station by a fellow from out of town. He saw potential as competition for the local pocketbooks by adding a small kitchen – which served only hamburgers, fries and hotdogs – along with gas, convenience items and a pretty staff of young ladies to make your change.

My Mistress got me a position just under her as assistant manager. We worked the same hours. Now she could keep a watchful eye almost around the clock on her last source of income, errr, grieving collar.

The only time I was out of her sight was at the funeral home. She had alerted June behind my back that I could be suicidal. Suddenly the hideous June began to appear and hang around most of my shifts when I was finally free of Mistress Ginger's constant presence. June tried to appear as if she was concerned for my mental health.

The truth is that June was watching and waiting for her chance to take advantage of the coming storm. I was unaware that she had been told by my Mistress of the secret sale. Hell, I didn't even know I had been sold since May. Not yet anyway. I never thought to question June's motives of appearing suddenly benevolent towards me. Likely, my lack of insight to what was happening with June was partly because of my grief over Matthew, partly because I was coming unhinged in prodromal, and my total trust that Mistress Ginger would protect me from that vile woman if she even dared to come at me again.

NOTE: *I wish I had realized this apparent over interest in my welfare was not because Mistress Ginger cared. It was because she feared Matthew had told me we had been sold. She was watching me like a hawk to make sure I didn't blow her deal with the buyer of my collar as Matthew had.*

She had told June about my collar being up for grabs hoping June would offer a counterbid. Mistress Ginger was trying to recover some of the money she had lost when Matthew died. The greedy Mistress had to return a minor fortune to Joyce when Matthew collar sale became null and void. My clever brother had cut that deal short by sending his unit to where it was of no use to anyone, even that pimp. Joyce could not afford the price Mistress Ginger wanted for my collar even with the money she had paid for Matthew, but she was scrambling trying to find a way. That is going to matter real soon so remember I said that.

June had initially told her no. June had figured out that without Mistress Ginger there to protect me as soon as the new buyer collected my collar in just one short month, she was planning to abuse her position of power over me at the funeral home. She figured she could get what she wanted without paying one red cent or providing any services in return. Plus, June was very aware I would never submit to her even if she did pay the price. June knew there was one shot as Keyholder. She had already used hers and lost her bid. She didn't want to deal with my disease anyway. She just literally wanted my ass. Yeah, get ready for the next chapters. They are going to be uglier than you can imagine. You will soon wonder to yourselves why I didn't take a nap at the wheel like Matthew did.

Now how did Mistress Ginger know Matthew had figured out we had been sold? Well, the collar in the box was his confession to her, but we are getting ahead of ourselves. The truth shall be revealed soon enough.

I continued to grieve for Matthew in silence. I pretended when in public everything was okay, that nothing at all was amiss. Especially when around my children and my Maiden Mary. I couldn't let the one's around me know how deeply I was affected. I feared that somehow that would allow them to see I was weak and vulnerable.

Any moment I had alone I would cry, wail or just sit aching in complete agony. Every day we were further from the last time we held each other, I felt more alone. I would watch the horizon hoping against all hope that somehow this was all just a joke. He would return and I would forgive him. I also would never let him out of my sight, never again.

I bargained with the Gods and Goddesses making all kinds of childish promises to them if they would let him come back to me from the Summerlands. I promised to give him all the blow jobs he ever could want, that I would never let the Mistress thud him again, and I would never call him a pussy if he would just come back to me. It was very pathetic what I was willing to do to have Matthew back for even a moment. It was also very human.

I also got angry for no reason, breaking shit at work on purpose when I saw happy couples holding each other's hand. I would spend hours cursing the walls of the outhouse yelling that the world should die because of my unhappiness and loss. It was so unfair. I never got anything I ever wanted. Matthew was such a small thing to have in the great scheme of things. Why could I not have his unit serving next to mine.

Mostly when I was alone I would dig up his collar and hold it to my unit weeping uncontrollably, telling him I was so sorry for ever calling him names, trying to get rid of him and any tricks I ever played on him in the beginning. My guilt was impressive. I blamed myself for letting him be collared in the first place. I blamed myself for not loving him faster and not telling him enough times (thought I did, it was all just the grief talking. He knew how much I loved him, trust me).

I blamed myself for letting him go that day. I was his head submissive. I should have tied him up. He was not supposed to leave the house by Mistress's commands. I never should have stepped aside to let him leave. I broke the directive and now it was all my fault he died. I began to believe I didn't deserve him since I was such a bad lover, sister and friend to him. If I had done my duty, he would have been alive, and I would not have a broken heart.

NOTE: *I was very obviously suffering the stages of grief: shock, anger, depression/guilt, bargaining, and eventually I would have to accept he was never coming back. I was a long way from the final stage. In the meantime, the buzzards were taking their positions to pick the corpse of what was left of me clean. I was a very easy target, even easier than normal. My mental illness was crushing enough without this deep and dangerous grief reaction going on.*

I must assume that Matthew never considered this possibility in his master plan to pay back our Mistress for her lies to us. I know damned well he loved me, so no way he left me in shambles on purpose. He was clever, but no one is perfect. His little plan had one big hole. I would have to discover the letter he left for me. It contained all he knew, and it even explained what I needed to know to defend myself. He hid it well knowing the Mistress would not find it, but he also made the mistake of assuming I would look there immediately.

He believed he had made it clear where to find his words to me if ever something happened to him. I had missed his instructions not even considering such a tragedy could ever happen. At the time, it seemed like such a little thing, just the usual romantic gesture Matthew was so known for when it came to our love affair.

If he had made it clearer that I look in that place if something ever happened to him, perhaps I would have gone there the second he was gone. Matthew had died peacefully expecting I would find his confession quickly. I did find it, but sadly, not in time to save me from what was coming. Who knows how this story would have ended had I found that suicide note before Mistress Ginger had collected the last dollar on the sale of my collar. We can only guess but never know for sure.

My Mistress has appeared to recover very quickly from the tragedy. She also appeared to enjoy her new job as manager of that small quick stop. In this new arena she was able to lord her powers over me as both my Mistress and my work better which brought her great delight. More than anything else she has a place to demand new public displays designed to humiliate me and feed her ever threatening emptiness. I of course never minded. After almost two years of playing her 'freak on a leash' there just wasn't much she could do to rattle my cage anymore.

Mistress Ginger would order me to stock the shelves backward (standing with my back to the shelf and putting up the items without turning around). She would order me to take all the orders for the kitchen while kneeling to the mostly surprised customers. These tricks would always cause a great deal of laughter from the vanilla and my Mistress alike. I just endured it trying to remember that if it made my Mistress happy then my place in her heart would be secure. She did appear to be having a great time. For the first time in a very long time, she didn't appear restless nor was she ignoring me.

When we weren't working, she began to thud again and sensually torture me. This time there was a new vigor in her behavior. By the middle of October, it seemed like everything was going to be okay after all. I still missed my brother collar like one would miss their own arms and legs, but my Mistress had become my world once more. Mistress Ginger had forbidden me to even say his name.

I tried not to worry about her strange grieving style regarding my brother. I just assumed it was her way of dealing with such a vicious loss. After all, she was keeping all her promises to Simon's Key as usual with her perfect return of my extensive service to her. She and I were rebuilding together, just as she said we would. In her household, and in the world outside, it was if there was never a gentle giant with a collar named Matthew. I decided that I was doing enough serious grieving for the both of us whenever I was alone anyway. He surely was being honored and missed in a way that would have made him proud. Besides, I was the one who really loved him.

Even as dense as I am, I understood my Mistress never loved him like I had. I was glad he never truly figured that out. I sure as shit wasn't going to soil his memory by telling him in my private discussions with him either. I was slowly starting to adjust to living with him only as a voice and memory, though my heart was still aching to have him serving at my side. If things had continued unchanged from this point on, I would have very little to tell you for many years to come.

Mistress Ginger was her old self. Matthew was almost like a brief detour that while pleasant was never meant to be. I had indeed lost my bid to become a forensic pathologist and maybe a college graduate. My yellow house was not lost, but my family was no longer unified. There was hope with people coming almost every day to look at the trailer that soon that would be repaired too. I was continuing to deepen in my psychotic shit, but that was my life. I would have cycles. Mistress Ginger assured me she was ready, and all would be fine just as it was the last time I had gone septic psychotic. I was blissfully unaware of the coming storm.

Then only one a half weeks before Halloween a new woman was hired by the quick stop shop. Her name was Leslie. Mistress Ginger was thrilled by this new hire. Leslie was weird as weird as it could be. Coming from me, that is something.

She was about five foot six with long brown hair and in her mid-thirties. She always wore a homemade dress that went down to her ankles. Leslie had big brown eyes and never wore makeup on her unblemished skin. Her hair was always pulled into a simple bun. Leslie had the strangest build to go with her odd withdrawn personality. She was rail thin, had chicken legs and a thin waist with no significant bust.

It was her backside that caught your eye. You couldn't even look at the woman without noticing her incredibly large and misshapen buttocks. It was not that having a big booty is that much a thing of oddness. It was that in every other area the woman was a waif. So, this freestanding ass made her look like she was carrying another person around her waist. Leslie's rear end was so large she knocked shit off the shelves when she walked by. It was obnoxiously large not just normal big.

Mistress Ginger, in her typical cruel fashion, enjoyed pulling me into the cooler to watch the hapless lady walking around. She would say horrid things and tell big butt jokes expecting me to laugh with her about it. I didn't like this behavior one bit.

Obviously, Leslie had a medical or glandular condition that was simply not her fault. Picking, bullying or making fun of someone's physical detriments – since I have a significant mental one – was low as one could go far as I was concerned. I got thudded at least twice, once we got home, for voicing my disapproval of my Mistress's nasty statements regarding Leslie's ass.

Poor Leslie was aware of her comical appearance. Customers who came in would often stop and stare at her. Some very rude ones would laugh or make fun of her. I would see her in the back crying sometimes when someone said something real horrid to her. To her credit she took the public's derogatory behaviors without complaint. She never brought it up to Mistress Ginger nor to me.

I tended to defend the lady running off the assholes, even refusing to serve a couple of teenagers who were incredibly cruel to her. I was not going to just stand there and take the constant pecking at the quiet and gentle Leslie. Within only a few short days Leslie appeared to understand she could depend on my fierce defense of her right to work without the hostility from the public. I would look up from my duties and she would be right there. Often when Mistress Ginger was pulling her old 'stock the shelves backward,' Leslie would run over and help me get the duty done faster appearing unaware of my reasons for doing it so bizarrely.

Leslie would only raise an eyebrow but said nothing when I would kneel to take orders in the kitchen. She never said a word when Mistress Ginger would make me stand behind her in high protocol while she made change at the register.

Leslie's lack of inquiry to my obviously odd behaviors did strike me as strange. Mistress Ginger was not hiding our very D/s relationship. Leslie had even walk into the kitchen to find my Mistress kissing and groping me like a lover.

Leslie didn't appear too startled. She just walked off saying, "Oh, pardon me."

When I wondered about it to Mistress Ginger, she told me Leslie was the wife of a Pentecostal preacher. That did nothing to curb my curiosity about Leslie's lack of interest in what the hell we were doing acting like that.

In fact, Pentecostals in my experience tended to be the worst kinds about judging the so-called sinful behaviors of others vocally. Mistress Ginger and I were very obviously engaging in a lesbian looking love affair in public, and I was kneeling to customers. Leslie had nothing to say about that. I found that more than a bit hard to swallow.

Only three days before Halloween and my big Sabbat in the Springfields, I was finally approached by the very demure Leslie while I was stocking the cooler. She opened the door looking around to make sure my Mistress was not around to see her speaking to me. Her anxious behavior caught my attention.

What the fuck was this about I wondered.

"Uhm Psycho, can I speak to you privately," said Leslie appearing satisfied Mistress Ginger was busy at the register and wouldn't notice she and I talking.

Quick Note: *Mistress Ginger didn't allow me to speak to anyone without her being present. Even Leslie knew about this strict rule. My Mistress had enforced this harsh regulation the whole two years of our relationship. If I spoke to anyone, I had to report the conversation immediately to her or suffer punishment. Even poor Matthew had suffered this isolation tactic. It is one of the reasons he and I had fallen in love in the first place. No one else could interact or speak to us so we only had each other to hold on to.*

I looked toward the front nervous myself, "I don't know Leslie. Mistr…uha Ginger is not here. What do you want?" I narrowed my eyes at the woman.

She came inside the cooler closing the door behind her. "Look Psycho, I see how Ginger treats you and it is keeping me up nights with worry about your immortal soul. I know that red headed woman is demonic, but I think you are different. I don't think you are happy with what is going on.

I have this Wednesday a meeting of women for empowerment through the word of Christ. I want you to come tonight. I really think you can be helped by joining our group." She handed me a piece of paper with her address on it.

I laughed. "Leslie, thanks but no thanks. You don't know a damned thing about me or Ginger. I have no idea what got into your head that I am different than her. Look at my face. I am wearing demonic makeup, sugar. See my clothing? Yeah, I am a whore darling. So, if I were you, I wouldn't get too close. I may rub off on you, stain your soul. Buh bye now. Run back to your nailed God. I have no time for this drivel." I shook my head sticking her note into my pocket but going back to my task of stocking the coca cola.

Leslie stood there looking at me appearing unable to grasp my words but finally left the cooler quietly as she had entered. She appeared disappointed. I found the whole idea rather insulting but then again, I was an active High Priestess of Wicca. Leslie had no idea who she was talking to, how could she? Not like I could visit with anyone sharing my life, my story or my religious affiliations. My fucking Dominant wouldn't allow such a thing.

Mistress Ginger never missed a trick. She had seen Leslie sneaking into the cooler to have that little 'come to Jesus meeting.' She waited until Leslie was busy elsewhere. Then she too came back to the cooler to ask me what was said.

I chuckled. "Get this Mistress, Leslie thought she could save my soul at some fucking woman's Jesus meeting. She wanted me to come to it tonight. Can you believe the balls on that chick." I was shaking my head at the absurdity of such a thing as I handed over the note to my Mistress.

Mistress Ginger looked at the scrap of paper then laughed hard. "Oh my God, this is hilarious, Psycho. You have to go. I mean what a fun thing that would be. You the High Priestess, schizophrenic, submissive with a bunch of dried up prudes talking about Jesus. That is a fucking riot."

I stopped laughing. "Wait, what? Uhm no way Mistress. I am not going to that bullshit. Funny to who? Not to me."

My Mistress also stopped laughing. "Are you telling me no, Psycho? I think you had better remember who you are talking to. Do you need a correction? If I say you are going, you are fucking going." She put the paper in her pocket.

I stopped and dropped to a kneel. "No. Mistress please don't make me go to this shit. I can't take this. Punish me instead. Pentecostals are insane."

She stomped at me. "Shut up Psycho. You are going, I command it. This will entertain me. So, you march right out there and tell Leslie you will be there tonight. No more argument. I will take you, drop you off and pick you up. You will tell me all about it and I will get a good chuckle over it. This is my pleasure. You want to serve your Mistress and make her happy, don't you?" Mistress Ginger crossed her arms still glaring.

I groaned. "Yes Mistress. As you wish. I apologize for my insolence." I wanted to brain Leslie for putting me in this position.

Mistress Ginger started tapping her foot. "Get up and go. I am waiting, damn you."

I got up and hurried out. Leslie smiled brightly as I told her I would be there that night. I shot angry looks at the cooler where I knew Mistress Ginger was watching the show.

"Oh, how wonderful Psycho. I will see you at seven sharp." Leslie reached out and hugged me suddenly.

I pulled away almost punching the dumb thing. "Uhm yeah, get off. Damn, I said I would come to your meeting. I did not say I was going to marry you, fucktard," I growled.

"Psycho, stop being rude to Leslie," Mistress Ginger barked as she left the cooler.

She had seen me get ready to plow into this weird woman. Had she not come out just then, I may have hit her. I am not very pleasant to be around in prodromal.

Despite my nasty outburst Leslie seemed thrilled that I as accepting her offer. This seemed very odd to me but then again, she was Pentecostal. I never could figure them out. I mumbled a half-hearted apology and went back to my work tasks.

Mistress Ginger was in fine spirits the rest of the afternoon often reaching out and slapping my ass. She continually teased me about my getting baptized and having my soul save before I would even know it. I must be honest, my Mistress was getting on my last nerve.

After work Mistress Ginger rushed us back to the trailer. She had me dress in the old zip all the way down black cat suit with red cuffs. She couldn't help herself but to grope and grab me while I tried to dress for this fubar meeting. I tried to keep it to myself, but I couldn't help but whine about being forced to deal with a bunch of church loons. Mistress Ginger threatened to thud me if I bitched about it one more time. I decided Leslie wasn't worth a beating, so I shut it up.

Finally, the dreaded hour approached. Mistress Ginger drove me to the address. Leslie's home was very large and expensive. Apparently preaching paid well. The home was a two story, grey with a black roof. It stood alone on a large lot of land with a two-car garage attachment. The doorway was arched and obviously of fine oak. The place reeked of wealth and vanilla Christianity.

In the drive way was at least five other cars. I rightly assumed these were the other meeting members. I looked at Mistress Ginger hoping for a last-minute reprieve.

"Please mercy, Mistress. This is just not right. I am a High Priestess of Wicca. This is a dead end and truthfully sacrilegious for their faith. I may not believe like they do, but I respect their religious preference. Don't make me go in there." I looked at the floorboard knowing that Mistress Ginger wouldn't hear me, but I had to try, damn it.

She chuckled. "Oh come on, Psycho. Are you afraid you may catch on fire when you enter that holy place? I would almost pay to see that. Stop whining and get in there. I will be back in an hour to pick you up. You will tell me all about it. We will have a good laugh and that will be the end of it. Now you get in there. The Jesus freaks are waiting for you. You had better hope they don't discover you have no soul." She pointed toward the door laughing hard.

I snorted. "Yes Mistress." I opened the door and headed for the hellish meeting of the High Priestess and the Pentecostal women.

I barely knocked before Leslie appeared. I heard Mistress Ginger pull out. I could almost hear her laughing at my most compromised position. I damned my disease for the millionth time. The preacher's wife grabbed my wrist excitedly pulling me toward the kitchen of this large home.

Sitting around a large rectangle table were five of the greyest, most dower looking ladies I had ever seen in my life. They reminded me of the dusty people I had seen years before at the Pentecostal church I was forced to attend when I lived with Mary and Bob. They were all around their late twenties to early forties. None of them were happy to see me in my wild black cat suit and six-inch platforms. My makeup was more demonic than normal, I did that on purpose, and it caused several to gasp at the sight of me.

I smiled diabolically. If I had to sit through this drivel, I was going to be sure no one made the mistake that I was joining their team. Believe me, there was not going to be any misunderstandings that night. These ladies knew I was not playing on their team under any conditions. Years before when I was a little child, long before Debbie's basement hell, or before I learned to kneel, I had watched a show called Sesame Street.

There had been a Muppet singing a song that was suddenly being repeated to me by the Looper, "One of these things is not like the others. One of these things is not the same." It made me smile even bigger. Sometime even my Looper has a great sense of humor.

Leslie introduced me to the group of sullen women. None of them were happy to see me. Most tried to keep from making eye contact. Likely they feared I would steal their soul with my icy blue demon eyes. It was very strange to me how little it seemed to bother Leslie that her friends were most unhappy about my being there.

She continued to chirp away happily as if she had not just brought the devil to their women's meeting. I sat back in my chair, kicked out my legs and crossed my arms just marveling at the whole obscene show. My life has always been fucking weird. So, why should I be surprised that on a Wednesday night just days from casting a witch's circle naked before the eyes of hundreds as the High Priestess, I would be sitting at the table with a group of heavily Christian woman who burned my type at the stake for fun? In my world, crazy shit like this happens every day.

I must admit, the hour dragged painfully slow. I almost fell asleep several times. I listened to the Looper sing me that damned Muppet song, and I tried not to yawn too often. It was beyond boring. I can't recall a fucking thing said to be honest. I believe Leslie was talking about the important role of woman as helper to her husband in the home. Something about finding Jesus through the meekness of subservience to a man, and children, oh well, I turned off my hearing at that point. I needed a lecture on being submissive like I needed another thudding by Mistress Ginger. I was already a true expert in that area.

Thankfully the hour finally ended. The other ladies started to get their stuff and I practically ran for the door. Leslie was hot on my heels. She grabbed my arm as I reached for the door handle to bolt from that horrid place.

"Wait please, Psycho. I need to talk to you privately for a second. I wanted to see you without Ginger hearing me or the other women," she begged.

I looked at her hard. "Look Leslie, I don't know what you damage is, but I have to go. Ginger is going to be here to pick me up any minute. She gets really pissed when I am late." I jerked my wrist from her grip.

She looked at the other ladies now all going out the door. "Please Psycho, I swear it will only take a second. Just have a seat there on the couch. I will be right back. I have to check on the kids real quick. Please, it would mean a lot to me." She actually put her hands together as if praying.

I shook my head. "Okay but you have to hurry Leslie. I really have to go." I went to the couch and sat down as directed.

The reason I did as she asked was twofold. First, I was pissed Mistress Ginger made me come to this thing at all. So, I was punishing her by making her wait a few more minutes. Second, whatever this was about I was curious to know. Leslie was truly weird, and I thought maybe I would glean some information that would explain her sudden interest in my fucking salvation from hell. I assumed it would be a quick conversation that could be justified with my Mistress after it was done. I sat there wondering how I always managed to get roped in by the fruitcakes of the world.

I heard Mistress Ginger's car pull up and sit idling. She didn't come to the door. That made me chuckle. I enjoyed making the bitch wait. Afterall I had to suffer the whole hour listening to bullshit about my place sucking a man's dick so I could get to heaven or something. I really wasn't listening.

When Leslie hadn't returned in a good ten minutes, I decided maybe I shouldn't push my luck any further. I had heard the car leave and return then leave again. Mistress Ginger was pulling in and then leaving going around the block and returning. Something told me that if I didn't catch her next pull into the driveway, I would be walking home. I stood up and started heading for the door.

"Psycho, wait, I am here." I turned toward Leslie's voice.

I could have been knocked down with a feather. There standing in front of the couch was Leslie dressed in a latex cat suit. Well, sort of. She had a latex shirt with a pair of latex assless chaps, yeah I said assless, on her very large

180

bottom. Around her neck was a ball gag hooked and worn like a necklace. She was holding a flogger standing there like a BDSM nightmare come to life. I just stood there with my mouth open in pure shock.

She smiled then made a creepy purring noise in her throat. "I have figured out your and Ginger's game. I want to play." She cracked the flogger loudly.

That was all I could take. I turned, then ran out that door so fast I am not even sure I closed it behind me. I was sprinting across her lawn towards Mistress Ginger's car that was now pulling out of the driveway.

I could see my Mistress looking at me. She sped up her backing out and I ran full boar chasing her with all the speed I could muster. She made me run almost halfway down the road before finally stopping to let me in.

I ripped open the door, jumped in and breathlessly yelled out, "Go, go, God damn it. Leslie is fucking insane." I turned around terrified the nutball had followed me somehow.

Mistress Ginger slammed on the brakes nearly sending me through the windshield. "What the fuck is wrong with you. I waited for over fifteen minutes. You are late. Why are you acting like a loon, Psycho. What is going on."

I continued to look over my shoulder nervously. "Look Mistress, Leslie told me to wait for a minute. She said she would be right back. She came out dressed in assless chaps with a fucking ball gag. She had a fucking flogger, Mistress.

What the fuck. Just what the fuck." I was sweating and about to puke from the terror of seeing that most bizarre sight in a place I would never have guessed it.

It was insanity, even for me.

Mistress Ginger's face fell. "Psycho, are you sure you are not hallucinating that shit? I mean you are slipping off the deck. Leslie in BDSM gear? No way."

I looked at Mistress Ginger hard. "Mistress, I was not hallucinating this. I saw what I saw. She said she had figured us out and wanted to play." I shuddered at the thought of that weirdo being involved with Mistress Ginger and myself in any capacity.

Mistress Ginger gasped then began to laugh hard. "Oh my God, I knew this was going to be a riot. Fuck me, that is funny." She started laughing so hard she almost couldn't keep the car on the road as she started heading back home.

I shook my head angrily. "It wasn't funny to me. Damn that bitch is scary. Never ever let her be alone with me again. I beg mercy Mistress. That woman is crazy."

Mistress Ginger snorted. "Fucking right you are to avoid her. I agree, Psycho. She is nuts. We can't escape her at work, but we will agree right now to keep her at arm's length. Assless chaps and a ball gag? What the fuck is she thinking?" She shook her head appearing disgusted.

I shook mine back. "Yes Mistress, you have my promise on that. I don't want to even guess what she was thinking.

Best to stay away from insane people. You never know what they may do."

Mistress Ginger started laughing again. "Psycho, I do love you. You are the craziest fucker I have ever met, and you fear the insane. Leslie is just like you, stupid. Maybe she has schizophrenia too."

I glared at my Mistress. "You need not be offensive Mistress. I may have schizophrenia, but I am not stupid. Leslie isn't psychotic crazy, she is normal crazy. Leslie is dangerous in a different kind of way. If I hurt someone, it is by accident because my disease fools me. She hurts people on purpose with full knowledge of what she is doing. That is scary shit."

Mistress Ginger sucked in her breath stifling her laughter. "Well now Psycho, I am sure Leslie is sincere in her bid to be a lifestyler. She just needs a little training. She likely saw you as the one who could help her out is all. Never mind, I won't be asking you to do shit like that anymore. So, let's just drop it shall we?"

I nodded. "Sounds good to me, Mistress." I tried to keep it off my mind as we pulled into the Mistress's driveway.

I was scheduled to leave for the big Samhain Sabbat at Springfields in only one day. I had no intention of stirring up my Mistress when I was going to be out of her sight for two days. Normally I would only go on the Saturday of a Sabbat but due to the loss of Matthew I had asked for the full two-day visit. I need to have time for grieving my lost love and I was eager to spend time with him at the dumb supper without having to rush my meditations. To my pleased surprise Mistress Ginger had granted me the two-day pass. I assumed she knew I needed this break, and maybe she did too.

When we got inside Mistress Ginger was unusually interested in my affections. She pulled me into her bedroom for our usual carnal congress then fell asleep spooning me, insisting I stay the night. It was rare for her to want me to sleep with her in the bed, but I was happy to be in her arms and not stuck in a dark lonely outhouse for the night.

The next day we went to work. Leslie was quiet as usual and tended to avoid being around us. Mistress Ginger would make faces behind her back which sent me into spasms of giggles. I knew it was wrong to laugh, but after that little scene I was more than happy to view Leslie as a joke too. I did my best to erase the memory of her most misshapen bottom in those latex assless chaps. I was mildly successful but every time I saw her knock something over with her big ass I felt sick to my stomach with the sudden vision of it. It sent chills down my spine on more than a few occasions. I was so happy to see quitting time I nearly forgot my protocol of walking behind my Mistress to the car. I wanted to be away from Leslie as fast as possible. I figured a few days at Springfields would re-invigorate me. All would be fine, I just needed to get away from my problems for a minute.

That night the Mistress again was amorous and again asked me to stay the night in her bed. Her sudden romantic behavior made me think that I should ask for two-day passes more often. I had never seen her so eager to spend quality time with me. She had even asked me to sit at the table and have dinner with her. I had not been allowed to eat at her table since the day she had tried to seduce Matthew into her bedroom so long ago.

It was a magical night and one I was hoping would continue once I returned from my duties as High Priestess. I missed Matthew more than ever, but my Mistress had done everything right to help me feel loved and cared for. I was beginning to believe once more that the collar and Key solution was the correct path to follow to find ultimate happiness. At least as happy as I could ever be given my illness and emotional limitations.

The next morning Mistress Ginger removed my collar as per our agreement for Sabbats. She instructed me to make sure to remember everything anyone said to me so I could report to her when I got back. She was eager to hear all about Roary but reminded me I was to remain monogamous to her. I chuckled telling her that it would be a hard one but that I never betray my collar. Mistress Ginger chuckled too. She went on to say I was a tougher soul than she because she would likely not be capable of minding that promise if Roary were her Priest.

The red van pulled up, James at the wheel as usual. Mistress Ginger followed me to the open door then as usual kissed me deeply while my members did their best to not pay any attention. I just let her play this old game. No one fell for this public display anymore. The shock of it had long since worn out.

Once she was finished with her tonsil hockey she whispered in my ear, "You will never know how much I am going to miss you Psycho." Then she walked back into the trailer.

I stood there thinking how odd a statement that was, but with my Mistress no one could ever be sure what she meant by anything. I got into the van and James took off for the Springfields celebration. Hidden inside my purse was Matthew's collar. I brought him to put on the table for the dead at the dumb supper. He was my guest of honor that year. I was ready to spend the next two days with him for the last time on this plane.

No one brought up his name or asked about the tall good looking fellow they all had seen me with for almost two years. I found that strange but since I had promised Simon not to mourn in public, I dared not ask why no one seemed to care what had happened to him. I guess they all thought we had just broken up. No one wanted to be the one to ask if indeed the breakup had been ugly. I suppose that is how normals handle situations like that. It hurt my feelings and made me think no one cared about him or me either. Amazingly, no one ever asked about Matthew ever again. To this day, I never heard a single member utter his name. It was as if he never existed at all.

When we arrived, I was notified my Priest Roary would not be attending. He had broken his leg in an accident at his construction job only the day before. It was the only Sabbat he would ever miss in the whole decade we served together.

I have always wondered if Matthew fixed it so he would be the only male with me that holiday. I spent the whole two days with his collar, meditating when not doing circle work for the Covens. I felt he was with me the entire Sabbat. I shed many tears and was in agonizing psychological pain.

However, this healing time finally brought me a bit of peace. I needed that quit time to truly deal with the loss. I am forever grateful for it. It was to be the last two days of peace I would find for the next twenty-four years.

I didn't know it, but the world I thought I knew had just come to an end. That Samhain I said goodbye forever to my brother, lover and my best friend.

I had not realized that the day I had left for Springfields my Mistress had said her goodbye to me forever too.

There would be another two times like this in my future but this horrible break up was the first. I was young, getting very sick, and had been living happily with a false life of peace for over two years.

The end of Mistress Ginger's reign was as sudden and terrible as the loss of my beloved Matthew. We shall never see her again. That was the last of her forever.

This Mistress taught me to never trust what you think you see or feel. Always ask the hard questions and never ever believe it when things seem too good to be true.

Chapter 39: The Key to Matthew's Heart
The Betrayal and Fall of Mistress Ginger, Part 2

Well we have finally arrived at the end of the red-headed, beautiful, heartless, Mistress Ginger. She was our greatest failure to that date. Not even Master Julie had brainwashed us as badly as this cruel woman had. During her reign we had found success, love, and trust.

Oh, sorry we were in error on that last statement. What we had found was delusion, lies, false dreams and grief. All of it had been fake. We were never anything but a meal ticket to get her the fuck out of town. Sadly, we had suspected that all along, but we refused to question our own better judgement.

In the end, a good heart went to a watery grave and we found our own cemetery hell. Broken, bitter, and without guidance we were forced to come to grips with the brutality of our position in life as a victim waiting to happen. Even our beloved Simon's Key couldn't protect us from this near deadly exploitation of our weaknesses.

We would have no time to mourn our stupidity, losses, or broken promises. We had a shit storm coming down on our head, and no shelter in sight. This is one time we would have to take the crap bath and hope the foulness of it would not stain our soul.

So, ready to meet our new Mistress? Oh, you already have. She is just as bad a match as one could ever be, so don't get too comfy kneeling before her. This Mistress will not last, we shall not submit to her collar. Mistakes will happen when greed is involved instead of our best interests. Too bad for her, very bad for us.

In record time our silver ring will slip through her clumsy fingers into the hands of one more vile, cruel, self-absorbed and worthless than any before her. Before this little trip is done, we will desire a perfect score as a diver in the Suicide Olympics. So, you all head for the old bridge, you know the one. I will be right behind you promise. I won't push or jump, trust me. I just want to look over the edge for a minute and wish for release.

"I have left you the key to my heart enclosed. I know you will guard it well and never betray me like Mistress Ginger did. Every day since I found out she sold us I have meditated with it over my heart putting my soul into it so I could leave a piece of me behind. My love, I know we can never be together in this life because of our collars, but this is one way we can never be parted. Please never forget how much I love you. I am now completely yours forever.

With all my love,

Matthew, Psycho's Pussy"
Final paragraph of Matthew's suicide note to Psycho, Dated September 27th, 1996

The return trip from Springfields was somber and uneventful. Linda was pouting as usual likely due to watching the seemingly passionate kiss that Mistress Ginger had planted on me before I left. I just sat there watching the world go by the window. Matthew's dented collar was back in my purse hidden from the world.

My heart ached that his beautiful heart would be forgotten, never mourned or celebrated. He had lived like me in our secret world of D/ss from everyone who would have cared about him. I again felt the tug of suspiciousness about Mistress Ginger's keeping he and me from outside communications during his time in her service. Lately, I had been questioning a lot of things about her motives.

I shook off the feeling of paranoia chalking it up to my oncoming prodromal psychosis. Yet, I could hear my brother among the voices of the Looper saying "beware."

He had said that a lot as of late. It was a strange word to hear him say because in life he never said it that I could recall. I closed my eyes trying to isolate his voice. I wanted to see if he was saying something more, but with my coming madness there was just too much interference from all of the Looper's messages for me to catch Matthew's clearly.

Linda's hand on my shoulder roused me from my engaging in listening to the voices. "Psycho, are you okay? You have been unusually quiet lately. I noticed you are not yourself in the last few Esbats either. Something is wrong? Do you need to talk?" She looked truly concerned.

My first instinct was to shrug but I thought of Mistress Ginger's command to always report any conversation. I didn't want to make Linda a target of my Mistress's nasty temper.

I shook my head. "Just tired, I guess. I am going prodromal again. It is nothing really. Thank you for asking." I looked back out the window to indicate I was not interested in carrying the conversation further.

Linda was not so easily shaken off. "Prodromal? Wow, you have been residual for a while now, right? Would you like me to warn Dennis and Boyd in case when you go acute there is trouble?"

I shrugged now irritated at that statement. "Ginger will take care of this business. No need to get the cops on my ass, Linda."

She shrugged. "Okay Mother. Have it your way, but I know Ginger had to call them in twice last time. Maybe you should stop assuming you have this handled. It is occasionally okay to ask for help, you know."

Now I was angry. "Linda I would appreciate it if you butt out. I am not some dumb teenager anymore. I got this handled. My girlfriend will catch my fall. You will see."

Linda looked hurt but didn't push me any further. I was so damned cock sure that Mistress Ginger could handle the budding problems since she and I had been through this before. I have no idea why it pissed me off so bad that Linda's offered to alert my beloved Dennis and Boyd. Maybe I just didn't want to face being helpless and crazy yet again after being well for so long. Maybe it was just the irritation of prodromal. Whatever the reason, it was not a smart move and one I certainly would live to regret.

The red van dropped me, Delilah and all the kids with Maiden Mary at her place. I had left the Motorpsycho there because I had a shift at the gas station with my Mistress in only one hour. We usually worked Sunday afternoons together. I would have to move my ass to be there on time. I went inside the house helping the girls get the children settled. I was looking forward to seeing my Mistress. I had truly missed her while I was away even though I did need the quiet time and break from harsh service. My life was very structured under Mistress Ginger. I no longer recalled a time when I was not kneeling, scrubbing, thudding or other under her watchful eye. It was a hard life but predictable. I had grown comfortable with it despite its many draw backs like not enough rest, no support system outside her house, and loneliness unless she had time for me.

I jumped on the bike smiling ready to tell her a few lies about Roary. I hoped it would incite her to invite me to stay the night with her in bed like before I left. It is always the little things that make life worth living you know.

I made it to the service station in record time. I noticed I did not see Mistress Ginger's car parked in our spot. That was odd, but I though perhaps she had car troubles. The vehicle would sputter from time to time. I assumed she may have put it into the shop again and caught a ride in. I went through the doors eager to see her smiling face and open arms ready to take me back into her bosom of watchful protection.

Leslie was behind the register watching me come in. She smiled and I shot a nervous smile back. Since the little scene at her house, she made me very anxious. I ran to the kitchen assuming Mistress Ginger was handling the cooking. Yet, there was no Mistress Ginger there. I was very confused now. I walked back into the main store looking at the cooler. Where was she?

"Are you looking for someone, Psycho," asked Leslie in a weird mocking voice.

I turned to look at her. "Where is Ginger? Isn't she on shift today? We always work the Sunday afternoon shift together. She is on the schedule."

Leslie smiled big. "Oh yeah she is on the schedule, Psycho, but she isn't coming in."

Now I was dumbfounded. "Huh? Why not is she sick?" I felt terror rising inside me as I worried that like Matthew something awful had happened to my Mistress.

Leslie shook her head. "No, she is not sick. She quit yesterday." She was still smiling and looking me up and down like a loon.

"Quit? What the fuck. Why would she quit?" I was beyond anxious now thinking something was very wrong here.

Leslie laughed, which unnerved me even more. "Oh I imagine it is because she didn't need the money anymore, Psycho. Not with sixty-five thousand dollars in her pocket." She leaned down reaching under the counter for something.

I shook my head with confusion. "Sixty-five thousand dollars? Where the fuck did she get that kind of money, Leslie? Did she win the lottery?" I couldn't wrap my mind around the very obvious, there was no lottery in the State.

Leslie stood back up. I felt the walls start to move in toward me as I realized she was holding my collar. She had a big smile on her face as I watched in horror, while she placed my Loyalty Dog and Simon's Key on the counter. She then spun my circle of silver around her finger like a handheld hula hoop.

"Well, she got the sixty-five thousand dollars from me. I bought this collar. I mean I bought you, Psycho. It took me months to pay it off but here it is and here are you. So, I think you are supposed to kneel and let me put this back around your neck. You can call me Mistress now." Leslie stopped spinning my collar then looked at me with a crazy look in her eyes.

I shook my head feeling as if I couldn't breathe suddenly. This was not happening. Mistress Ginger would never do this to me. She couldn't have sold my collar, not to this thing. Months? No that couldn't be right. This was a prank that was all. Mistress Ginger was watching from afar laughing at this little cruel joke of hers, right?

I looked around but Mistress Ginger didn't pop out saying 'gotcha Psycho' while laughing her ass off. I suddenly realized this was real. Mistress Ginger had sold me out to Leslie the Pentecostal. No fucking way.

Without another second's hesitation I rushed over to the counter snatching up my Loyalty Dog, Simon's Key and grabbed my collar from her finger with brute force. "Give me that bitch. These are not yours." I tore out the door pushing the items into my pockets putting my collar on my wrist like a bracelet.

I took off towards Mistress Ginger's trailer. She was going to answer for this bullshit. If she was unhappy with my service, she should have told me. After all she had taken my Loyalty Dog. I deserved to have an explanation. There was still time to give back Leslie's money. If the Mistress wanted me gone, fine. She could sell me to a decent match. This was not going to do.

I pulled up to the trailer realizing in moments it was devoid of life. My Mistress had packed up her stuff and skipped out of there in record time. Even the curtains were gone. It looked like no one had ever lived there before. I ran to the door anyway to find it locked tight. I looked through the windows seeing that all her furniture and everything else was gone. It took me a few moments to realize I had been abandoned. I sat down on her steps starting to cry as the truth of my predicament finally started to sink into my daft brain.

Mistress Ginger didn't love me anymore than she had loved Matthew. I was just a paycheck to her. She had pretended all those months to love and care for me only to keep me from realizing it was over. The betrayal hit hard. I wailed as hard as I did the day I was told my brother was never coming home. My heart was breaking for the second time in only two months. I sat there grieving heavily for hours, unable to get up and face my fate. I didn't think I could go on without Matthew, I knew I couldn't live without Mistress Ginger. I had no idea what to do.

Then I suddenly thought of the yellow house. Maybe Mistress Ginger had moved back there. Maybe the money was from the sale of this trailer and I was being misled by a bad joke. The crazy idea seemed to work since I was unwilling to face reality. I jumped up off the steps running for the Motorpsycho but almost fell when I tripped over Mistress Ginger's signature crop laying abandoned in the yard. She must have dropped it while packing. Thank the Gods, I had found it for her. She would have been broken hearted to lose that. I picked it up then headed out for the yellow house. I was sure the reunion would be wonderful. This was all just a bad dream.

I arrived at the yellow house with my heart feeling heavy once more. No one had been there in two months. Mistress Ginger's car was not waiting in the parking lot. I killed the bike and went inside hoping against hope, that she was there waiting for me. Inside it was cold, dark and empty as the grave that held my brother's unit. I walked in turning on the lights calling out for Mistress Ginger, my tears and grief beginning to break up my voice.

I went to her bedroom and it was empty save for the clothing she had made Matthew wear still hanging up waiting for a unit that would never return. I grabbed one of his outfits and fell to the floor with it cuddled in my arms sobbing in agony. I dropped her crop next to me laying there with what was left of my D/ss family. One was dead, the other had abandoned me to a fate worse than death. I couldn't catch my breath from the utter despair of it all.

I wailed and sobbed until I finally fell asleep from sheer exhaustion and grief. I never intended to get off that floor again. This was too much for even the strong Psycho to take in. My happy, structured, secure world was gone in a matter of months without any notice or warning. Even my vicious disease was more merciful about letting me know my goose was cooked. This was the cruelest thing that had ever happened, next to Debbie's eighth birthday surprise. To know love and happiness when you never expected it only to have it ripped away. Well there are no words for the pain.

Just know I was broken to pieces by it. I loved Mistress Ginger as much as I loved Matthew. This heartbreak caused me to seriously consider taking my life rather than live without them. Thankfully when I awoke, my brother was there one last time to save me from doing something very stupid.

My brother the sun poured through the window into my face causing me to stir from my slumber. I looked around at the near empty room. My sights settled on Matthew's outfit and Mistress Ginger's crop at my side. I suddenly recalled the horror of the day before. It had not been a nightmare. It was real. I was alone and my family was gone. I decided to end my life once and for all.

In my prodromal mind I thought it over and believed it was all my fault this had happened. My not following the rules had let my brother get killed. My Mistress obviously had blamed me too. She must have been unable to stand looking at me. To punish me, rightly so I believed, she had sold me off to the horrible Leslie. Then she left wanting to start over where she would not have to suffer the pain of seeing her worthless Psycho ever again.

That had to be the answer. Understanding all that, I knew that I didn't deserve to live. I had murdered my own happiness by being a poor submissive to them both. It was only right that I die for what I had caused.

I got up to get a knife and open a vein or three. Just as I entered the kitchen, I heard Matthew's voice loud and clear.

He said, "No matter what ever happens if you ever miss me or worry that I have forgotten you, open this book and read this. This is the truth Psycho. It will always be the truth. I will never love another for the rest of my life. I never loved anyone before you either. I thought that I did, but now that I know what love really feels like, I know the difference."

I stopped and thought of the Advanced Genetics Book where my love had written "*Matthew loves Psycho forever.*" He was telling me to get that book.

I went into the kid's old bedroom and dug into the closet. It was easy to find sitting on the top shelf along with other old books from my classes in forensics. I took it down then walked into the living room to sit and look at his words to me one last time before I died.

When I opened it up instead of the words I expected to see I found an envelope with the words: "*Psycho please read this*" taped over the statement of love Matthew had written inside the cover. I pulled the envelope off careful not to rip away his love words. Inside I found a five-page suicide note written by Matthew to me dated September 27th, 1996.

It began like many suicide notes. "To my dearest Psycho, my one and only love." I read on hearing the words of my beloved brother Matthew as he told me of Mistress Ginger's scheme.

I read on in horror as his letter informed me that from the very beginning our Mistress was planning to sell my collar to finance her trip back home to California. That he had accidently come along, and she had seen a chance to double her profits. Matthew had discovered that she had used me to train him so his collar would be worth at least a good chunk of change while she robbed and stripped him of his life savings and daily income. Worse still, her enforcing us to have sex and public humiliations was all a way to slowly inoculate him to a life of prostitution, to an endless string of kinksters at the end of Joyce's leash. He told me that we had been sold in May, and that he had never heard the name of my buyer but knew it was for sixty-five thousand dollars. Matthew stated the amount was so high the buyer would have to pay it out. Our transfer date was November 1st.

Most sinister of all Matthew told me that our Mistress intended for us to fall in love so that when we were separated the grief reaction we demonstrated would make us more compliant for the new owners.

The letter went on to discuss the fact that our entire life together as a D/ss family had all been a sham designed to polish us up and buy time to auction us for the most money possible in those small one horse towns. Mistress Ginger used us, abused us, robbed us, and in the end was going to abandon us to our fates.

Matthew shared his plan to thwart our greedy Mistress in his very own "Rim Job." Matthew said he couldn't really hurt her completely, but he could put a kink in her master plan by taking some of what she had stolen back. He planned to do this by causing her to lose the money to Joyce on his collar. He said she would then have to sell her trailer too rapidly to get what it was worth. Matthew thought she would believe she needed to run before my collar was paid up and collected or suffer my wrath.

He said she would run like hell afraid I would retaliate by having her accidently burn up in her home. Why does everyone think I am going to burn them up? Hee-hee! He also explained he had to do it the day he wrote this letter since a chance to run had appeared that would seem plausible. He had a real family emergency come up suddenly. He surmised if he left right away it would force our Mistress to return Joyce's cash. He apologized that he would have to leave one month earlier than he had originally planned. This was unavoidable due to this one irrefutable opportunity to escape her clutches. Matthew went on with many lines of romantic statements that mourned the loss of thirty more days in my arms.

Matthew confessed he couldn't live with the truth, the devastation (that I was just now discovering) and even though he loved me, he didn't want the life that was coming for us now that our Mistress was false. He couldn't give up his collar but couldn't imagine a life in it either. So, his choice was death. He asked me to forgive him for his weakness. Matthew told me I had been right all along. He didn't have the strength to live life as a submissive. Yet, he didn't have the ability to live vanilla ever again either. Mistress Ginger had fucked up his psyche too much. The brainwashing was too complete for him to go back. He made it clear this was not my fault and there was nothing I could ever have done to stop him. Matthew reminded me that in our life as a submissive all we have are choices. He had made his and that was his right.

In the last few paragraphs, he gave me his heart and soul locked inside a key that was contained in the letter. The key was an exact duplicate to Simon's Key. He asked me to keep it with me forever. Matthew reminded me of our promise to never pair up again with another submissive. We were a pair for life, monogamous in the only way a submissive can be to another. Matthew asked me to live on for him, the children and all the Psychos out there because he believed in my strength. He wanted me to become a psychologist and help make the world a better place for the unloved, unwanted, mentally ill and different. He reminded me that he had never asked me for a thing in life but my love. Matthew made it clear he was demanding I return his service of loving me by showing my love back and respecting his wishes.

He ended his letter with a last single twist on his secret passion with me for oral sex mixed with my propensity to call him a pussy. I laughed with tears in my eyes at this very classic 'Matthewism.' My beloved brother had just saved my life with his words to me. I held up the key understanding the importance of what he had asked me to do. My heart was broken in a thousand pieces crushed to dust. I really wondered how I could do as he asked me.

Yet, my clever brother knew how to put things to me in a way I could understand. His favorite Aunt Maggie had been schizophrenic. He had learned how to speak our language. Despite my terrible grief I got off that couch. I went into Mistress Gingers old room and collected the only outfit that truly belonged to him. The one he arrived in the day he was collared. I also collected our Mistress crop, the pictures Julie gave me, several photos of me and Matthew, the suicide letter, the Advanced Genetics book, and his collar.

I packed the whole lot on the Motorpsycho. I put his key on a chain around my neck and said goodbye forever to the yellow house. I drove away chuckling at the memories of the wonderful times he and I shared despite all that I had learned of the truth behind it. We had fallen in love, and no matter what the greedy Mistress Ginger had done, she could never steal that away from us. I knew I would sell the house as soon as it was paid off by the middle of the next year. I would never return, nor collect the items inside it. I never wanted to see it or anything from that past ever again, and I never did.

I drove to Darlin and put everything but Matthew's collar, Mistress Ginger's crop and the collar she had given me inside the outhouse. It was all I would have for many years to come of my brother and the life we shared. His words to me and happy face in the photos would get me through many lonely nights in the darkness of my cemetery home.

I got back onto the bike and headed for the bridge that Dude had once pushed me off when I was first getting sick with my illness. Once I arrived just at dark, I took out the master key that I had stolen from Leslie when she was demonstrating her purchases to me. I unlocked Matthew's collar than my own. I closed them on each other locking them both together forever. The circles now formed the symbol of eternity. I marveled at them for a few moments then tossed them together over the side of the bridge into the silent water below.

Now, Matthew's collar would never be collected by the pimp Joyce. Now he and I were symbolically a submissive pair locked for all time in the collars Mistress Ginger had put around our necks. We had kept our vows to her and each other. No one could break us apart.

To this day somewhere out at the bottom of that lake there is a big collar locked into a smaller one. Sleek and silver, the big one with a dent from a silly attempt to cut it off the owner by the other. They lay silent and proud and tell the tale of a forbidden love of a brother and sister. Two hearts that once beat as one serving side by side. Ours was a special kind of love that can never be separated, not even by death.

I watched them sink together into the murky waters below. I held on tightly to Matthew's key. I could hear him telling me we were safe now, that he was with me always. I closed my eyes and wept because I wanted to go into the water with them and never come back. It was not the life I wanted, but it was the life I got.

Once I had gotten myself recomposed, I took Mistress Ginger's crop to a field full of cows. I bent it across my knee. Then I threw it into the freshest pile of cow shit I could find. That is what she had given to us, bullshit. So, it seemed a fitting place to put her so called weapon of authority. I smiled and could even hear Matthew laughing with me. He would have appreciated that little joke no doubt.

I drove back to Darlin for the night. I had lost my job at the service station no doubt. I didn't care. I only worked there for Mistress Ginger. I already had a job at the funeral home. I would have to return there the next night and deal with the awaiting June. I had by now realized what she was up to hanging around like that. I would have to do some serious tap dancing or she would use her position of power over me for sexual favors in a most foul way. I had big trouble on my plate without Mistress Ginger there to protect me.

Once the word got around that my powerful Mistress had sold me to a nothing I would even have to fear kidnapping by Joyce and her goons, and perhaps Circe who was still seeking revenge. I didn't have time to be maudlin or grieve. Not until this mess with my new Mistress was settled. I had misgivings about her. Since she had purchased my collar, I really had no choice but to give her the interim position to see if this could work. If it didn't there was no time to waste getting a new holder of Simon's key. I couldn't allow Joyce to get enough time to gather the needed funds to purchase my collar if Leslie didn't work out. I already knew she had forty thousand of it. I didn't want to find out how long it would take her to get twenty-five more. Or worse if Leslie would be willing to let her pay out the rest as Mistress Ginger had let her do.

I decided to have my own 'come to Jesus' meeting with the odd Pentecostal Leslie the very next day. I had already wasted enough time fooling around with shit that couldn't be changed or fixed anymore.

The dead do not come back and neither do Mistresses who fear reprisals. I would have to forget the D/ss family or suffer further extreme consequences. I swore that night as I watched our collar sink together to never breath Matthew's name or talk of our secret until a time came that I could mourn him properly. Only when I could be honest about what happened would I ever tell his story. So now you know it. He can finally be laid to rest at long last. Just know he is gone but never forgotten.

As for Mistress Ginger, there are no words foul enough in my vocabulary to say what I think of what she did to Matthew and me. She murdered my poor brother just so she could make a buck. I am accustomed to being exploited and abused. That is my lot in life, but Matthew was a vanilla, sort of normal. She used me to trap him in a world he should have never been involved in. For that I can never forgive her, and for that I believe nothing she will get will be bad enough. If I ever saw her again, you can bet your bottom dollar, she will get everything she has coming and so much more. However, she was never that stupid. She knew that, and that is why she ran like hell. I will never see her again, nor do I desire to.

Now on to the rest of the story.

Master number eleven: Mistress Leslie (Key, no collar) Reign November 1st to November 15th, 1996 (two weeks-refused submission). *Forever known as the Mistaken Mistress.*

The next morning, I got on my bike and headed to the service station with two things on the agenda. One I went to pick up my final check and two to deal with this new Mistress. Leslie saw me pull up and came running outside immediately.

"Psycho, you know you are fired right? And you have my property. I want that collar back. I bought you fair and square." She had her hands on her hips and was visibly angry.

I snorted. "You didn't buy me Leslie. You misunderstood. You gave Ginger money for a collar that I can say no to. Bet she didn't bother to tell you that did she? I am not a fucking slave. You can't just buy people." I walked over to her and handed her Simon's key and my original collar that Julie had given me many years before.

She looked at the items. "There was a little dog too, and this is not the same collar Psycho."

I shook my head. "The dog is for Loyalty and is only granted after a successful year reign, Leslie. As for the collar, that is my collar. The other one belonged to Ginger. I sent it back to her. This one is mine. That is what you bought so deal with it."

Leslie looked at the items again. "Okay, fine. So now what do I do?" She was trying to open the collar not even looking up at me.

I sighed loudly. "Jesus Christ, didn't you and Ginger discuss this at all, Leslie. I am a service for service submissive. You and I provide services to each other. If you do your job then I do mine. I provide many services, but you don't even have a clue as to what they are, do you? Hell, do you even know what you are supposed to do for me in return?" I grabbed my forehead feeling I may faint from the disaster that wanted to hold Simon's key standing in front of me.

She looked up at me. "Services? Uhm, no. You better not use the Lord's name in vain again, Psycho. I won't put up with that. Ginger said I can whip you for misbehaving. I am making that a rule right now. Do it again and I will whip you." She glared.

I rolled my eyes. "You can't do shit Leslie until I submit. I am not collared, nor do I think I ever will be by you. We need to discuss this somewhere. When are you off work?"

Her eyes went wide. "I am off whenever I want. I quit. I only took this stupid job to get a look at you and see how it all worked like Ginger suggested I do."

I stopped and glared back. "Fuck you Leslie and fuck Ginger too. You both should be drowned from your sneaky bullshit. Never mind. We need to go somewhere private to talk. Any suggestions?"

She smiled. "Let's go to my house. The kids are at school and my husband is off at a meeting for the day."

I nodded. "Okay Leslie, you take off and I will chase after you."

She giggled. "This is going to be so much fun." She ran to her car.

I just groaned but got back on my bike and followed her back to her house. I looked at the big house thinking of how awful the housekeeping was going to be. Oh well, tough shit for me. It wasn't until I was following Leslie's large rear end inside, I suddenly was gripped with terror. What if she wanted to use the special services of the collar. Yikes!

I calmed myself remembering she was obviously devoutly Pentecostal and straight. Hell, she had six kids. Surely, she would be like my last Pentecostal Master Anita and never request that service from me. Once inside however, I realized I was fucked or potential was going to be fucked and in the worst of ways.

"So, do we go to the bedroom now or does that come after I put this thing on your neck? Ginger said I could do whatever I sexually wanted to do with you." She blushed and covered her face.

My jaw fell and I nearly tripped over it. "Uhm, Leslie, I am a woman. I am not hiding a dick in my pants sweetie. My voice is low, but I am all girl."

She laughed loudly interrupting me. "I know that, Psycho. Gosh, I mean I am not sure how to go about sex with a woman, but Ginger said you can teach me and know things that will make it amazing. I have been waiting for months to see what secrets you have." She turned even redder.

I felt I may faint. "You are moving a bit fast here, Leslie. We need to discuss the rules here. I am not submitted so there is not going to be any services especially that one provided till I understand that you understand this arrangement." I practically fell into the sofa terrified at the thought of having to sleep with this very odd woman.

She sat down across from me with a frown on her face. "Okay, I am listening. Let's hurry this up please. I want to get to the sex before my husband gets home."

I just shook my head in disbelief that this was actually happening. Somehow, I had fallen into yet another fucking dimension of shitville. I really needed to get some heavier medication. This couldn't be real. Could it?

I began the long process of explanation and Key rules. Leslie sat there nodding her head, asking questions and eventually appeared somewhat concerned. When I finished,

I asked her if she was willing to try it out for a bit before trying to collar me in case she couldn't handle the job.

She looked at the ground. "Yeah, maybe we had better wait on the whole collaring business. I didn't realize how involved this was going to be. I have a husband who would frown on your being here all the time. I have six kids to care for already, and to be honest I thought I was going to be able to keep this thing a secret from everyone. If the church knew what I was up to they would have a fit, maybe toss me out."

I let out a sigh of relief. "Okay great. I see you are finally understanding this is not going to work. So, if you will just give me back the Key and collar, I will take care of it myself."

Leslie looked up angrily. "Oh no you don't Psycho. I paid a lot of money for this. I am not letting it go till I get what I paid for. It is true I can't do what you want me to do, but I know you need this to survive. Ginger told me so. So, here is how it is going to work. My hubby is off in meetings for the next two days. You will come here every day and let me play the way I want then on the third day when he comes back, I will find someone to buy it and get some of my money back."

I sat there flabbergasted. This so called righteous, church going, Christian lady was blackmailing me to get some twisted sexual fantasy played out. Wow! I have seen a lot of trash in my day, but this took the cake.

I glared at her. "You have me between a rock and a hard place Leslie so here is the deal. I will do what you want for two days, but I will never submit. I also will allow you to sell the Key and collar to recoup what you can of your money, however, with a stipulation. You will not sell it to a woman named Joyce or anyone affiliated with that cunt. Nor to any women named June or Circe. If you try to screw me over on this I will return and tell your hubby and everyone in your church was a fucking vile demon you really are. Do you hear me, Leslie? I am not joking here. I am truly horrified at your lack of humanity. How could you be such an asshole. I can't believe I ever felt sorry for you."

She laughed at me. "Grow up, Psycho. I live like a fucking nun here. I pump out babies for a man that wants to have sex in the dark. I have never experienced anything but my husband. I wanted to see what it would be like to have wild sex, and they don't get any wilder than what Ginger told me about you and her. I have been reading up on this stuff. If I can only get two days of fun in my whole drab life, then so be it. I will follow your instructions and for the next two days you will follow mine. Fair is fair. So, do we have a deal or what?" She stuck out her hand to shake on it.

I grimaced wondering if I could still run and just abandon the Key and collar before dealing with whatever horrors this monster had planned for me. Instead I took a deep breath then shook her hand looking at the floor damning Mistress Ginger and my mother for having my sorry ass in the first place.

She stood up squealing like a child. "Yay. Now let's go to my bedroom. There is something I have been dying to do since I first started paying on you."

I stood up almost falling down while the blood rushed from my head. "Sure whatever you say, Leslie."

She looked back at me as I started following her to her bedroom. "I want to be called Mistress like you did Ginger. Can I have that too?"

I shrugged. "Sure, Mistress. Whatever you want."

Mistress Leslie squealed out again appearing very pleased by this silly request. Once in her room she had me stripped down completely. She looked me over remarking on how tiny I was without my platforms. She then began to tie me up with simple square knots binding me arms to arms, knees to knees and ankles to ankles.

Once I was completely roped up, she sat me on a small stool and went into her bathroom informing me she would be right back. I just sat there miserable trying to lock into my mind the wonderful sexual congress with Matthew and even Mistress Ginger so that I could escape this sure to be horrid scene of sexually pleasing Mistress Leslie.

Within only about fifteen minutes Mistress Leslie reappeared dressed in the same outfit that had caused me to run from her home less than a week earlier (including the assless chaps). I have to say in my life following Simon's Key, I have seen and dealt with many horrid people and sights. Mistress Leslie in a pair of assless chaps is number two on the list (wait till you hear about number one in 2004.). She turned around demanding I get a good look at her humongous derriere.

Once she was sure I had taken in the complete horror of that ungodly vision she said, "Psycho, now your Mistress wants you to describe how small and beautiful my ass really is. I want you to use different words and they had better be sweet and wonderful too. If you fail, I will beat you with this flogger until you get it right." She cracked her flogger at my unit just nearly catching my left arm by the many knotted ends.

I almost puked at the very idea much less the ability to perform such a task. "Mercy Mistress, I am afraid I don't understand your command."

She laughed hard then got right into my face with that elephant man like ass wiggling it hard. "Yeah, you understand just fine. Tell me how beautiful and small my butt is now Psycho or else." She cracked the flogger at me this time catching my right arm.

I let out a yelp. "Uhm, it is as small as a bead box, Mistress?"

That made her chuckle. "Keep going Psycho."

I thought rapidly. "It is as beautiful as a smiling child?"

She squealed in delight. "Now you are getting somewhere. Keep telling me how glorious my ass is. I want to hear all about it. Worship it Psycho. Now." She thudded me again this time hitting my right thigh leaving a welt.

I will not go into more detail. There is no need. For the next hour she thudded the shit out of me while demanding I make positive statements, all untrue by the way, about how small, perfect and gorgeous her rear end appeared. It was of all the things I have ever been commanded to do the strangest and trust me I have had some weird shit requested by Dominants, of them all.

Somehow, I did manage it. However, no one told Mistress Leslie you don't thud someone who is doing the fucking requested task correctly. In short order I was covered in nasty welts, some bleeding and others deep enough to tell me this idiot had never been trained to handle a flogger.

By now I was a bit scared of this loon. I suffered terribly already from the damage wrought on my unit by the untrained evil clique. I didn't need to add any further permanent injury to my list from an overzealous religious nutball. I began to beg and plead she stop thudding me immediately.

Mistress Leslie apparently thought that part of the game. "I never knew this could be so fun. Okay, I am going to untie your arms but not your legs. I want you to show me what you did for your Mistress Ginger."

I swear to the Gods I was ready to chew through my ropes. I had just had to look at her lumpy ass for that hour while being struck heavily. I never wanted to see this woman again, much less see the intimate parts of her any closer. Despite my best efforts I began to cry like a fucking child as she hauled my still bonded unit to her bed. That seemed to confuse her a great deal.

"Why are you crying Psycho? Ginger told me you love doing this kind of thing. I thought you said you are a whore to me in the cooler that day I asked you to come to the woman's meeting. Don't whores like to have sex with strangers?" She looked at me hard.

I shook my head. "I was just being an asshole when I said that to you. I am always an asshole, Mistress. Please don't make me do this. I am not interested in you like that. Ginger was lying too. I just want to go home. Please I am begging you untie me and let me go. Keep my fucking collar if you want and the key too. I am done with this shit." I began to wail unable to keep my head on straight at the thought of having to endure this humiliation with her and God knows who else after her two days were up.

Mistress Leslie sat on the bed next to my weeping unit. "I am sorry Psycho. I really thought you were into this stuff. I can see Ginger was lying to me. You really did love her, didn't you? I suppose she didn't tell you she had sold off your collar and led you on. I can't even imagine what that must be like." She reached out and petted my face catching some of my tears appearing truly sympathetic.

I just sobbed keeping silent on my heartbreak. I understood this was part of my job dealing with nasty shit like this. My recent heavy losses should have been of no consequence. If I couldn't get my shit together now, I was doomed. I closed my eyes reaching deep inside seeking the strength to curb my outward despair. I had made a deal with this vile woman, if I kept my end, she would sell my collar to someone who could do the job. If I failed, she owed me nothing. Mistress Leslie had paid a lot of money to get what she wanted. Even if I didn't see a single cent, not giving her what she thought she had paid for would still equal my being blamed for the bad deal.

I finally calmed my sorrow then swallowed my tears. Opening my eyes, I looked hard at Mistress Leslie taking a deep breath making sure I was ready to do my fucking job and stop acting like a coward.

"Untie me Mistress. I won't run. I can't give you what you want incapacitated like this. I will need to be able to move about freely." I shuddered with residual anguish but was slowly getting myself back into my usual cold demeanor.

Mistress Leslie raised an eyebrow. "You promise you won't run away?"

I nodded and flashed a bitter smile at her. "A deal is a deal. I won't run, and you will keep your promise back, right?"

She smiled brightly. "I will Psycho, I promise." She then untied me.

Now I wish I could say that it turned out that we were wonderfully compatible and despite her most heinous physical attribute I got over it. However, that would be a terrible lie. Leslie was horrified when I applied my abilities of lovemaking on her. She had somehow expected it to be like that of being with a male. I had to calm her down several times when her unit began to respond to my, uhm, techniques. She had apparently never orgasmed before and it frightened her. Yeah, it did amazingly when she encountered the natural response to pleasure.

She screamed and tried to push me away yelling, "I am having a heart attack. Oh my God I am dying Psycho. Call 911."

I stopped my uhm, task, and tried to calm her down. "No you are not dying Mistress. That is normal. You are having an orgasm, just relax and enjoy it."

She screamed again grabbing me and pushing me back again, "Stop, I am dying. Something is wrong with me. Help, please help."

I stayed back this time watching the insane woman writhe, then for the God damned life of me to my horror she began speaking in tongues. I really couldn't handle this weird shit. I sat up on her bed watching her have this little religious moment feeling somewhat humored and somewhat horrified. I never did understand fucking Pentecostals.

Two things I can say about this incident in my horrible life. One, some brag they can cause a religious experience in the bedroom. Well beauties I actually did once if you can ignore that it was with a nutball to begin with so I suppose there is some bragging rights there. Though somehow I never felt it was a thing to brag about. Two, if you pay someone sixty-five thousand dollars for a fuck, you should see God and all the saints. In that respect, I had done my damned duty. She was getting her money's worth from what I could tell.

Mistress Leslie spoke in tongues, rolling around as if possessed for several minutes. I started to think I would have to repent to some God somewhere for this most beastly display during orgasm. I feared that at the very least I would need to apologize to her husband. I doubted Mistress Leslie was going to be okay missing out on this kind of connection with her Lord from that point forward. She finally came out of her odd behavior. Without hesitation she then demanded I do that again at the threat of another thud from her flogger. I groaned realizing the next many hours were going to make me wish I had jumped in after those collars after all.

I wasn't wrong. Mistress Leslie made use of my talents for the whole two days only breaking for food and bathroom breaks. I think the woman had been more sexually repressed than the average gal. Now that she knew there was a joy button, I thought she may push it till it broke the fuck off. Any needs I may or may not have had were ignored. Not that I cared. I was in no mood for getting any more intimate with her than necessary to perform the services she demanded in return for her tossing my collar to a qualified buyer.

I must guess she had hired a babysitter and cleared her schedule for this most degrading situation over the two days agreed upon. I never saw her kids nor her husband the whole time. She also didn't allow me to go into my job demanding I stay with her the entire time. She forced me to call in sick or face her holding my collar indefinitely. I felt like a damned prisoner and thought of Matthew often during this forced situation. This was the life he was facing on a leash to Joyce's kinksters. I only had to tolerate two days with a

218

single client, I couldn't fathom a lifetime with new idiots daily. No wonder he drove off the bridge. Yuck!

I had to tolerate forty hours of gibberish speaking, writhing, and the biggest ass I have seen on the smallest frame to this very day. She demanded I tell her how small her ass was on at least three more times. By the time this fubar was over I was covered in cuts, welts and bruises, my psychological health was in the toilet, I wanted to put out my eyes with a red hot poker, and to be honest I think I sprained my tongue and most of my fingers. Sorry, but just being honest even if it is a bit too much information. Nurse, medication over here.

Like I said, weird shit like this happens to me all the time. By now I had been very accustomed to it. Mistress Leslie was a sixty-five-thousand-dollar fuck job, literally. True to her word she cut me loose on the third morning free at last to escape her big ass. Before I left, she promised to have the new buyer contact me at Maiden Mary's phone number just as soon as one was found. I reminded her not to sell to Joyce, Circe or June. She smiled assuring me she already had someone in mind who could afford her price, would appreciate what I offered and could return the services required.

I asked her for a name and was told simply, "my friend Katheryn would be perfect for this kind of thing."

I didn't recognize the name so I agreed if this person could do what I needed then I approved the transfer. Mistress Leslie waved goodbye as I backed out on my Motorpsycho trying not to wince from my screaming injuries all over my unit. I just smiled at her bitterly then drove away forever. Buh bye Mistress Leslie. Now that was two days of pure hell.

I went straight to Maiden Mary's house to check on my children. Mary was worried since I had been missing for two days. She had heard that Mistress Ginger packed up and ran in the night. I assured her I was going to be okay and had a new potential Keyholder on the line. I don't think she believed me, and given the way I must have looked, why should she.

I was losing weight fast, was bruised up and very tired. However, there was no time for rest. I had called in sick for two days. If I lost my remaining job at the funeral home, I would lose my investment in the yellow house when I could no longer make the payments. I also had to find a way to buy time with the courts regarding my guardianship issue.

Mistress Ginger was gone, I needed a new guardian fast. I asked my maiden to stand in. She humbly accepted. I made her my guardian and she held that spot until December 1997. The day my next great Master would take possession of my collar. However, this was November 1996. I had a long haul till I found stability for Simon's Key once more. That is a story for another day.

That night I had another problem brewing. June was aware that my Mistress had abandoned me to Mistress Leslie. She had already determined that this new Keyholder was not able to protect me the way Mistress Ginger had. I hadn't even made it through the doors when June came into the embalming room to attempt to give me a new job description full of hideous tasks of fulfilling her twisted desires. Worse still, I noticed that Pat and the owner Julius had thrown their names into the sorted demands. June had told them the secret of my collar and key delusion. I couldn't believe my bad luck. This was not going to happen, so without even feeling a pang of regret I threw the paper into the floor and walked out.

June chased me into the parking lot screaming, "You will have no choice, Psycho. No one else in town is going to hire your loony ass. When you come back be on your knees, bitch. You will do what you are told around here, you'll see."

I got on my bike. "Fuck off June. I will starve to death before I ever take it up the ass, eat crow or your pussy skank." I tore off into the darkness feeling more despair than even during the days of Debbie or Master Julie. This nightmare was spreading like a cancer in my world. I needed help getting my employers, my budding psychosis, and my world back into order.

As I laid down sobbing yet again in the outhouse while holding on to Matthews key tightly, I damned Mistress Ginger for doing this to me. However, I knew it wasn't her doing. She just was smart enough to use Simon's key to its full power. I would need to be much more careful in the future on who wielded it and how they wielded it. If there was any future everything depended on some woman named Katheryn.

Below is a recap of Mistress number 10, 11 and Matthew's "Ultimate Rim Job" of Mistress Ginger for those who want to see the facts in one spot.

- *Mistress Ginger reigned from September 2nd, 1994, until November 1ˢᵗ, 1996. During her reign we trained and lost our only brother/sister collar to this date: submissive Matthew, January 1995 until his death August 27th, 1996. She sold our collars in May 1996 but never collected on Matthew's sale due to his death. She turned over my collar to Mistress Leslie on October 30th, 1996, then skipped town never to be seen or heard from again. I hope she rots in hell for what she did to Matthew and me, but to this day, I don't know her fate nor do I care to know.*

- *Mistress Leslie took possession of my collar that she had 'paid out' from May to October 30th, 1996. She paid a whopping $65k for my collar. She wanted the pleasure of owning her own submissive without any knowledge of the lifestyle or understanding of what exactly she had purchased. Leslie was demonstrating what is known as 'bored housewife syndrome' and was looking for something exciting and different. It was a match made in D/s hell. She would fail as Mistress when I refused to submit to her collar when I demanded she 'toss it' only two days after her purchase. Her reign lasted only two weeks in November. She managed to sell it rapidly gaining back her lost cash to another Mistress.*

- *Matthew's collar had been sold to Joyce's house for $40k. Mistress Ginger had to return the entire amount* *when Matthew outfoxed the greedy Mistress by taking his life on September 27th. Mistress Ginger was forced to flee leaving without Matthew's$ 40k and sold her trailer for a measly $15k due to the unexpected derailment of her plans. She had intended to keep me worried about the safety of Matthew in Joyce's possession. She thought I would be too busy trying to save my brother to come after her, so she could sale that trailer at her leisure. Well, that is what she gets for being a cunt. Her trailer and land were appraised at $30k. She lost $55k of money she thought*

She would be living off in California thanks to Matthew's death and the anxiety driven sale of her trailer. I am sure wherever he is he laughed his ass off when she had to flee with barely enough cash to survive half a year wherever she fucking ran to. At least he didn't die for nothing. He did indeed pay her back for what she did to us. He did it in the only way she truly could understand, in her pocket.

Chapter 40: The Narcissistic Lawyer
The Rise of Mistress Katheryn

Things are looking grim for Psycho in the winter of 1996. Seems like she took a gamble with her heart and lost everything. She has been abandoned, unemployed, almost homeless, separated from her children, without a Keyholder, without anyone to love her, dropped out of college, back to the outhouse. Wow! Mistress Ginger did a double tap on the poor schizophrenic's future didn't she? The greedy red head went so far to sell her collar to an unworthy nothing in a literal type of 'kiss my ass' goodbye message.

Now, you see Psycho has learned a big bad old lesson here. Love is for suckers. It makes one weak. Thankfully, she will not fall for that bullshit anytime soon, like for decades. Good thing too since no one is going to even pretend to care for her a long time to come. She will encase her heart like Matthew did in a place where it can never be broken again. Instead of a key, she will put hers inside a metal circle and wear it around her neck instead of inside her chest. She will close her ears to the words such as forever, love, adore, care and loyalty. Psycho is never fooled twice.

The bizarre Leslie has found a buyer for Simon's Key in record time. The new Mistress will not bother to try to fool the hapless, helpless, broken Psycho with promises of adoration forever. No, Mistress Katheryn loves herself so much, she needs no one else.

In a dry business, cold transaction the collar will pass into her uncaring claws. Mistress Katheryn knows exactly what she wants, and she will hear no pleas for mercy. The color of gold means nothing to this lady. She only loves her reflection in silver that does whatever she commands.

Mistress Katheryn has the law on her side. She speaks the secret language of the competent. In her reign, she will set the records straight. She however is anything but straight. Mistress Katheryn's nose isn't the only thing crooked about her. This hateful lawyer knows how to own a person, make them march to her drum, and never gets business mixed up with pleasure.

Her short reign will be marked with clashes regarding the definition of equal service for equal service. In the end, her cruel lack of care will send Psycho's collar into another toss up like a discarded wedding bouquet at a divorce hearing.

Ready to meet one of the most irritating people on earth, errr we mean our twelfth Mistress? Awesome, you go on ahead. We are going to linger back here at the bridge a while longer. We are still wondering if maybe we should have jumped when we had the chance.

"Psycho you look like hell. You had cleaned up your life and were doing great. Now here you are getting arrested repeatedly just like back in the bad old days. I have heard a rumor that you are living in Darlin again and have quit school. Look, normally I don't stick my nose where it

doesn't belong. But I want to know what the hell happened.
It can't just be the schizophrenia doing all this, can it?"
---**Dennis questioning Psycho during her arrest for**
Disturbance of the Peace, December 1996

Three days had passed since Leslie had cut me loose from her headboard and commands of ass worship. I was unemployed, not in school, without a real home, without purpose and there was no Master there to make me get up off the outhouse floor. I laid there reading Matthew's letter to me, looking at our pictures, yearning for our life together to return. The weather that November, reflected my emotions, grey, cold, bitter, and bleak. My future was dust, my love was dead, and my Mistress was a lie. It seemed like things couldn't get any worse.

I should know better than to assume shit like that. Since Mistress Ginger had abandoned me to my fate, I had been skipping meals and my medications. It had been far to long for me to recall what happens to a loon like me when I suddenly stop taking my meds. On the fourth day of laying out like a corpse in that outhouse hovel I had a nasty reminder.

It started with a sudden crashing noise just outside the walls of my poor shelter. The noise was impressively loud or I wouldn't have bothered. I had become so depressed that nothing short of nuclear war likely would have stirred me from my near catatonic slumber. I sighed but got up to see if maybe one of the trees had finally fallen into the cemetery yard.

I had to rub my eyes several times to make sure I wasn't seeing shit. There pulling backward off the iron gate was Mary's old Station wagon. For a few moments, I flashed back to the late eighties. All around me the air changed to that of days long since past when I was just a confused teenager dealing with a big disease and no support other than the hateful mother of Debbie, my creator.

I looked around at the past scenery wondering how the fuck I had managed to go back in time like that. Hell, if I could do that, then I could maybe go back only a few months instead of years to find Matthew and stop Mistress Ginger. But my thoughts were interrupted by the shrill sound of Mary herself. This was not a hallucination, she was actually there, and she had just crashed into the gates of Darlin.

"Psycho, I knew I would find you here. I heard downtown you were back to your old haunt, you ghoul. I need to speak to you. Get over here now," Mary demanded standing next to her car, not entering the now bent gate I noticed.

I stood there unsure if I should run like hell, go to the gate or just stand there staring like she was an apparition of my imagination.

Mary walked to the gate, slipping a look back at the front of her car to see how much damage she had caused. "Damn you girl. Are have you gone as deaf as you are insane? Do you not hear me talking to you?" She glared at me from her position of safety.

I nodded. "Yeah bitch, I hear you. What the fuck do you want." I growled back, not really interested to hear what it may be.

She grimaced at me. "Foul thing. Sinner. Trash. Whore. How dare you call me a bitch. You of all creatures have no right. I came here to help you out and that is what I get? Well I shouldn't be surprised knowing the hellish thing you are." She stood there eying me through the slightly bent bars.

"Oh, fuck off Mary. I am done with this conversation. Crawl back to hell where you came from. Send my mother all my hate will you? Come back here and I will do worse than break your pelvis, and if she comes, I will bury the fucking hatchet once and for all in her God damned skull." I turned to go back to the outhouse and lay back down as I was already tired of my company.

"Psycho, wait." I heard Mary come through the gate.

Now she had my attention. I turned back around ready to fight. If that old heifer thought she was going to drag me back to Debbie she had another thing coming.

Mary saw my sudden stance of aggression "Wait, I don't want to fight with you Psycho. I came here to offer my help. I know you need a guardian. I am here to offer to take that before you get into trouble. Do you want to go to jail again?" She backed up ready to run.

I began to laugh loud and long. "Are you fucking kidding me? Have I pissed off some powerful God somewhere? I am fucking sorry. Do you hear me? I am sorry," I yelled at the sky holding up my hands towards the heavens in true apology.

Obviously, I had done something heinous. If I had not broken some cosmic law, then just what the fuck was going on? Mary offering to take guardianship? I am living in the outhouse again? I obviously was slipping off the deck big time this time. Surely, the straight jacket and leash would be required for this little trip into the rabbit hole.

Mary appeared somewhat disturbed by my strange calling out to the Gods. "Psycho, I think you are very sick again. Look let me take you to see your psychiatrists. Your kids need you. Mary tells me you have been missing for four days. Even Timmy is worried sick. Dennis and Boyd have been looking for you."

I interrupted her by running for the old hag. She saw my sudden aggression and ran to her car slamming and locking the door on me just as I got through the gate. I jumped onto her hood and just as I had in years past began bashing the windshield with my bare hands in a fury of pent up hatred and rage.

She threw the car into reverse but this time I held on as she took off down the dirt road trying to shake my unit off her car. I held on to almost the schoolhouse before I finally lost my grip and was thrown from the car. The force of it bounced me off the gravel road as I rolled into the deep drainage ditch with a hard thud. I was knocked out though I have memory of the drop.

Apparently, Mary thought she killed me. She stopped the car, and in a panic rushed off and called 911 from the first house she encountered. I came to at the bottom of the ditch to see a small group of people staring down at me and sirens in the distance coming closer. I got up realizing I had broken my left arm just below the shoulder. Still in a panic I took off running down the drainage ditch holding my busted limb. Behind me I could hear the gasping and surprised yells of the small throng of people who had been staring at what they thought was my dead unit.

The sirens were what scared me. I thought it was the cops coming to haul me to jail for attacking Mary's car. I had lived in Darlin for years in the past, and I knew these drainage ditches like the back of my hands. Not far up from where I awoke, I knew there was a less steep slope that I could, even with the broken arm, crawl up to free myself and run to safety, or so I thought. I managed to reach it and despite my severe injury and got out back onto the road.

Without a second of hesitation I took off running away from the approaching ambulance and the familiar squad car of my dear friends Dennis and Boyd. I was planning to run back to Darlin and collect the Motorpsycho then head to Maiden Mary's house to escape my pursuers. I ran at a full sprint sparing none of my available energy to get ahead of anyone who desired to stop me.

However, fast as I may have been, I can't outrun a police vehicle. Boyd easily overtook my stride in the car and pulled in front blocking my exit to the cemetery. Behind me was the ambulance and crowd. In front the cops, on each side a steep drop into the ditch with no way out. I was trapped like a rat in a cage.

I stood there glaring at Dennis who was getting out of the squad car. "Psycho, now you just hold still. You have been in an accident. You have been injured. Those folks are here to help you. Stop running and let them look you over. I don't want to have to knock you down and cuff you, but you know that I will," he said as he walked around the vehicle looking at my very obviously broken arm.

My prodromal mind was paranoid as hell. I was sure the cops had been sent to haul me in for weird experiments or something. I couldn't recall exactly but something was wrong here. I looked back at the crowd then back to Dennis. I decided to try to break through them instead of him. If they wanted to cut me into pieces for their thrills, they would have to catch me first.

I turned and fled right back toward the now very frightened group of rubberneckers. Dennis was hot on my heels yelling for me to stop immediately. I heard him but wasn't going to listen. I approached the group of people they scattered in every direction. A few got in front of Dennis tripping him up, buying me just enough time to outrun the usually very fast officer. Boyd had begun to follow but he too was stalled by the straggling nosy town folk.

I ran right past the ambulance and confused ER response crew. I had reached the school property. I tore across it knocking down surprised students who were on their way across the school yard from the parking lot. It was apparently morning. I had been unaware due to my days of laying in despair while not paying attention to the time. Dennis had not given up the chase and was still right behind me. I felt my lungs were going to explode in my chest from this drawn out foot race. Wait, wait what the fuck am I running for?

I stopped suddenly just before crossing the main road unsure what I was doing, what had happened, and why my arm was not working. Nothing was making sense. I must be hallucinating again. I turned around only to be knocked to the ground by Dennis who was unaware that I had now become aware once more.

I let out a scream as my broken limb was sent crashing into the ground with the force of Dennis's weight. He didn't hesitate despite my pleas of agony pulling both arms behind me and cuffing my unit. I supposed I had that coming. He was full of adrenaline and fear that I was about to run into the road traffic like I had done in the past. A broken arm was better than a broken head, which is likely what he was thinking. Well I hope that is what he was thinking anyway.

He was red faced and out of breath as he now gingerly lifted me up. I was sobbing in pain. Having a broken arm pulled behind you into cuffs is not fun. He appeared genuinely sorry as he stood there waiting for Boyd to catch up. He was stalled behind the masses of students blocking his path to pick us up.

Dennis looked at me appearing concerned then said breathlessly, "What the Sam Hill were you running for

Psycho? You could have gotten yourself killed. Are you not taking your meds again?"

I didn't say anything. I just stood there looking at the ground crying as my left arm screamed in holy terror pain. I didn't really care what Dennis or anyone else did to me. I just wanted to die anyway. Surely, this was going to kill me or at least put me where someone could tell me what to do next. I was just so lost without anyone to guide my next move or help me figure out how to fix the mess that Mistress Ginger's departure had left me in. In jail, Mary, Circe, Joyce, Leslie, June nor Debbie could reach me. Things could certainly be worse, oops there I go again. I am just never going to learn.

Though I had run from the scene of my own accident and tried to evade the police, I really had not broken any significant laws. I was released by Dennis into the ambulance custody just as soon as Boyd managed to pick us up and haul me back to the ER vehicle. I noticed Boyd was looking at my neck strangely and raising an eyebrow. I had forgotten he and Dennis knew about my secret. The lack of my silver necklace and my sudden bad behavior got my old flame thinking of things he should not have considered.

I was hauled by ambulance to the hospital. The break was clean, so no plates were required. They set the bone and put my arm in a caste. Luckily, I am right-handed. My left arm was useless for at least six weeks but then again, with no Master to serve, and no job it really didn't matter. I was treated and released to Maiden Mary who came to pick me up and take me back to her home.

Just before we headed back, I had her stop at the courthouse. I transferred Ginger Kirkpatrick off my guardianship papers to my Maiden Mary. I must admit that taking her name off my papers hurt. Despite all she had done to me and Matthew, I still loved the bitch. She had lied the entire time, but she had granted me a stable two years and two months. It had been the hardest but happiest time of my life. Remember my bar is real low here. Saying goodbye forever was harder than you can imagine. Try as I might I simply could not erase the longing to be with her and Matthew from my heart.

Mistress Ginger may have been a sham, but she was a damned good one. She had demonstrated (maybe not so cruel and without all the brainwashing bullshit) that living in a purely D/s household is what I needed to function correctly. I needed the rules, rigidity, and structure. That was very evident since anytime I had too much time to do nothing and no guidance, I tended to get arrested, break arms attacking cars and ended up in mental institutions.

I had no illusions that I would ever know any happiness like that ever again in my pathetic existence. The torture at not being able to find a place to truly belong was worse than any pain I had ever known. I understood what Matthew meant when he said he could never go back to vanilla now that he had become a lifestyler. I too was trapped forever by it, even if mine had started as a delusion and not brainwashed like his.

NOTE: *I know you may already know this but let's brush up, shall we? Vanilla versus lifestyler was not just*

234

about sex despite what everyone seemed to be misunderstanding. Though sexual congress is part of the entire package it is a minor part of the entire story.

Lifestylers follow a strict code of conduct, and every person knows their place and role. Punishment is handed out when the behavior of either the D or s is out of sync with previously agreed upon regulations of behaviors in all realms of the relationships.

Vanillas do not have such rules, and are free to love, work, choose, and live without answering for their behaviors. They don't have pre-agreement contracts nor do they do anything with enforced deterrents when they don't meet certain standards.

The behavior of Leslie and the interims before Mistress Ginger, taught me an important lesson. If a Keyholder was not part of the true D/s lifestyle, I would be misunderstood as a slave or whore or likely both.

This was painfully demonstrated by continued misunderstandings of my service for service submissiveness. My needs were being continually ignored and only my sexual abilities coveted by the filthy people willing to purchase my collar. These idiots truly believed they had paid for a private, personal sex slave and if I would wash the dishes too, even better but not that important.

None had understood that I did not sleep with them for kicks. The special services of the collar are just a service like any of the others. It is provided so the Keyholder would have time to look out for my needs rather than having to find a fucking date every weekend. I didn't enjoy providing that service any more than I did providing wake up service or bath service. It usually, depends on how the Keyholder approaches this one.

It seemed everyone was just looking to buy a hooker who couldn't tell you no. Joyce had proven there was a huge market for it and my poor Matthew had taken his life to avoid that fact. I was beginning to fear I would have to join him soon if too many more of these so-called collar holders pulled the same shit Leslie, Tammy, June and others had already pulled. In a sentence, I was very fed up with the bullshit.

Maiden Mary would not allow me to leave once we got to her house. I was one-armed and very sick now with malnutrition, on setting psychosis, and grief. I was in no condition to fight her off. I transferred my laying around mourning from the outhouse floor to her couch. I never got up except to pee and often refused to eat. Mary was getting seriously worried she would have to have me hospitalized when November the 15th finally rolled around. That day a phone call came in that would set me back on my rocky road to controlled exploitation and accidental success from it.

She came to me on the couch saying someone was on the phone demanding to speak to me. I moaned and told her to take a message. Maiden Mary told me this woman was saying she would not leave a message. She was demanding I come to the phone at once and speak to her.

I laughed bitterly. "Who does she thinks she is, my mother?" I rolled back over and told Maiden Mary to hang up on the bitch.

Mary was left to tell the woman I would not take the call. She hung up and we both let it roll since the idiot wouldn't leave her name or message for me. I went to sleep forgetting about the whole thing. Until suddenly I was rolled off the fucking couch onto the floor.

I was startled awake. I looked up ready to kick the ass of whomever was the fucker who dared to pull me off my couch. Standing above me was a woman in her late thirties with short brown hair. She was five foot six but appeared taller due to a very straight posture. Her face was pointed, and she had a nose with a very prominent lump in it. She was average in build, nothing stood out about her other than her hawkish nose and deep brown eyes that appeared vicious.

This stranger was tapping her foot appearing quite angry with her hands crossed glaring down at me on floor.

"Who the fuck do you think you are," I growled looking around for Maiden Mary thinking this must be one of her idiot friends.

The woman narrowed her dark eyes. "I am your fucking Mistress, Psycho. I told you to come to the phone, but you didn't mind. I was told you weren't taking calls, so I came to collect my property in person thank you very much." She started tapping her foot.

I shook my head. "I don't have a Mistress, lady. You need to bugger off. Where is Mary?" I got up off the floor sitting back down on the couch looking at this snotty woman suspiciously.

The woman reached out and grabbed my ear pulling me to my feet. I let out a yelp and hit her wrist knocking it off me.

She growled then backhanded the hell out of my face. "You fucking bitch. How dare you. Keep your fucking hands off me unless I tell you otherwise. Get up. Get your shit. We are going home now. This shit needs to stop now Psycho. You will mind me, or you will have two broken arms by nightfall." She reared back to hit me again but Maiden Mary came running.

"Katheryn, stop it. Psycho, get up. Look she is your new Mistress. She has the collar. Katheryn show her please. Stop hitting her, my kids don't need to see that shit." Maiden Mary pointed at a fine leather purse sitting just at the doorway with my collar hanging off the strap.

I looked at the woman. "Your name is Katheryn?" I suddenly recalled Leslie said her friend Katheryn would likely purchase my collar from her.

The woman who was scowling at Maiden Mary now looked back at me lowering her hand. "Yeah, Mistress to you Psycho. Now I am not going to say it again. You are wasting my time. Get up, let's go. Now," she growled.

I shook my head. "Whoa, hold your horses. I haven't submitted to you. There is an interim period, Katheryn. You can't just buy people. I am only going to say this once, I am not a fucking slave," I yelled at the most foul woman.

Katheryn started laughing. "No you are not a slave, and no you can't buy people, which is true. However, I could make your life pure hell if you try to screw me over on what I was told I have paid for. I paid a pretty penny for your services as a submissive to my household. Don't fool with me about petty interim bullshit, Psycho. I am a lawyer. I know how contracts work. I also know what you are, what you do, and what you expect from me in return. I bought out your contract from Leslie, who bought it from a Ginger. You now owe me the services provided by that contract. If I must stand here another minute, I will take that damned collar and sell it to Joyce who keeps calling me. Apparently, you are very popular. She is also looking to purchase your contract. Look, this is already getting on my last nerve and I don't like being seen in this neighborhood. I didn't realize you were going to be such a pain in the ass. So, get up or fuck this. I have better things to do." She stared at me hard.

I heard that loud and clear. No more arguments from this schizophrenic. I got up grabbed my purse and a few changes of clothing and followed Katheryn out to her Ranger pickup truck without saying another fucking word. I didn't like this asshole, but she wasn't Joyce. My agreement not to sell to that pimp was with Leslie. Katheryn now owned my collar. I did not have an agreement with this woman not to send me to that prostitution hell. Katheryn had me in a position where argument could lead to my worst nightmares come true.

We drove back to the town where my yellow house was located. Katheryn drove through the town and into the fancy suburban outskirts where all the finest housing subdivisions were located. She pulled into a large two story, modern home. Her yard was well manicured, obviously by professionals. Katheryns home was on a huge lot of land and I could see the signs of an inground pool in the privacy fenced in back yard. This lady was upper middle class and lived in the snootiest of all the neighborhoods in that town. I felt my heart sinking. This was going to be terrible, no doubt at all. I was used to a more liberal type of dress, expectations and orders. I now was pretty sure I would be expected to wear a maid's uniform. Yuck!

She pulled into her garage then hit the automatic button closing it behind us. "Get out and follow me."

I nodded then did as commanded. She took me through a door that led into the spacious laundry room. Then like a rat in a maze I followed the brisk woman into a huge kitchen with a center island and all the latest in modern conveniences of the time. From there she took me into a living area with modern but modest furniture, then into a small entry with three steps down. She opened the door and ushered me into a small den complete with a fireplace and two small windows. The furnishings were much less formal than in the main part of the house. I could tell this was a place of relaxation, pursuit of hobbies and other pleasures for the household occupants.

She closed the only door in or out behind us and told me to have a seat on one of the easy chairs in front of the fireplace. I did as she told me to do wondering just how long I could tolerate this snotty bullshit before I did jump off the old bridge.

Katheryn took a seat beside me then looked me up and down. "Well, you are at least handsome enough. I worried you may be ugly or deformed. You'd look better a bit taller. Your bosom is far too large for that frame of yours as well, but no matter. You'll do, I suppose. I will say I am not happy to see that broken arm. It had better heal fast. I have a lot of work for you to do, but that is okay, you can start by going over cases and jotting down important notes for my upcoming court cases. I was told you are bright. We shall see. I doubt it though considering how damned close together your eyes are."

I sat there staring at the floor wondering just who the hell this woman thought she was. However, for now I had no idea what exactly was going on, so I decided to keep my mouth shut.

She stood up grabbed her purse and took my collar off her strap. "I don't like this collar. It is bulky and ugly. I have another one on the way. In the meantime, it will have to do. I want to see your papers before I collar you."

I looked up surprised. "You want to see what?"

Katheryn growled low, "Your fucking papers saying you're disease free. Where are they?"

I rolled my eyes. "Oh those papers. They are in my bag. I was just cleared again when I broke my arm." I got up and retrieved my proof of free of STD notice.

She looked the paperwork over then put it down looking at me again. "Okay, so I have talked to Leslie who says you can provide personal services of all kinds. I already am aware of what I want, and I am aware of what you expect in return. I need a list of prescriptions, doctors, psychiatrists, and I want your dietary restrictions, medical and psychiatric records pronto."

I sat there almost knocked out by the forcefulness of this very business-oriented woman. However, she at least wasn't mistaking what I do for what I do not do. I shrugged then retrieved all the folders that Mistress Ginger had put together during her reign about my treatment and care.

Katheryn took them and studied them closely. I sat there quietly expecting any moment she would call Joyce and say no deal. Instead after about an hour or so, she put down the files and sighed.

"Okay, seems like a pretty simple and cost effect deal I am getting. Not sure it is worth what I paid, but then again, we shall see what you can do soon enough. I will now hear the services you provide. Then I will accept your submission and we can go from there." Katheryn grabbed a pen and paper to take notes.

I shrugged then began to call off the services I had been trained to provide. She demanded to know what level each service could be categorized as, such as novice to master of the task. I had not had to provide such detailed information about my abilities since the days of Debbie and my German teachers. I watched as Katheryn wrote down each one then put stars or lines through them as I rattled them off.

Eventually I got to the special services of the collar. I stopped to see if this woman would desire I go into detail on this service too. If she would not require it, I was happy not to discuss it. I already didn't like her so not having to sleep with her was fine by me.

Yet, like all before her, this service caught her attention and she demanded to know in detail what I could provide her in that realm. Of course, in that area I was expert. My stomach soured as she demanded full on details about all possible and plausible sexual acts, I could grant her. I noticed she put several stars next to that service. Oh well, it sucks to be me.

Finally, I got to my discussion of leashing, and my denial of Master interference with the Green Temple or my children. Katheryn didn't seem to disagree with either stipulation. Once she felt she understood my requirements, abilities and regulations she looked over her list carefully.

"Well, I have to admit I thought at first I had gotten a bum deal. However, this may have been a lucky purchase after all. If you can do half of what you claim you can this may just work out well for both of us. I am ready to take your submission now. Let's get this over with, you have wasted enough of my time already. This ugly collar will do to the new one gets here next week." She dropped the pad and picked up my collar.

I looked at her hard. "I don't see the Key. Without the Key you are nothing to me. I follow the Key, not the collar, Katheryn."

She snorted. "Oh that dumb thing. It is here." She dug in her fancy purse and held up Simon's Key for me to see.

"It is not dumb, Katheryn. It is the Key you purchased. It would be wise for you not to forget that," I growled most unhappy about this rushed and forced collaring.

Katheryn chuckled "Okay whatever. Now get over here and kneel. I am ready to submit you now."

I shook my head. "It is not you who allows it. It is me who does. It is my choice not yours Katheryn."

She growled. "Then fucking make your choice. You are irritating me again. Not smart. Seems to me you are in no position to argue with me over trivial shit like that."

This lady had some balls. I suddenly remembered something very important. "Katheryn, before I agree to this, you don't have Borderline Personality Disorder, do you?"

Katheryn looked at me laughing hard. "No. Of course not. I have Narcissistic Personality Disorder. Who told you I had Borderline Personality Disorder?"

I just looked at the ceiling. "No one did, Katheryn. I assumed something had to be wrong with you or you wouldn't have paid sixty-five thousand dollars for a fucking collar."

She laughed even harder. "I paid sixty-five thousand dollars so I would have one fucking person do what I tell them without saying 'You don't own me Katheryn.' I am sick to death of hearing it. Now I finally have someone who can't fucking say that to me because I do own them. Now, kneel and let's do this."

MISTRESS KATHERYN (Collar and Key)
Reign: November 15th, 1996, until May 20th, 1997

I shrugged and knelt before the lawyer Katheryn. She promised to protect and defend the collar. She promised to provide equal services for equal services. She requested almost all my services except for driving, yard, and housekeeping. She had others already hired to do the yard and house. She preferred to drive herself, but she maintained cooking and food serving services. She demanded monogamy but not chastity. She herself would not be monogamous but reported her only other sexual partner was in a fifteen-year marriage with her. He was to be kept unaware of my existence as her submissive and not to be made aware of any administration of special services of the collar. I was essentially her secret affair on her husband, blah. She would manage my income but would not take any money for any of her services. Instead I would keep her confidence in the reading of legal reports and special services of the collar, a way to not flaunt myself as her lover in case you missed that, as equal service in return. She demanded the title of Mistress Katheryn.

She finished her promises, then demanded I make my own. I said my usual, then warned her about tossing, selling or trading the collar. I also made it clear that lying to gain service, misdirection of my service, mismanagement of my service, obtaining a second collar, demanding that I train another collar and lack of equality of service (chronically meaning I had to caution more than twice) would result in forfeiting of our verbal agreement. In short, an automatic collar toss.

Quick Note: These new rules were created because of the brainwashing and cruelty of Mistress Ginger. I would never tolerate such bullshit again. If you want to sell me say so, don't sneak, God damn it. I also would not tolerate being used to hurt another ever again either.

Mistress Katheryn clumsily opened the collar. I felt the tears begin to rise in my eyes like they always did. It had been more than two years since I had to deal with this realization of failure and a honeymoon night. I was more than a bit despaired this time. I didn't like my Mistress, was still grieving and this time, I was without any choices.

She finally got it open then clicked it around my crying unit appearing irritated that it took so long to work the old collar.

"I will be glad when the new one gets here. This thing is a mess," she said as she finished bonding me to her Will in submission.

My tears were not even noticed by the very self-absorbed Mistress. She looked at the clock then at me sighing.

"Well, my husband will not be home for about an hour. I wanted more time for those special services. So, I think I will wait until tomorrow to try that out. For now, I have to ask what your work schedule is so we can manage our time together more efficiently." She looked at my collar again appearing disgusted with it.

I was still weeping over my collaring. "I don't have a job anymore. An old Mistress told everyone there about my collar. When Mistress Ginger skipped town, they started demanding sexual favors or I was not able to work. I left rather than comply, Mistress. I am unemployed."

Mistress Katheryn smiled evilly. "Ah you mean old lesbo June, don't you? Well, well, I have waited a long time to get that old bat. Now, I cannot have you unemployed. I will not pay your way. So, you will go into your shift tonight and take this letter. Give it to June. Then you will get your new work schedule and bring it to me tomorrow at my office at eleven when I am on my lunch break. I will give you the address. Don't be late. If anyone asks, you are my new field office worker." Mistress Katheryn wrote something down on her pad of letter head paper then got up and retrieved an envelope with her stamp on it.

She handed it to me. "But Mistress, if I go in June will expect me to have sex with her."

Mistress Katheryn growled, "I told you to give her this letter, then you do your job only. You are not to fuck anyone else but me. I am disease free, you are too. We are going to stay that way. Got that, Psycho?"

I nodded my head still sniffling. "As you wish Mistress."

She smiled. "Good, now where is that damned Motorpsycho of yours? You need to get out of here before Roy gets home."

I looked up at her. "It is at Darlin, Mistress. How did you know about the Motorpsycho?"

She chuckled telling me to follow her so she could take me back to Darlin.

"Psycho, I am Crystal's Aunt Katheryn. You remember Crystal, don't you? She sure remembers you." She continued to laugh hard at that statement.

I almost fainted as I walked behind my new Mistress realizing I had just been collared by a fucking relative of a member of the evil clique. No wonder she seemed to know so much about my situation. Crystal was there when the fucking delusion was created by the evil Master Julie. She had been at my horrid tortures both time in the cemetery and the day of the now infamous shock collar incident. Mistress Katheryn was privy to my creation history through that blasted girl. Fuck me. See, I told you I should never say, it couldn't get any worse...

Mistress Katheryn told me on the way to Darlin she had been hearing tales of my abuse for the last eight years. She said that Leslie had been a client of hers a few years ago in a lawsuit regarding a minor car accident Leslie had caused. They had remained friends since my Mistress had won the case for her.

When Leslie had contacted her out of the blue the week before asking for a private meeting about a sensitive subject Mistress Katheryn has quickly agreed to see her. My Mistress told me she was a bit more than intrigued to find out what the devote Pentecostal could possibly be wanting to keep a secret. To Mistress Katheryn's humor she was offered the collar of the most notorious Psycho for purchase by the preacher's wife.

My Mistress chuckled at the irony of finally having in her possession the very person she had heard so much about over the years during many family get togethers with her sister and her sister's daughter Crystal. Apparently, Mistress Katheryn had been contacted several times regarding my case about the sexual sadism of Master Julie against me. It made sense since Crystal had also been a probable target of reprisal by the angry Julie for spilling the beans about the evil clique to the cops.

I just sat there listening in disbelief as she told me all about the hellish incidents of my past in gory detail. She was completely correct. There was no doubt it had been given to her by Crystal's own mouth. Only someone who had been there in those days to witness the horror could have reported it so accurately.

It really bothered me that Mistress Katheryn was very aware of my sorted past and of the torture at the hands of those disgusting bitches. Yet here she sat proud and laughing that she now possessed the very thing the entire trauma had created. In fact, she made it very clear she thought I was the greatest thing she had ever treated herself to by purchasing my collar (she actually said that "I was a treat to herself. Well happy fucking birthday Mistress Katheryn. Sheesh). I was already beginning to regret having submitted to this black hearted woman before reaching the iron gates of home.

Mistress Katheryn dumped me off outside the cemetery never raising an eyebrow of concern at my current living conditions. She merely warned me that I had better show up at her office the next day, on time, bathed and in a clean outfit. My Mistress didn't give two shits how I accomplished it, but failure would result in a stiff punishment at her discretion. After that warning and without another word, she left me there speeding off down the dirt road never looking back. I stood there wanting to cry over this most horrible new situation. I found I couldn't. A new empty feeling was inside my chest. I suppose eventually one can cry out every tear left inside. Apparently, I had reached my limit.

I just shrugged then went to set about the tasks of getting my life back on track or at least trying to anyway. My grief time had expired, it was time to get back to serving and scrapping. I believed I would receive no quarter or sympathy from this most unkind Mistress. As usual, I was absolutely correct.

I examined the gate Mary had run into with her car. It was slightly bent in the center but still worked okay. I decided to leave it be. As long as it closed there was no reason to try to try to fix it. Knowing me I would only manage to break the damned thing. I had decided it was as tough as I was. We both were a bit worse for wear. However, we both still managed to do our fucking jobs despite the ravages of the insensitive, uncaring and time itself.

I went to the outhouse and grabbed a few items of clothing from the days of Mistress Circe's reign. I had already thrown out the heavy BDSM bullshit catsuits from Mistress Ginger's career as Keyholder. I hated that look anyway. One of the only things I didn't miss about her was her shitty taste in clothing. I loaded everything on the Motorpsycho including the letter Mistress Katheryn had given to me for my funeral home show down. I got on the bike and with much difficulty managed to drive to Maiden Mary's house with one arm in a caste. It was not easy, nor fun, but manageable with some caution.

My Maiden was very upset when I came inside. She noted the silver bulky collar right away. "Oh no, Psycho. You didn't let that horrid woman collar you," she said sounding exacerbated.

I nodded while sighing. "I didn't have a choice Daughter. She was going to sell me out to Joyce. It will work out, I think. She is hateful and self-absorbed, but she seems to understand the job. Only time will tell. For now, I need a shower, to change and I am headed to work."

That made my Maiden pause. "Work? I thought they told you not to come back unless you fucked them?"

I chuckled. "Yeah that is what they said but Mistress Katheryn wrote June a letter. I have no idea what it says but my Mistress swears it will end the bullshit. I need the job Daughter, and I have to do what Mistress Katheryn says, so we shall see." I headed for the bathroom to bath leaving Maiden Mary shaking her head mumbling about mean people in the world.

I was happy that Maiden Mary had accepted the guardianship when she did. I told her to keep all my checks for the kids care and for herself to compensate her for giving them a safe, stable home. Maiden Mary was an honest, trustworthy soul. Many of you may wonder why I never let her become a Mistress. Well I had considered it. In the end, I never allowed her to take Simon's key simply because she already had enough trouble with her own kids and helping with my own.

Maiden Mary was not well educated and, to be honest, not very bright. She was useless at reminding me to even take my medications, much less navigating the very complex problems my disease created (such as legal issues, psychiatrists and chronic inpatient treatment). I loved her like a sister, but I knew that even the job of guardian was above her head. I would have to find someone more suitable in time. For now, she had saved my ass from commitment to a mental institution for non-compliance with court ordered guardianship. For that I am forever grateful to her among the many little things she always did for me.

I got myself cleaned up for the first time since the abandonment of Mistress Ginger over fifteen days before. I put back on my plain black button up shirt, black pants and long black coat that had been my old standby for years. I reapplied my signature white makeup and black eyes. My blond hair had gotten quite long, though it was still horridly thin. I noted that it seemed to be darkening at the base. Perhaps, I would become a dirty blond like my lost brother Matthew in time. For now, I was still pretty tow headed. I noticed my back appeared violently bruised. It could have been the road rash from the fall off Mary's station wagon or long-term injury from Mistress Ginger's habitual thudding. Not to mention Leslie's most inappropriate ones only a few weeks before. I realized I had rarely, if ever, looked over my own unit while I was so busy looking after everyone else. I had never bothered to notice my own existence, oh wait, that is why I wear a collar and follow a Key. I don't recognize my own reflection half the time. It was this strange fact that had me deep in thought when Maiden Mary came banging on the bathroom door wildly yelling that a woman named Joyce was out front demanding to see me.

I felt a chill go down my spine as fear made biscuits on my soul. The horrid Joyce had tracked me down. Then I looked back at my reflection when the silver collar caught the light sending a prism of collars across my vision.

I smiled at the strange person looking back at me from the mirror. Joyce was too late. I was already owned. Mistress Katheryn was not giving up my collar to this pimp for any amount of money. She wanted the pleasure of total control over. Gold didn't matter to her. She had plenty of her own. I may not like Mistress Katheryn, but her strength was already being mirrored within me. I confidently walked out to calm my Maiden and deal with the devil Joyce.

Joyce stood next to her Fiat smiling as I walked out the door. Maiden Mary was pleading with me to stay inside and call Dennis to send this harpy back to the pit where she belonged. I decided I wanted to face the witch whose cruel intentions had sent my lover to his grave. It was the least I could do for my brother. I wasn't scared of this unwrapped mummy.

I smiled back. "So, what brings you to these parts, pimp? Oops, where are my manners. I apologize. I forgot my protocol. I meant what business do you have with me Madam Flesh Peddler."

Joyce's smile faded to a scowl. Geez, I was being polite damn. "Well that is not very nice of you to say now is it, Psycho? I came all this way to offer you a deal and this is the thanks I get." She crossed her old, spindled arms.

I snickered. "A deal you say? Ah, well now I am all aflutter to hear what an old cow like you has to offer the likes of me. If I were you, I would hurry it up. It is likely the drug dealers in this neighborhood may decide to make you pay for the huge debt of your stable of addicted whores. Though I would not mind watching them put a bullet in your dusty old head. Hell, I would help them aim straight."

She shifted uncomfortably., "Psycho there is no need to be nasty about this. Your Mistress is gone. Good riddance to the idiot I say. She sold that big cocked male collar of hers to me but refused to offer me yours for a decent price. I need an old school collar like yours to train my unruly slaves and snotty submissive collars. If you sell that collar of yours to me, I can make sure your children never go wanting for their entire lives." She trailed off as she began to reach into her purse.

I was beyond furious. Matthew was a human being, a good heart, a beautiful man, and not some big cocked male collar. I was sick to death of her references to people as nothing more than breeding stock or pieces of beef. I felt my feet began to rush toward the old Dowager Mistress with murder most foul on my mind.

However, strong arms grabbed me around my upper arms, even the broken one. "Whoa Psycho, stop now. Hey lady, get the fuck off my property now. I have called the cops. You leave or I will press charges for trespass." I heard a male voice I recognized as Ronnie's (Circe's husband and Maiden Mary's live in boyfriend) yell out from behind me.

Joyce looked up surprised. She saw my obvious attempts to break free of Ronnie to beat her ass, and his very serious look of you had better get the fuck out of here. The old pimp decided not to push her luck. She got into her little sports car and sped off without saying another word. I was now yelling obscenities, describing in gross detail what I was going to do to her when I saw her next. I will only say I was not promising to fix her hair or take her out to a friendly lunch.

Ronnie finally let me go when the old hag had driven far enough ahead, I could never catch her on foot. I shook off his touch then looked at him angrily.

"This was none of your business Ronnie," I growled at him.

He smiled then said, "Mary is the best thing that ever happened to me Psycho. I am not going to let your murdering some old cunt in the front yard cause her to be strapped with your kids to raise too. You need to calm down and think before you go smacking people around. You are a mother now. Think of your loved one first and your anger second. That old bitch will be dead soon. She is older than dirt. You would have gone to prison for what? Think on that a bit. I am going to see what Mary made for dinner." With that Ronnie walked back into the house leaving me to calm down my rage alone.

Ronnie was so different than Circe it was as if they were from two different planets. It was no wonder Maiden Mary fell in love with him so hard. He was calm, easy going, quiet, and an honest hard worker. He was only in his early thirties compared to Circe's advancing age of over fifty-five. I never understood the whole marriage to that old witch, but I never pried either. My own life and relationships were more crooked than an old lady's spine. I was happy for Mary that Ronnie brought her so much joy after her own husband had abandoned her and the kids.

However, Ronnie had one fatal flaw, he worshipped the demon alcohol. One rarely saw him completely sober.

During this time in our lives Ronnie was still a functional drunk. In the years to come he unfortunately became more enslaved to his addiction until eventually, well that is for another story.

For now, just know, Ronnie saved Joyce's life that day. Had Mary not alerted him to step in, I would have killed her over her derogatory description of my lost Matthew. Ronnie was right. She was not worth it, though I didn't think so at the time. I would never see Joyce again. She died of heart failure three months later. Good riddance to that old cunt. She was not worth years in prison for murder when only three months later father time did the job for me. It was something that I would not soon forget the next time I wanted to kill someone who I believed had wronged me.

I would never attack anyone again – but I will attack some trust me, damned schizophrenia – without asking myself: "is this asshole worth my suffering in a cell when maybe life will kick their ass for me in time?"

NOTE: *Now, that you know Joyce died three months from the day that Mistress Ginger was to transfer our collars on November 1st you must realize had Matthew held it together till February his collar would have been free of that nasty bitch. He didn't have to kill himself. Maybe he could have handled the short time. That fact has always haunted me to this very day. It is why I told this little side story here. It is not always easy to remember, but life is going to be what it will be. Trying to take control by losing control or hope is never the answer. Nobody can know what the future will be or what is in store for us* *unless we live to experience it firsthand. Sometimes using patience by waiting to see if you are stronger than you thought, or they will get theirs without your getting into trouble, is the right thing to do. The inability to trust fate cost Matthew his life needlessly and me many hours in a cell confined by a leash to the floor.*

If I had not learned this most powerful lesson very young, I would not be talking to you now. My life has been very hard, brutal and extreme, but in the end, I have always had faith that I am going where I am supposed to be even if I am not happy with the destination in every case. Worrying about what others do, have done or what fate has in store for them (unless you must defend yourself) only threatens your own journey on this plane of existence. It is always best to leave punishment to Karma and mind your own road. Unless you get a chance when no one is looking to burn down their house, errrr, thump them.

That night as my Mistress instructed I drove to the funeral home after calling Julius to tell him I was coming back to work. He told me fine by him. Likely he was thinking about getting blow jobs like he had demanded on my work list. What a pig. He said to make sure to check in with June right away when I came in. I of course told him she was exactly the one I intended to see first. He told me how happy he was to hear I was returning to work. That everyone had missed me. Yeah, I bet they did.

When I pulled up into the parking lot, I saw June standing in the corpse receiving entry smiling a gotcha smile. I smiled back then retrieved the letter Mistress Katheryn had commanded I give to the nasty woman. She backed out of the doorway apparently desiring to give me plenty of space to walk into her awaiting trap.

I came through only to be grabbed and slung into the wall by the vile creature. June pinned me to the inner wall by the door with her arm around my neck while groping my crotch roughly. She then started giving descriptions of what she expected me to do to keep my job. I almost couldn't get her attention to hand her the letter. She ignored the envelope I was pushing into her face. June was almost incoherent to anything outside her fondling my unit.

"Let me go, damn you June. I have something for you. Please take it and get off me," I squeaked out barely able to breath from June crushing me with her body weight against the wall.

June cooed, "Oh I am about to let you go Psycho, right to your task. I told you that next time you came here I would put you on your knees." She began trying to force me down continuing to ignore my attempts to hand her the letter.

I fought her but finally fell under her weight still holding up my Mistress's words. I had become desperate since I was almost helpless to fight her off with only one good arm.

"June, I will do what you want if you will take this letter and read it first. Please stop this," I groaned out as she started to undo her pants.

She finally noticed the paper I was holding. "What is this shit, Psycho? You want me to read a letter from your doctor? Or your momma maybe? Fine, give it to me. We have all night, and I intend to use every hour of your shift to pay you back for making me wait so long to have you all to myself again. There is no Ginger here to protect your loony ass now is there."

I just moaned in horror at having to deal with June's disgusting carnal desires yet again. Once was already one time too many. The woman was beyond gross. I sat there on my knees looking at the floor wishing I had just stayed in the fucking cemetery and taken Mistress Katheryn's punishment. No matter what it was it had to be better than this shit.

I miserably supposed I would lose my house after all. June may have had me trapped this one night, but I would never make this mistake twice. I also wouldn't stick around to deal with the repugnant Pat nor the odious Julius either. There was no doubt in my mind I had just quit this job for good.

However, June suddenly zipped up her pants while she read the letter appearing more upset with every word. I looked at her confused. She seemed afraid. What was going on?

June finished reading, folded up the note, then reached down and pulled me back to my feet. "Okay, sorry about that little misunderstanding, Psycho. No need to tell Katheryn about it, right? I mean if you can keep it between us, I will be willing to drop my charges for supervising your work this month." She looked at me smiling nervously.

I narrowed my eyes. "You won't charge your monthly fee if I don't tell Katheryn you tried to rape me is what you are saying? No, I think you won't charge me a monthly fee for good or I will tell her and even add a few details June. You will also call off Pat and Julius and never let me see your ugly face here when I am working again."

I wasn't sure what was going on but shit if she feared whatever Katheryn had threatened in that letter, fuck if I wasn't going to use it to my advantage. Besides she had been planning to rape me. So, I may as well get what I could from this nasty situation. I assumed I wouldn't get any of my demands, but didn't hurt to try, right?

To my shock, June readily agreed appearing grateful that I had not asked for more. "Yeah sounds fair, Psycho. You keep your mouth shut about this little mistake and I will stop charging a fee, tell the boys to fuck off and I will work the day shift so no problem not being her when you work. Deal?" June held out her hand to shake on it.

I reached out and shook her hand still eyeing her suspiciously. This was just too fucking easy. What was in that damned letter. Now I wished I had read it before handing it over. However, I dared not let June know I had no idea what was really going on. My ignorance could get me pushed back to my knees. Instead, I decided to stand my ground pretending I knew what had just happened.

June let out a sigh of relief. "Okay, great. Now Psycho, Mr. Roberts is waiting on the table for prep. I believe you have the rest under control. Have a good night. See you around." She hurried through the door almost tripping over her own feet she was rushing so fast.

I stood there for several minutes flabbergasted that I was saved by my Mistress from losing my house and total financial ruin. I could now afford to go back to college and best of all I didn't have to tolerate rape, degradation and sexual harassment from June, my boss and other employees. Mistress Katheryn was my new hero. She was pushy, cold and self-absorbed, but hell, as long as she kept me safe from others and myself she was awesome in my book.

I worked the rest of the night without further incident. June, Pat and Julius didn't come at me again and I went back to my tasks peacefully. June kept her promise and withdrew her monthly fee from my paycheck on her court ordered supervisor appointment. Since I worked the graveyard shift, my job became quiet and comfortable once more.

The next day I arrived at my Mistress's Law Office exactly at eleven o'clock as she had commanded. Mistress Katheryn was talking to her secretary when I came inside the brownstone, very regal looking building. Her waiting room reeked of money, greed and lies. I started to sit down in one of the fancy chairs in her waiting area when Mistress Katheryn called me back to follow her into her office.

I got up and took my place right behind her as she literally pushed me into the room. She closed the door then locked it. I looked at her a bit nervous about this strange behavior. My Mistress closed her blinds then went behind her desk and sat down in her rolling office chair. She was wearing a houndstooth dress suit without panty hose or panties as it turns out. Uh oh, how do I know that?

Mistress Katheryn smiled at me standing there with a dumb look on my face. "Okay, so I have always wanted to do something kinky. I am calling in my special services of the collar right now. I want you to get over here under my desk, kneel and take care of my needs. While you do that, I am call my friend Grace and bullshit about last week's barbeque."

My eyes went wide. "Special services of the collar, here? Now? Huh? You can't be serious Mistress."

Mistress Katheryn glared at me. "I am not joking. I will want a better demonstration later after work but for now I want to test your skills. If you fail to please me, then I still have time to rethink this whole contract. I want to see how you perform under pressure before I see how you do when there is no chance at getting caught at home. The bonus for me is the allowance of multi-tasking and efficient use of my time. You will get your lunch, she chuckled at that most foul misuse of her serving me by making sure I eat, sheesh), I will get my phone calls in, and I will get a fantasy fulfilled all at the same time. Now, did I stutter? Get over here and do what you were told." She pointed at the empty space under her desk where she would normally pull her chair in.

I shrugged realizing that this is my fucking job like it or not. When the Mistress tells you to perform oral sex on her under her work desk while she chit chats with girlfriends, you do what you are told. I had done worse with Mistress Ginger no doubt and a few others I wished to not recall.

I approached then knelt pushing myself into the small alcove while the Mistress hiked up her skirt. She picked up the phone and called her friend. However, she cut the phone call to Grace short appearing more than a bit satisfied with my, uhm, service. Apparently, she was the one who couldn't work under pressure.

So, we have a nasty Narcissist this time. How do we keep getting so fucking lucky eh? Well she will not be a fun one, but of all the Keyholders she will be the only one that after her reign is done, we still stay in contact from time to time in a cordial fashion. What? Why? Well, you must read the story to find that out. Now, in a small town sooner or later we were bound to run into relations of the evil clique members, but this was a real shocker. Very shortly our deep dark past will come back to try to haunt us once more. Yeah, we are unlucky all the way around in many ways but lucky in others.

Chapter 41: Idol Reflections and Four Letter Words
Mistress Katheryn

Looks like the mirroring has begun in force. Now exactly how does one reflect one that is so self-absorbed? Well, when someone is having that passionate love affair with a looking glass, it is best not to get in the way. Silence may be golden, but duct tape is silver. We must be seen and not heard by this most narcissistic Mistress.

Mistress Katheryn is pleased with her service for service contract. It was a much better deal than she could have imagined. What a wonderful gift she has given to herself. It is about time. The Mistress believes she deserved a bit of pampering. She had grown tired of those around her not recognizing the amazing, incredible, perfect creature she truly is. With her personal Psycho, there is never a dearth of compliments. She of course doesn't really need them. Mistress Katheryn knows how great she is. Yet, it is very nice to have someone close by to stomp on, errrr, help give her a lift when others forget to give the proper respect.

It is not important that her latest acquisition is getting sicker by the moment. The white, cold season of winter is in full swing. Psycho is now slowly becoming static, and not the stationary kind. She is reuniting with old support systems. She is visiting old friends, and dancing with her Prince Val once more. Somethings just never change. A heart has been re-ignited by a misdirection and a missing collar.

Fate, love, hate, loss, and idol are all four-letter words that are whispered into the schizophrenic ears by the Looper. The Lord of Misrule reigns over the shaky future of the broken-hearted Psycho. How unlucky can one person be? Ah, that is always the question.

Ready for the next sorted tale of 'no fucking way that happened?' I hope you all brought your memory for paths already traveled and old dog-eared maps to navigate this journey. You see it will be a lot easier to get where we are going this time. We have been here before. If we recall correctly, and we do, we were in a hurry to get the hell out of here last time too. So, you go on ahead. Don't worry this time we won't get lost, we already know the way..

"I noticed you aren't wearing a collar Psycho. I wanted to ask you a question about that." **---Boyd to Psycho during overnight jail stay, December 1996.**

Mistress Katheryn was unable to finish her phone call to her friend Grace thanks to the perfect employment of my requested services. In fact, she nearly got caught by her secretary, called Carla, in a most compromised position thanks to her underestimation of my expertise level and her response to it. Her inability to keep silent alerted her ever vigilant Carla to strange goings ons in her office. Thankfully, the Mistress had enough forethought to lock the door or there would have been a lot of explaining to do.

Mistress Katheryn signaled me to end her service immediately as the knocking at the door became almost as frantic as her moaning in pleasure. She had yelled that all was well, but my Mistress did not follow that statement of well-being with even an attempt to shut her fucking pleasure noises up. I was beyond frustrated with her over this madness. Granting special services of the collar in her damned office with a waiting room filled with clients and a secretary was humiliating enough. I believed there was no need to add the indignity and danger of alerting the whole lot of them about it.

If my Mistress couldn't keep down her racket, then why not just go and call the fucking police on me herself. Carla was sure as shit about to anyway or so she said through the locked door. She had been eyeing me suspiciously before Mistress Katheryn pulled me into her inner office. I could tell Carla thought I was an unstable criminal client. She likely thought I was strangling Mistress Katheryn or worse. Well what I was doing was worse in some ways. Protect and defend bitch.

Mistress Katheryn yelled out to Carla that calling the cops would not be necessary just in time. She then directed me to take a seat in the chair in front of the desk while she went and opened the office door to calm down her now terrified secretary.

I sat there fuming and trying to fix my disheveled makeup wondering how the fuck I kept getting into these horrible situations. I wondered how much time one would get in jail for practicing oral sex on a lawyer in a law office without a license, hahaha. I was pretty sure that is breaking some law, public indecency maybe? I was completely unsure. I made an internal bet with Simon that Mistress Katheryn was more than aware.

I won't lie, I was beyond pissed over the whole shady scene. Not only was my Mistress slipping around on her husband with me, but she was also using me to thumb her nose at the very regulations that she swore to defend. I will lay no claim to being a perfect law-abiding citizen or even a good person in the great scheme of things. However, this situation regarding the use of the special services of the collar by my new Mistress was too much hypocrisy even for my demonic ass.

As she settled down Carla and her awaiting clients, I decided she and I were going to have to discuss my misgivings about her marital cheating and semi-public demands of carnal congress. She and I had far too much to lose to take these unnecessary risks. She was not Mistress Ginger. She had a good reputation, a very lucrative career and a very trusting husband. Getting caught with her skirt up would be a career ender and a ticket to her own divorce hearing no doubt.

It would be equally bad for me since I had such a slippery hold in those small town already. For the moment, my bad behaviors other than the psychotic shit, was all rumor and conjecture. No one could prove the rumors about my sexual activities. Getting caught with the politically powerful Mistress Katheryn would put me at risk from assholes far worse than June, Pat, Julius, and Leslie. I was already a target for the dark fantasies and twisted ideas of many an evil heart in those little communities. I did not need any help making that worse.

I was like poor Bobby, a decent looking gal that was too small and frail to defend myself from attackers. Unlike her, I was without family protection and daft in the brain most of the time. It was just not a good thing to be. There was no dearth of predatory males and females around looking for a chance or excuse to force me to make their hideous dreams come true at my expense as this story has already proven.

I was very upset since considering Mistress Katheryn knew my history and the rumors, she had decided to ignore the obvious outcome of demanding my compliance in this matter. All the above are the reasons for my refusal of her order when she finally came back into her office, locking the door once more and demanding I continue the service.

She glared at me while sitting down. "You are telling me no? Psycho do I need to remind you we have a contract agreement. I am holding up my end, now you are refusing to pay me back?"

I looked at the floor feeling very nervous. "Yes Mistress, I mean no Mistress. I mean I am refusing to grant special services of the collar here in this office. I will do whatever you want in the privacy of your home. Just not here. It is too dangerous. Forgive me Mistress."

She laughed dryly. "Well. I didn't realize that you had the right to choose the venue or set parameters on my demands for the services you promised. This is a wrinkle that will never do. I suppose if we are going to start that bullshit then I can start to set parameters too. So, if your needs are too much trouble or not to my comfort then I will decide where and when and if you get them." Mistress Katheryn was now starting to write shit down on a pad of paper.

I felt my throat go dry realizing this bitch had me dead to rights. I had not specified that there would be any denial of requests of any service to her when she requested it. Only that service would be denied if she did not perform her own promised duties to the collar. In that respect, Mistress Katheryn had done her job. Now, I was going to be forced to return the favor or be in breach of my own rules. Damn it.

I blew out my breath. "I apologize for my knee jerk insolence, Mistress. You will need to correct my bad behavior. I will not disobey you any further." I got up and went back to her desk kneeling before her.

She smiled in victory. "That is better. Now, as punishment, you will come here five days a week at eleven and do this for me. Any further arguments, and I will sell your collar to Joyce or give it to Crystal to be very cruel. Got that?"

I almost choked at that threat. "Yes Mistress. I understand. No more arguments."

I couldn't believe this nightmare. Every weekday I was going to have to come to her office and repeat this indignity. I was ready to jump off the fucking bridge right behind my brother. His solution was making a lot more sense every day.

As I went back to my task, I thought of Matthew and Mistress Ginger and the life that was yawning before me without them. I didn't think I could do it. Endless days of servitude to hateful vanillas only interested in forcing me to fuck them or forcing themselves on me. When they were not acting as if I were a whore, they would treat me like a piece of furniture that had no needs, thoughts or emotions. I was condemned to nothingness, pain, and crushing service without any hope of happiness.

I did my best to hide my tears from the Mistress as I continued with the agony of my thoughts running nonstop through my mind. Not that she bothered to notice me anyway. I was just a fucking masturbation machine to her, not a lover. I could have wailed like a mother who lost her child and I seriously doubt she would have noticed. She instead went back to her loud moaning and panting.

When she was finally sated, she told me to again fix my makeup. Then she gave me a stack of legal records. I was directed to a small desk in the front waiting area and told to go through the cases and find inconsistencies, patterns and pertinent information to prove each client as innocent or guilty according to the evidence presented.

I took the large stack and began my task when the Mistress came up smiling holding a very large book. "Oh you will need this since I realize you are not very bright or educated." She dropped a dictionary into my lap and walked into her office laughing at her insult.

I rolled my eyes while dropping the dictionary on the floor. Fuck her. I was more educated than she ever expected. I was very aware that Crystal had likely told her I was retarded or slow. Perhaps she assumed I was dumb because I was insane. It didn't matter. My Mistress could think of me as a monster for all I cared.

Mistress Katheryn had made this clear it was going to be service for service without any kindness or even basic human decency between us. Fair enough. She would get none in return. She was not going to play lover or even friend. She was playing slave driving boss. Got it. At least she wasn't a fucking liar like Mistress Ginger had been. I wouldn't have any misunderstandings about our relationship this time for sure. I wondered if maybe this would be for the best in the long run. After all, my little unreality trip had cost Matthew his life and me my future as it had been. My life following Simon's Key was never meant to be pleasant. That is not why I was doing it. I do it because my only other choice is death.

My life was going to be brutal. I sat there realizing that enduring not love is what I would have to engage in from that moment forward. I did my best to refocus my mind, harden my heart and stay on the task ordered. My precious emotions gleaned from my beloved Matthew would have to be buried along with his collar and unit deep inside. I locked away my hope of happiness with it. It was distracting me from my goal of survival at any cost. It was going to be the tough to repress the very things I thought I had lost and wanted so much.

NOTE: *However, these things were forbidden someone like me. I was a reject, defective, unimportant, diseased, useless, and unwanted. It was sort of laughable that I had even believed I had found those things in the first place. I wonder what the fuck I had been thinking. If I had been paying more attention Mistress Ginger would have never fooled me so badly. I knew better the whole time, but I had chosen to ignore the truth and live the fantasy. It landed me in the worst danger I had been in since Master Julie's bench.*

Trusting that red-headed bitch was beyond stupid. I admit I had allowed her to brainwash me for the third time in my life. When was I ever going to learn? When a Keyholder says they love me, they are lying. No one who is willing to put a collar on another human being and make them do shit against their will is demonstrating love. They are using and abusing me, and I am agreeing to it to control the guaranteed exploitation caused by my disabling symptoms. I should never trust a Master. If I was hurt, it was my fault for forgetting that most obvious fact.

I was rapidly going through my prodromal, but never had I been saner than that day in Mistress Katheryn's office. I had finally gotten my head back on straight. Had I not, likely I would have committed suicide by the end of the week. It was just time for that reckoning, I guess. It was not the life I wanted, it was the life I got.

The truth be told, thanks to Debbie and her poisonous trick, I was lucky to have any life at all. Too bad for me if I was unhappy with the terms of my escaping the reaper. I would just have to get over myself. I had been living in a dream, and it was time to wake up. I was completely in sync with reality for the first time in a long time. It sucked it had taken me so fucking long to get there. Maybe, had I been a bit faster, Matthew would not have died, and Mistress Ginger would have been sent to hell by my own hands.

However, I didn't figure all this shit out till it was far too late to change a damned thing. They say better late than never, but this is one time that maybe it is not so true. Since we shall never know, we will now just go on with the story understanding I was no longer under Mistress Ginger's bullshit spell of adoration for a Keyholder. It would take a miracle and a lot of hard work to ever reach my dead heart again, but that is still twenty-four years in the future. We have a long way to go.

I sat there all afternoon pouring through Mistress Katheryn's cases. Everything from DWI's to divorce petitions was in that stack. I found it easy to see the connections in the cases, the lies told, the misdirection and even the weakness in some pieces of claimed evidence. By the end of her office hours, I had finished them all. I was sitting there quietly waiting for her next instructions.

Carla continued to watch me with a stink eye. I could tell she didn't like me being in the same room with her much less on the same planet. I didn't bother to even look at her directly but kept my guard up in case she pulled shit on me. I no longer trusted anyone. It seemed everyone around me wanted to stick a foot or some part of their unit up my rear end. I wasn't taking any chances.

Mistress Katheryn approached me asking for the pad I had taken all my notes on. She looked at them, nodded then pursed her lips.

"Well you are not as stupid as I assumed. This looks very adequate. I see you have put the case number and name. Hmm, I guess you will do until I tire of looking at you. Your contract is secure for now. Keep up the work and I will keep your collar." She took my notes into her office without saying another word.

I shook my head at her arrogance. I had already submitted. She acted as if I were doing an audition for her. What an asshole. Oh well, at least she had said she would keep the collar. I decided to ignore any of her little jabs at my abilities and attributes. It was becoming clear she intended to put me down in every aspect she could find. Apparently, she was one of those people who liked kicking others when they were down. Baby, you couldn't get any further down than I was. So, her insults were basically a waste of her time. Calling me a loser was like calling me Psycho. I was painfully aware both were truth.

The date was November 16th, 1996. The next day was a Wednesday. Mistress Katheryn's husband was out of town on Tuesday and Wednesday due to his job as a buyer for some retail company. She had me follow her back to her house for the night. Once there I was instructed that each week on those two nights I would stay at her home and provide all requested services without fail or argument. I was also required to work out my own work schedule to have those days off so I would have no excuse to be available for everything from wake up, to bath service on command. This Mistress was aware of what she wanted, how she wanted it and would not tolerate any excuses.

That first night two things happened that led me to believe I had indeed found a new level of hell. One she demanded special services of the collar once again and demanded all my abilities in this area be provided. Second, she had bought a new cat o'nine tail thanks to Crystal's story of my situation years before with it. After she was done making me feel like a whore, she refamiliarized me with it. Not that Mistress Ginger didn't use this thudding tool commonly. It stands out in my memory because Mistress Katheryn was no more trained than the damned evil clique had been with it. She didn't understand safe zones. My back, upper arms, and backside were whipped mercilessly despite my pleas that she stick to safe areas.

This punishment was handed out thanks to my initial denial of her command to get back to my task under her desk. My Mistress assumed my begging was just a way to get out of the correction she had chosen. It took me many weeks to get her to understand that thudding was not my problem. Her beating me in areas that could kill me or permanently injure me were not okay. The *back is not a safe zone. You can break a rib, damage the kidneys, and as I had already suffered destroy the shoulders, elbows and nerves of the back easily. There is no meat there to protect the nerve bundles, soft tissues, organs or bones. Think about it*.

I was beginning to see why Crystal had been such an asshole. This woman was likely a good representative of what she had to model from as a little child. Mistress Katheryn thought she was the smartest, prettiest, and most experienced person on earth. No one could tell this bitch anything. The more I tried to explain why she shouldn't hit me in some spots, the more she hit me there and harder too. It was counterproductive to try to correct this narcissistic cunt. She was a know it all, self-absorbed, belittling person in every respect.

Not that knowing this new information changed my mind about Crystal or her place in my history as a scum bag. Crystal not only helped Master Julie and those girls torture me, but she kept her mouth shut until telling the story did nothing but hurt me further. I was more than fearful I would run into the stupid bag of shit and end up punching her out. That would surely lead to my arrest with my own Mistress calling the law to have me hauled away. The only persons in her life that she considered as good as she was, were her immediate family. Crystal included. To hear Mistress Katheryn tell it they were all descended from the Gods themselves. A truly blessed family of absolute perfection in every way. I had to listen to my Mistress brag about the mediocrity of her various nieces, nephews and daughter as if they were a family of blue-ribbon champions.

Not since Cindy and Master Julie had I heard so much ado about nothing. Crystal was going to a community college and was barely passing to become a legal aid. Mistress Katheryn's oldest daughter Mindy was a college drop out with two children and a divorce looming. She had never worked a day in her life and was living off my Mistress. Her house rent was paid by her mother.

Colleen the second daughter, and one I knew far too well, was working in a nursing home laundry. She had one child and didn't even know the paternity of the child thanks to her catty antics. Colleen was also living in a house rented for her by my Mistress.

I would listen to the bragging and roll my eyes.

Especially, when my Mistress would say shit like, "Well my Colleen is smarter than you Psycho. You are just a common whore. She is special and that is why she needs many men to keep her happy. If she wanted to make dean's list in college, she could but she is an artist blah blah blah."

NOTE: *I may have been a homeless, loser, schizophrenic but at least I did plan my kids and know who the father is. I even married him.. I didn't expect something for nothing in this world either. Sheesh. I resented my Mistress calling me a whore and saying her daughters who were fucking everyone in sight were not whores but were artists. I have had my share of sexual experiences and there is nothing artistic about it. Any fool can get the job done.*

If you get a lot of sex because you like it and don't lie about loving it, good for you. You are not a whore, you are promiscuous and that is fair. If you don't because you don't believe in sex with a lot of different folks, good for you. If you don't like sex or only like sex with one person you are not a whore. You are asexual or monogamous and that is fair.

If you trade it as a service for survival you are a type of prostitute. *Yeah, okay I just called myself a prostitute, but truth is truth ain't it? I provide many other services too but that is the one everyone seemed to want so call it whatever you like. Just being honest is all.*

However, if you lie about your reasons for fucking everyone in sight such as calling yourself an artist who needs a lot of dick to feel excitement and fill the emptiness, you are a Borderline Personality Disorder and a whore. There is a fucking difference between a whore and a prostitute.

By Thursday morning I was filled to my limit of endurance of my braggadocios Mistress. I simply couldn't get away fast enough. I even tripped over my own feet trying to sprint through the front door for my Motorpsycho to be shut of my company with her. Not since the beastly second Master had I been more in a hurry to escape the notice of a Keyholder. I swore if I heard one more depreciating comment about myself or one more unwarranted boast about her own worthless kinfolk I was going to cut her throat to shut her up once and for all.

I ran out the door not even looking where I was going. My paranoid looking back to make sure Mistress Katheryn was not following me running that diarrhea mouth of hers is the direct cause of my head on colliding with none other than the horrid Colleen herself. The useless girl was coming into the front door as I was flying out it. We both went sprawling to the ground with a loud thud.

Colleen recovered first. She was getting up brushing dirt off her pants looking at me with what appeared to be awe. "Holy shit. Psycho, here in my mom's house. Am I dreaming this?"

I got up off the ground quickly feeling discomfort rising within at running into an old fan. "Yes you are. Go back to sleep Colleen." I headed for my bike ignoring the starstruck girl.

I started the Motorpsycho and tore off down the driveway leaving Colleen standing there with her mouth open, holding her chest as if she had just smacked into an angel on Earth. I shuddered despite myself. I really hoped my Mistress would be able to distract this nutjob from interference with my service to her.

Colleen had been enamored, without reason I may add, with my so-called bad ass reputation for many years. She had once asked me for my autograph in the bathroom when I was still selling lawn weed with my old friend Kick Start. Then when I had returned to high school the second time, she was the ringleader of the throngs of admirers that had taken on my signature makeup and dressing style. Colleen had been the one who pushed the idea of making the cafeteria into a Darlin cemetery for my graduation party. Her misguided claims of inside familiarity, all lies, had essentially ruined my special day.

Worse of all she was the ground zero stool pigeon that had helped Master Julie keep tabs on Crystal's movements that fateful October in 1989. This meant she did have inside information into my situation with the bench, the evil clique and of course likely had heard all of Crystal's stories just as Mistress Katheryn had.

It seemed that every time this horrible girl showed up in my life trouble was sure to follow. How much of it was being manipulated consciously by this idiot I was not sure, with the exception I related above about the graduation party. However, I had no intentions to engage her in another opportunity to fuck with my journey through my brutal existence. Colleen had long since been identified in my shattered mind as a shit stirrer and threat to my safety.

I returned to Maiden Mary's home to visit briefly with my children before they took off to school and pre-school. Getting to spend quality time with them had been very hard since the loss of Mistress Ginger. They didn't seem to be any worse for the wear. My daughter was now in first grade and my son would start kindergarten in the fall. They were both very popular with their classmates and teachers despite their notorious mother's reputation. My kids smelled, looked and acted like the local town folk. The people in those communities readily accepted them as one of their very own. It helped them a great deal that I kept a low profile. I avoided overly public appearances to deal with the paperwork of their educational needs. My second trip to high school had also erased some of the natural fear that Psycho was a loon to be reckoned with.

Not that from time to time my daughter didn't come to me or Maiden Mary. She would cry while relaying stories she had heard about my misbehaviors many years before her time. I would calmly set the record straight doing my best not to tell too many lies. Both children were aware their mother was ill. My constant inpatient treatments had to be explained to them as a natural occurrence because of my terrible disease. When it came to the schizophrenia, while withholding the information about how that came to be, I was mostly honest with them from the start.

However, I hid my delusion and Keyholders (my lifestyle). It was a well-guarded secret. I did this by keeping them away from it since the departure of Mistress Ginger. I would never mix them with any Mistress or Master again thanks to their age of full awareness. Had the red head kept Simon's Key, I would have dealt with the truth when the kids could understand. Since she had left in the night, I had a much harder time explaining the sudden departure. This loss of Aunt Ginger and Uncle Matthew had hurt them deeply too.

Thankfully they were so young, that to this day neither child recalls Mistress Ginger. My daughter vaguely recalls Matthew, but she only remembers him from his gift at her sixth birthday party just before his final few days of life. I suppose that is both a blessing and a curse. He did love them both so much. It saddens me they don't have the memory of his adoration of them. I suppose it must be enough that I will never forget.

The tragedy of losing my D/ss family had taught me a valuable lesson. My collar would be tossed chronically as proven over time so getting the kids involved was detrimental to their stability. Maiden Mary and I had made a pact that December in 1996 that she would always behave as the children's temporary guardian when I was put away. She kept her agreement with me until the day came that they could handle themselves.

I of course always made sure she was well paid, and the children had need for nothing. Since I didn't require much, all my money went to their care or to pay for the yellow house. I borrowed the shower at Maiden Mary's and slept in the outhouse. I had very few expenses. I rarely ate and never engaged in pleasures or hobbies. I left such triviality to those who enjoyed freedom of choice and to my normal children.

All in all, my kids successful thriving kept me from feeling like a total loser. They were everything I had never been. Most of all they were happy, secure, safe and loved. In this life, there is not much more you can ever desire. As a mother I was doing well with a little assistance. If I could have been, I would have been proud of them. Sadly, Simon owns that emotion.

Instead, I felt gratitude. I was able to redirect the abuse and cruelty away from them. It did mean I had to suffer in their stead but any mom worth her salt would have done the same. You may look at this story and say wait, how did you suffer in their place? This is a righteous question to ask yourself.

However, if you think on it a moment you will understand. My survival promised them the safety and stability in my choice of home at Maiden Mary. I was surviving the only way possible for one with no support. If I died they would have gone into their father's custody or worse my own mother's. My very life breath blocked that horror. My choosing a secure home to place them and constantly guiding their care in that home allowed them to never know the terror that waited just outside the door. I didn't want to live my cursed life, but if I pussed out like my brother Matthew did, my kids would pay for my weakness. That is something I simply couldn't do to them. Yet as November was coming to an end, my resolve to continue was weakening.

Mistress Katheryn's chronic derogatory statements and disregard for my input was undermining my already tanked psychological wellbeing. I felt more helpless and minimized daily. She continued her demands for boxed lunch meetings in her office. She also used Tuesdays and Wednesdays to further unravel my self-image by constant negative criticism. It seemed nothing I did for her or around her was ever good or done fast enough.

Except the sex, that service she never bashed once. She also never attended any of my needs in that area. I was made to feel like a brainless sexual plaything that she directed. I was not supposed to have any feelings, needs, or compunctions regarding her twisted interests. If I dared to voice discontent or offer resistance I was thudded immediately and dangerously by her untrained hand.

It more than angered me that this clumsy, untrained vanilla seemed to believe that she had more expertise than myself. I already had more than seventeen years of impressive service. To top that off she was officially my fifteenth Master (this is if you include Debbie, Julie and Shannon). I was her first and only submissive collar. Her arrogance was beyond idiotic. Often her corrections of my implementing requested services got her or myself harmed. I had suffered many indignities, torture and punishment to learn proper protocols for all items offered to her for a reason. Doing some of the things I do the wrong way is not only dangerous, but it can also even be deadly.

The more I tried to tell her that the more damned cock sure Mistress Katheryn would be to command them done in her errored way. When the service failed because of her novice experience she would punish me for the failure she had ordered. This constant passive aggressive behavior was wearing on my last nerve. All she was managing to do is convince me that very soon I would call her contract null and void.

Then as December rushed in two things happened. Mistress Katheryn removed my collar. She had purchased a new one that had yet to arrive. Her reason for removal of the old one was she could no longer stand the clanking noise it made during her boxed lunch sessions. She found the noise distracting. Go figure, damn. My collar was missing though I was indeed owned. The lack of feeling the silver circle but still being made to mind or suffer was confusing to me. My delusion is very strong. Removal of a collar unconsciously signals emotions of being lost without a Keyholder. The collar is like a security blanket as well as a reminder of my promises. Mistress Katheryn ignored my pleas to wait until she could replace my symbol of bonding to Simon's Key. It was removed and I was told to get over it.

Second, she demanded I stop wearing my signature makeup during the weekdays. This was also due to her lunchtime nooners. My having to fix my makeup before working in her office the rest of the afternoon pissed her off too. I was now left without direction in dressing. My official protection, my mask, had been banned. This was due to nothing more than the cost of a few moments of Mistress Katheryn's precious time. Without my mask, I felt naked and vulnerable.

These two mistakes were cruel assaults on my unstable psychology. They are directly the cause of my turbulent ending to one of the most tragic years of my young life. Mistress Katheryn never forgot to remind me to eat, take meds, or bathe. She failed completely at understanding the importance of keeping her foot off my defense mechanisms.

Like a spinning top now uneven in weight distribution I began to spiral out of control. My prodromal was rapidly morphing into a deep psychotic break. Mistress Katheryn who was always too busy watching her own reflection, missed all the warning signs that Psycho was about to live up to her name. Though my cycle was inevitable the harshness, this one could have been mitigated by something as simple as a compassionate ear and a tiny bit of empathy.

The first Friday of December, I awoke from the ground in the outhouse feeling odd. I could hear the residents of Darlin whispering about me to each other. I tried to ignore them, but they were all talking at once. I looked toward the horizon above the belly of the sleeping giant, but my vision appeared to be winking in and out. First too bright, then too

286

dim. I believed somehow, I had short circuited my wiring in the darkness. Maybe I had gotten to close to a magnet, or perhaps something had come loose from Mistress Katheryns severe thudding two days before. Whatever the reason, my sensory capacity was compromised from the malfunction.

I looked about for something sharp. The only way to fix this error was to locate the cause. That would require exploratory investigation under the skin suit. I held up my arms to the strengthening sun realizing that the branching system of veins looked broken in many areas. I sighed with irritation. This was going to take tools I was not in possession of at that moment. I went to the Motorpsycho to head to town. I would need a knife, electrical tape and possibly even a few extra yards of proper copper wire. It seemed my tasks were never ending lately. Damn it.

I drove straight to the local hardware store to pick up a repair kit. I had never attempted such a thing before but I seemed to recall reading about electrical work in a book somewhere. The important thing is to stay grounded so to avoid death by high voltage shock. The young man behind the counter came over to ask if I needed assistance. I could hear his thoughts. He was a foul creature looking down my shirt thinking I could not see his trick. I growled that I knew exactly what I required.

I bought a package of razor blades, several feet of copper wire, electrical tape, heavy leather gloves and a rubberized mat. I even picked up a package of automobile fuse replacements. It seemed those should do the trick. I was ready to fix my damage before the eleven o'clock lunch date with Mistress Katheryn. She surely would not be happy if I showed up in the automated meltdown I was demonstrating. I tore out of there and headed back to Darlin ready to practice as my personal electrician without a license.

However, as I arrived at the iron gate, I notice a grey Chevy waiting there. The occupant was still sitting at the wheel. My fury was unprecedented. I parked the bike behind the shitty vehicle and walked around to the driver's side ready to pull the person out by their neck. To my utter horror a smiling Colleen opened the door before I could reach the open window to do my worst.

"Psycho, I heard I could find you here. Wow, you look great without make up," Colleen said as she slammed the car door closed behind her.

I stopped just staring at her unsure what to do. I didn't like this intruder near my home, but this was my Mistress's daughter. I doubted she would be happy if I buried her in little pieces in shallow graves like I wanted to do.

"Why are you here Colleen," I growled quickly looking toward the ground in case she could read my mind.

Colleen squeaked as if thrilled I had said her name correctly, "I told you I was looking for you. Ever since I saw you at Mom's the other week, I have asked her what you were doing there. She finally said you work for her. How cool. The one and only Psycho works for my mom. Wow, just wow." She stood there looking me up and down like I was novelty she had never seen before.

I spit on the ground now very irritated. "Yeah and so? I asked you a fucking question. Why are you here? Speak then get the hell out." I shot a vicious look at her then looked back at the ground.

She laughed. "Oh my God you are so fucking cool. I am here because mom said I should come and take a look at where you live. She wanted me to see how uncool you really are. Isn't that just like mom? Well, she doesn't understand bad ass, does she? It is okay Psycho because I do get it. I think living in a cemetery is beyond awesome. I mean you are not just a poser. You are the real deal."

I looked up in shock. "Are you stupid? Oh, what am I saying. Of course, you are stupid. Leave Colleen. I don't have time for your bullshit fantasies. I have no idea who or what you think I am, but you are wrong. Your mom is right. I am a loser Colleen. Now do run along and play elsewhere. I have important shit to attend and you are in my way." I walked back to the Motorpsycho started it and left her standing there in her own shock at my most rude statements.

I had other places to do my work. Darlin was just the best known. I headed for my old family plot cemetery up from Master Julie's old place. I decided the bed grave would work as a makeshift field surgical table. I was in a hurry to finish my job before my time was up. I was driving at speed limit when I noticed Colleen's grey car following me in my review mirror. I let out a breath of anger. The girl was like herpes. I couldn't get rid of her.

I sped up rushing past Night's station. I was so busy watching the tenacious Colleen keeping pace I forgot about Dennis and Boyd's speed trap. I flew past the sleepy cops just a few miles over the limit. Normally these police officers would let that slip, but Dennis recognized my bike and assumed if I was rushing somewhere there was trouble afoot. He is damned paranoid if you ask me. He directed Boyd to pull out and follow me for a bit to see where the fire was that I was rushing to or away from.

The sudden appearance of the squad car and Colleen's continued trailing me sent me into panic overdrive. I decided to lose the lot of them by making a rapid turn onto a dirt road. Too bad for me this time I was not as lucky as I had been in past hairpin turns. Likely my left arm still in a light caste had a bit to do with my failure to make this turn without incident. I hit the embankment sending my unit over the handlebars. The Motorpsycho continued right into a group of trees crashing into a twisted mess. My final Motorpsycho was destroyed in that paranoid driven mistake.

As for me, I was wearing a helmet for a change. I landed on my back stunned but only mildly injured. I had sprained my wrist, reinjured my arm, and pulled a kneecap. That too was unlucky for me. It would have been better if I had at least been knocked out. The sudden realization that I had wrecked my bike because of being stalked by this group of nosey assholes sent me into a blind rage.

The officers stopped to see if I was okay. They had witnessed the terrible crash that now left me without wheels. I flew at the squad car kicking the shit out of the tires and ripping at the windshield wipers screaming obscenities. I was demanding to know why they were harassing me as I began to pick up rocks from the dirt road pelting them at the front of the squad vehicle.

I was unable to do any damage to their ride, but the fit I threw was phenomenal. I was not so stupid to attack Dennis himself when he got out of the car to try to calm me. However, I was loudly cursing him and Boyd for being born. He warned me to shut up my shouting and stop throwing rocks or he would have to arrest me. I ignored him only ramping up my volume daring him to do his worst.

There was a house just behind the group of trees that had taken out my Motorpsycho. The occupants heard my loud ranting and the crash itself. They came running to the scene rubbernecking. That angered me even more. I began to threaten the middle-aged couple and pelted a few rocks their direction. All my projectiles landed a safe distance from their intended targets.

However, my continued neglect to heed his warnings had Dennis pulling out his cuffs to make an arrest for Disturbance of the Peace. He likely had figured out I was going septic psychotic since this was the second time I had come onto his radar in well over a year. I was screaming irrationally and acting aggressive. I really can't be mad at him for doing his job now that many years have passed. That day it was a different story. I saw him pull those cuffs and the fight was on.

Dennis had to knock me down while Boyd aided him to cuff my struggling unit. I was not going quietly. I swore, spit, tried to head butt, and even got one good kick into my old friend Dennis before the two officers were able to successfully subdue me. I watched Colleen's grey car drive passed and keep going as Boyd lifted me off the ground pushing me toward the awaiting backseat of the squad car. I was headed for a night of three hots and a cot until this could all be sorted out. Boyd started the vehicle as Dennis got inside shot gun before speeding off to take me to the white cell.

I watched my mangled Motorpsycho shrink in the distance. An era had finally come to an end. I would never buy another bike. I was a mother now. I needed more seats for the tiny backsides that would soon require my transport services anyway.

However, I admit, my heart ached as I said my final goodbyes to my old trusty Metal God. It was my final tie to my brother Matthew. We had shared secret romantic rides together. It was my only real freedom and my long-time symbol of survival at any cost. I had gotten my very first Motorpsycho from Mary in trade for my life and to keep Master Julie from busting out my teeth. Now that I understood the time had come to grow up, I did shed a couple of cold tears for the memories lost forever in that crash. Somehow, I knew I would never ride with the wind in my hair again. That was surely worth a moment of grief. I went ahead and took two.

Colleen had of course also seen the accident. She rushed to her mother's office to inform her of my misfortune. Mistress Katheryn was at the jail house before Dennis could even start my intake process. I heard my Mistress and Cathy arguing about my charges and rights to legal counsel. I could say a lot of nasty things about Mistress Katheryn but one thing I cannot say is she was a shitty lawyer. The woman was a bear when it came to her area of specialty.

I gigged while I listened to her legalese banter as she ripped Cathy and Dennis a new asshole in dispatch room. I had been cuffed to a desk chair in the intake room next door. I was brought there for my fingerprinting, mug shot and Linda's gloved examination. Dennis has left me there to deal with my Mistress who had come in like a spring thunderstorm, raising all kinds of hell over my unwarranted and trumped up arrest.

As the verbal argument grew into threats of Mistress Katheryn calling her judge friends, Boyd silently entered the room. He looked at me then listened at the door for a moment until finally satisfied Dennis was going too busy for a while handling my Mistress's complaints.

I watched him with a baleful eye. I didn't like his shady behavior. It seemed to me he was sneaking around fearful of being caught. By whom and what he feared he would be caught doing made me more than a bit nervous.

He took a seat on the desk across from my cuffed unit. Boyd looked at my neck appearing to study it deep in thought.

"I noticed the last two times we have picked you up that there was no collar around your neck, Psycho." He pointed to his own neck to make it clear what collar he was referring to.

I narrowed my eyes and shrugged. "Yeah so?" I had no idea why it was any of his concern.

He crossed his arms then looked at the ceiling. "Well I wanted to know how one goes about getting your collar. I mean I know you have to have one, or at least that is what I seem to remember."

I shook my head. "The Keyholders are given the collar dumbass." I lied assuming this was a trap to prove I was selling myself, you know, the prostitution angle again.

He sucked in his air. "Oh? Who gives it? I mean where does someone sign up to get the Key and collar?" He looked at me then toward the ground appearing sheepish.

I shook my head in disbelief. "I don't know. Look I thought Dennis said what I do is not illegal. Why are you trying to trap me into saying it a criminal act? I have the right to follow the Key Boyd. So, drop this shit."

I was beyond angry that he was trying to get me put away for good. I had thought Boyd liked me once. I could now see he was just a shitty cop after all.

Boyd winced. "No Psycho, I am not trying to get you to admit to illegal activity. I just wondered how the whole thing worked. Like right now you don't have a collar, so you need a Keyholder, right? How does one become a Keyholder and get a collar on you?"

Dennis walked into the room. Boyd jumped off the desk appearing startled.

"What are you doing in here Boyd? Don't you have paperwork to do? Psycho has been advised by her lawyer, Mrs. Ronald, not to speak without her presence." Dennis glared at Boyd appearing suspicious.

Boyd looked at his shoes. "Oh yeah, I just was seeing if Psycho needed anything is all Dennis. I will get right on that paperwork." Boyd rushed out of the room like his ass was on fire.

Dennis watched him shaking his head. "What do you do to my officers, Psycho," he chuckled.

"I keep them employed Dennis. They are just grateful for the job is all," I said bitterly.

He laughed at that as he began my intake process. I was then taken to my old familiar white cell to wait for Linda's search of the unit for hidden contraband such as rifles, switchblades or master keys to jail door locks. Okay, I'm being a bit dramatic here, but since I didn't expect to get arrested what exactly did they think I was shoving up my coochie to sneak into my cell? Sheesh!

Linda came in and relieved Dennis of his guard duty. She seemed overly concerned for my welfare.

"You look awful and your covered in bruises again. Damn, what is going on. I heard a rumor that Ginger left you and I heard that you are living back in Darlin. I know you have trouble asking for help but Psycho you are more than just my Priestess. You are also my friend. Please talk to me." Linda looked over my very welted back appearing disgusted.

I snorted. "Just do what you came here to do, Linda. Ginger is gone that is true. So what? I have a new lover now. I have lovers lined up around the block. Maybe if you hurry and take a number, I will get to you by the end of this millennium."

Linda glared at me hatefully. "Now that was not fair, Psycho. It was also uncalled for."

I shook my head feeling bad for being so rash with my Goddess. "Yeah, you are right Linda. I apologize. It has just been a trying day. I have no right to take it out on you. I am fine. No problems here. Just cycling again as usual, I suppose. Ginger is gone, but it is for the best. She was misleading me. I am glad she is gone. Kept me from committing a felony." I chuckled at that very real admission.

Linda popped her glove then looked at the floor as if uncomfortable suddenly. "I am afraid that I heard a rumor about those so-called lovers of yours like Ginger. I didn't believe it, not at first. Then I went back and read that old file on Julie Sloan. I also did some looking into Miss Kirkpatrick. Psycho I need to ask you something. I want your honest answer."

I stopped undressing feeling a twinge of cool ice float down my spine. I could read it in Linda's eyes. She had discovered the secret of Simon's Key and collar. She was always too clever for her own good, or mine. Linda had truly missed her calling as a detective in some big city solving crimes. She had the nose of a German Shepard and the memory of an elephant. It is a real sad thing her amazing gifts were wasted in those little nothing towns and on an unimportant schizophrenic to boot.

"Linda, whatever you think you know keep it to yourself. I don't want to have this conversation with you." I shivered realizing I had feared this moment for years now but always knew it would happen eventually.

She shook her head no. "Psycho, I can't let this one go. I see you are not wearing that silver thing I have seen around your neck since the days of Julie. Rebecca told me whoever puts that thing on you is your lover. Ginger was the last one. She is gone and so is that necklace. She also told me it is a BDSM thing. Look, it is not my business, but that is what is with the bruises, isn't it? You get into that stuff? Enjoy it, I mean sexually?" She again looked uncomfortable.

I chuckled. "Oh you are so way off base here, Linda. I don't enjoy being beaten any more than you do. My necklace is at the cleaners. BDSM thing? What is that exactly," I said trying to appear ignorant.

Linda looked at me angrily. "Stop playing dumb, Psycho. It is not very attractive on you. I believe Rebecca's rumor a hell of a lot more than your bullshit denial right now.

It is not my business but then again it is. You are not able to recognize reality half the time. People like Ginger could easily take advantage of your sickness. Maybe even make you believe they own you?"

I looked down at the floor feeling the walls closing in. I was not sure what to say to my dear Goddess. If I lied now, I knew she would not likely believe me ever again. However, I was unsure how much Rebecca had found out from Mistress Ginger and how much she then had shared of it with Linda.

"I suppose people do what they have to do to survive when no one cares about them, Goddess. You can believe as you wish to believe. I do not enjoy what I do. It is not a sexual thing, nor are others taking advantage without my agreeing to it. Voluntary exploitation of one is better than ending up with multiple rapes, robberies and murdered by the public. I merely redefine the parameters of what is considered rape or robbery. Murdered is what will eventually happen to me no matter what I do. What I am doing is only slowing my debasement down, keeping the number singular but linear, nonetheless. It is just my lot. Life is not so simple for some of us. In fact, for me it is downright hellish." I looked back up at her to see if she heard what she needed to hear.

Linda sighed appearing very sad. "Yeah I understand Psycho. More than you know. I am truly sorry I didn't realize it sooner. The horrible things I said and accused you of, I was wrong. Please forgive me. I can't even imagine what it must be like to face what you must face every day. I don't want to imagine it. Your solution is clever, but I agree it must be a real nightmare. Circe? Christine? Ginger? Anita? Who is it now? Let me guess. That horrid lawyer out front raising hell, right? Oh Psycho, she is a monster. Not that the others were anything less. None of those women are worthy of shining your boots. Yet they took everything you had, didn't they? Ginger set that up the day in the hallway. She did that to punish you for loving me like you do. Didn't she?"

I nodded but didn't look up at her. She had figured it out without my adding fuel to her fire. As I said, Linda is a smart gal. Mistress Ginger had a big mouth. The combination was bound to end up where it did. That day, my Goddess finally understood why we could never be together. She would never have used me like those others did. She also had figured out she could never bear to exert such control over my life to be effective enough to save me from me.

Since I had to follow Simon's Key, I could never belong to anyone but one who bonded my collar to them. It broke my heart to know she had to finally see the dark reality of my demonic existence. Yet, it was a relief to know that she would never make a play to try to collar me. The sheer disgrace of her knowing the truth was almost worth that peace of mind.

If nothing else she would stop asking about my welts, stripes and bruises. I was not a scared, helpless teenager who needed her protection anymore. I was an experience, professional submissive. Linda would have to come to terms with my choice to survive the way I do any way she felt comfortable. In the end, she promised to never revel my secret to anyone else. To this day, she has kept her promise (that I know of).

I spent the night in the white cell, but I was not alone. Thanks to the mercy of my beloved Goddess, the ER doctors were called in. I was introduced once more to my handsome Prince Val. He rode in on his white horse.

Amazingly, he this time resembled my lost brother Matthew. My Prince has always been very conscientious and full of romance. That is why I will adore him till the end of time. He rescued me from the ghastly cell of white and he whisked me away.

Generously, he granted me the fantasy night in his arms I had been longing for since I had lost my real Matthew. When the morning came the beautiful spell was broken. I wept with the bitterness of once again awakening in the coldness of reality. There was no doubt my biggest problem despite the lack of any quiet thanks to the Looper's many voices. I was dangerously lonely.

Mistress Katheryn sprung me from my padded cell the very next day. Once in her truck she made it clear she would hear no explanations or excuses for my insolent behavior. I wanted to remind her that my arrest was not for any infractions against her or our contractual agreement, therefore I was not insolent toward her. However, I could tell by her foul mood arguing my point of correction at that moment would be ill advised.

We made it back to her place where she continued her berating. She accused me of failing at my service contract to her since I had not been capable of servicing her at her office the day before. I was forced to kneel before her, keeping my eyes down and mouth shut as she hurled insults, complaints and accusations. Most were about my being a pain in her ass so quickly after submission.

Had the bitch let me answer, I would have told her schizophrenia didn't care if she was a new Mistress. My disease was unconcerned that she didn't believe she had been fairly repaid for the psychotic mess that was coming soon. I also would have reminded her that the whole reason she had me kneeling before her was because of this very problem. It was impressive how little these assholes wanted to return the service for the many services they always had taken in advance.

I was not granted the right to defend myself. Instead I was punished severely with a nasty thudding. Then she demanded that I employ special services of the collar right after. I understood what Matthew meant when he told me how pissed he was the day Mistress Ginger had beaten the shit out of him for being misled to attempt a rim job. He had said he did a shitty job at providing the special services to her after because she had beaten him mercilessly. That day I did the same. To my surprise, Mistress Katheryn didn't even seem to notice. She was so into herself she was able to orgasm just at the thought of being in total control of someone else.

After this totally obscene situation my Mistress decided to throw one more cruelty in my direction.

I was running the water for her bath service when she walked in looking at me oddly and said, "Tomorrow is Sunday. I am ordering you to spend the day with my daughter Colleen. She will pick you up from Darlin where I am dropping you off later today. You had better be there, and she had better enjoy her day hanging out with you. If she isn't happy then I will make damned sure you are punished severely. Do you understand me?"

I looked up from my task almost choking in terror. "What? Mistress, mercy please. What am I supposed to do with her all day?"

Mistress Katheryn smiled, "Whatever the fuck she wants to do Psycho as long as you keep your monogamy promise to me. I could give a damn less what the two of you do all day. For whatever reason she adores you. Tomorrow you will adore her back or so help me I will make you sorry for it. Don't test me." She stepped into the tub pushing my kneeling unit out of her way as she got in.

I didn't bother to argue with the vicious Mistress any further. I knew it would make matters worse, and it would fall on deaf ears anyway. Colleen was her princess. The last time I had tried to stop a princess, Cindy called Master Julie that remember, I had not fared well. This was fast becoming an unmitigated disaster. I had just been leashed to the horrible Colleen.

Oh boy now that is really not good at all.

**To be continued in Book Six of the
"27 Masters" series entitled "Minute Mistresses"**

About the Author: Alexandria May Ausman

Alexandria May Ausman in her 16th year was diagnosed with Schizophrenia. She was quickly abandoned by her foster parents. While still only a teen, she was forced to battle this devastating illness alone.

Alexandria has struggled with lack of a support system, numerous psychotic episodes, exploitation, homelessness, and an uncaring mental health system.

Alexandria raised two healthy children. After obtaining her bachelor's degree in psychology she worked as a child abuse investigator and became a diagnostic psychologist while acquiring her Master's in psychology. Alexandria never forgot the experience of 'slipping through the cracks.' Her life's goal is to help people suffering abuse and/or mental illness have access to necessary services. By accident, she became a model of 'gothic attire' and the World Goth Queen.

She began writing a fictionalized account of her life experiences after a catastrophic return of psychotic symptoms. Today, Alexandria is retired, and homebound due to crippling symptoms of Schizophrenia. She currently lives in Tallahassee, Florida, with her loving husband and a loyal support dog.